Caribbean Adventure Series
Book 7

AFRICAN WATERS

A Rick Waters Novel

ERIC CHANCE STONE

LOST AND FOUND
PUBLISHING

Printed in the United States of America

ISBN: 978-1-959020-05-9

First Edition

10   9   8   7   6   5   4   3   2   1

AFRICAN WATERS

FIND THE OFFICIAL SYNOPSIS MUSIC AT:

ERICSTONE.GUMROAD.COM/L/
AFRICANWATERSMUSICFREE

CHAPTER ONE

"Jules, I guess we're going to Zambia."

Rick and Jules had just solved the murder of Ava, the daughter of a wealthy businessman in South Africa. The case had been covered by mainstream media all over Africa and was one of the most publicized cases the country had ever seen. In the hotel, they and Gary had been ready to take a breather and then get out of Africa and out of the spotlight—until a young black man by the name of Junior Dlamini knocked on the door and offered Rick another case. His father, Bandile Dlamini, had been killed in what was officially ruled a "hunting accident." But Junior was certain he had been murdered.

"My father spent most of his life protecting animals from poachers," he'd explained. "He made many enemies." Shortly before his death, his dad had become aware of a large stash of illegal elephant ivory. "The biggest collection in all of Africa. There is a seventeen-million-kwacha reward for finding the ivory and delivering it to the government to get it off of the black market. That's the equivalent to a million US dollars. My father found the stash and stole it. He hid it somewhere near the Zambezi River near the Kafue National Park. He told me if anything ever happened to him, that the proof of his death would be found with the ivory. He gave me a map to it, but it was destroyed when my dad's Toyota Land Cruiser was fire-bombed. He had just given it to me when his new Land Rover Defender arrived. I think the men who blew up my Toyota thought my dad was driving. I was lucky to get out alive. I have terrible burns on my arms." He lifted his arms, which were both covered in bandages. "When the truck blew up, I had just opened the top and I was able to climb out before it burnt to the ground. The map was in the console. It was completely destroyed. Two days later, my father was shot in the back and died alone beside his new overland truck. There's no way it was an accident. No one would shoot that close to a vehicle accidentally."

Junior had told Rick that because the local police were corrupt and had failed to solve his dad's murder, the case had gone cold. "Please, Mr. Waters, you must help me." He'd stared at Rick plaintively, his dark eyes behind his glasses begging for help.

After careful deliberation, Rick had decided to take on the case. Even if there wasn't compensation for returning the ivory to the government, he would've taken the case anyway. It was the right thing to do. For now, Florida would have to wait. He just didn't know how to break the news to his crew, Johnie and Possum, back in Key West. He'd figure it out. This was too important.

"Junior, I'll help you. By the way, this is Jules, and over there is my partner, Gary. We'll need to fly to Zambia. What is the closest airport to your area?"

Junior nodded and smiled at the other two before answering. "That would be Lusaka. It's about a six-and-a-half-hour drive to my camp near Kafue National Park. I have plenty of room for you and your friends."

"You can fly with us. Gary has his jet here at the airport."

"Heck yeah," chimed in Gary. "You are totally welcome to fly on my jet. I've never been to Zambia, but I've heard the wildlife is extraordinary."

"Thank you, Mr. Waters. I just need to return my rental car. I can give your crew a ride to the airport when you're ready."

"Sounds good, Junior. We can be ready in about fifteen minutes."

Jules began to pack the luggage, and Gary returned to his room to pack his own things. Rick made a call to his first mate Johnie in Key West. Before Rick, Jules, and Gary had traveled to South Africa to try and solve the murder of Ava Giovanni, they had thrown a substantial amount of Mayan gold overboard after their boat was attacked by Venezuelan pirates. They hadn't had any choice because it wasn't exactly legal to have it in their possession. Possession was nine-tenths of the law. They had sunk it not too far from Key West and saved the GPS location just before the US Coast Guard escorted them back to dock, because of the damage done to the boat by the pirates. Johnie and Possum had stayed behind in Key West to oversee the repairs to Rick's boat, *Nine-Tenths*. Possum was Rick's old high school friend, now a part of his crew.

"This is Johnie. Thanks for calling *Nine-Tenths*. How may I help you?"

"Hi, Johnie, Rick here. How's the repair going? Are we on schedule?"

"It's going good, Rick. I was just about to call you. They have repaired the bow. I had them strengthen it more than it was when new. They're not sure if they can match the paint exactly. Do you want to just repaint the entire boat or try and match it? If you wanna repaint it, what color?"

"Can we do a wrap instead of paint?"

"Great idea. We can use it like a floating billboard. Let me check with them. May have to take it somewhere else for that."

"Okay, we have to leave for Zambia. It's a long story. I'll catch up with you later. Hopefully we won't be here for more than a couple of weeks. I wanna get out there and recover that gold."

"I did some research on where to buy an R.O.V., and you can't just go pick them up at Costco. There is a research/treasure-hunting ship for sale in *The Mariner* magazine. Let Gary know I emailed him the link. It has everything we'd ever need. An R.O.V. and a suction dredge. I called them to see if we could rent it."

"I'll let Gary know. You know how he feels about renting. I'll keep you posted."

"Okay, Rick, y'all be careful out there. Let us know if you need anything. Possum went into town. I'll let him know you called."

Gary walked into the adjoining room, as if he were a psychic, as soon as Rick hung up.

"Hey, Rick, you wanna buy a ship?"

"How much? I assume you're referring to the one Johnie emailed you?"

"Yep. That one was listed for $2.3 million, but it's already off the market."

"Oh, it's sold, huh?"

"Yep, I bought it."

"You what?! Oh my God. I haven't even seen it."

"You will. It's up near Annapolis. I'm gonna have it delivered to Key West. We may need to hire a captain with a larger tonnage license," said Gary.

"I know a guy named Larry Lane. I met him when I was working as a Tankerman on the Houston Ship Channel. He was first officer on one the Norwegian ships I was discharging. He's from Tennessee and a super funny guy. He invited me up to the captain's dining room for coffee one day after I'd been working on the barge for three straight days. I've stayed in touch with him for years. Last time I talked to him, he was close to retiring. He also has the treasure-hunting bug! I'll text him."

Rick texted Larry as they got in the car with Junior. He got no response, but it wasn't unusual for Larry to take time to get back to him. Rick figured he was either in a honky-tonk in Nashville or underwater somewhere with his metal detector.

Junior let them off at the executive side of the airport and then went to return his rental car. Gary's pilot Clay had already fueled up the jet and it was ready to go. Junior arrived about fifteen minutes later, and they were wheels up shortly after.

As the jet made the approach to Lusaka, everyone including Rick was plastered to the windows looking out at the vast African lands. Junior had gotten his SUV replaced by the insurance company, and it was waiting at an office for him to sign the papers.

Rick and the crew stayed back at the airport and waited for him to pick them up. Gary treated them to admission into the Pearl Lounge inside the airport. It was a swanky waiting area for international travelers with free drinks and snacks. They all had a Munkoyo, a traditional beverage in Zambia. It was a brewed drink made from the Munkoyo root. It was nonalcoholic at first, but the older it was, the more fermented it became, and it could turn into a strong drink. The first ones they had were freshly brewed and tasted like thinned vegetable juice with a mild nutty flavor. The next one was less sweet and packed a punch. The lady in the lounge told them it was best if the drink was brewed two to three days before so it could ferment a little.

Rick's phone pinged. "Junior's waiting for us at the curb," he told the others. "Let's boogie."

Junior had received a substantial amount of money from his father's life insurance policy and for his scorched Toyota. He'd used some of the money to purchase a four-wheel-drive Mercedes Overland truck. It was a massive diesel-powered beast with twin eighty-gallon fuel tanks. They would easily be able to make it all the way to the national park without even slowing down at a fuel station.

"Holy shit! I gotta get one of these!" exclaimed Gary.

"You just bought a ship, dude. Are you crazy?" asked Rick.

"That's what they say! Ha-ha!"

Once inside, Junior gave Rick a file folder on everything he'd been able to find out about the poachers. The leader and an original person of interest was Kelvin Marcus, a ruthless man who had been tried for murder twice and acquitted. He had a long rap sheet for poaching and trespassing crimes. He had been in and out of jail since he was a teenager. His gang was large and he seemed to never be convicted of any major crimes. Rick figured he had to be greasing some inside politicians and local authorities. To Rick, everyone was a suspect, including Junior. After all, he was related to the victim and had received a large life insurance settlement.

Junior's Overland was comfortable and expansive with a full galley and lounge. Rick spread the documents out on the lounge table. Both Gary and Jules took some to look for any possible clues. Rick knew he'd be working closely with Junior over the next few weeks, and rather than delay the inevitable, he just had to get it over with and ask Junior a question. When they stopped at an overlook, Rick waved him aside.

"Junior, as uncomfortable as this is, I have to ask."

Before Rick could continue, Junior piped up and said, "No, Mr. Waters, I didn't have anything to do with my father's death."

"How did you know I was gonna ask that?"

"My favorite TV show is *Dateline*. I'd be concerned if you didn't ask me. I knew I was automatically a suspect. I have the motive and means, but I swear to you, Mr. Waters, I loved my father. He was my hero."

Rick wouldn't rule him out completely, but he had a gut feeling he was telling the truth.

"What can you tell me about Kelvin Marcus?"

"I hate him. He is a bad man. He has threatened my father before. He is extremely dangerous and runs with a ruthless gang. He is the number one suspect in my mind. My father ran into him many times out in the park and reported him for poaching. He has never been convicted, but he has elephant blood on his hands. I know it!"

That moved Kelvin to the top of the list in Rick's mind as well.

They resumed their trip and arrived at Junior's camp just before sunset. His property was about five miles from the southern entrance to the national park. Once they got to his place, Junior showed them inside and handed them all sidearms with holsters.

"Never leave the camp without your weapon. We have big cats nearby. The national park is only five miles north, but I have seen two lionesses here and several leopards. We also get packs of wild dogs. And see that river? Don't even think of swimming in it. It's full of crocs. Other than that, enjoy yourselves," said Junior with a huge laugh.

They all liked Junior from the start. No matter how many times Rick asked him to call him Rick, he continued to call him "Mr. Waters." He also called Jules "Miss Jules" and Gary "Mr. Haas." He was respectful, kind, and pleasant to be around. He had many photos of himself and his father on the walls of the camp. It was apparent he loved his father. Junior's camp was not fancy or opulent. But it was clean and well stocked. He took pride in his place and had a broom in his hand many times.

After the sun went down, they had dinner. Junior prepared a dish called maafe, which was a traditional Zambian stew made from chicken, peanuts, onions, and peppers. It had a similar taste to butter chicken. After dinner, they settled on the expansive front porch and smoked cigarillos that Junior hand-rolled himself. Even on the porch, he insisted that everyone have their sidearm with them.

"Listen, Mr. Waters. Did you hear that?"

"If you insist on calling me 'Mister,' can you call me 'Mr. Rick'?"

"Okay, Mr. Rick, listen."

They all got quiet and heard a sound similar to a house cat purring but way lower.

"That's a leopard. He is close."

"Is it purring?" asked Jules.

"No, big cats can't purr. It's more of a rumble. It is a good sound though. The leopard has a full belly and is content when you hear that sound. If we stay quiet, I can identify any sound you hear. I've been doing it since I was a boy."

"Okay, let me see if I can stump you," said Rick.

They all listened carefully, then Rick chimed in, "Those are crickets, right?" referring to the constant chirping.

"Yes, Mr. Rick. They are armored ground crickets, to be exact. They are good in a stew but have to be cooked for over a day's time to remove the toxins. Otherwise, it will affect your urination. You won't be able to pee."

"Uh, I'll pass."

Then Rick heard a guttural sound, low and deep.

"What's that?"

"That is a big croc. The Kafue River is teeming with them."

They all got quiet again and heard a sound similar to a cow.

"What's that?"

"Water buffalo. What do you think the most dangerous animal is in Africa, Mr. Rick?"

Rick thought for a moment then said, "Oh, I got this. Hippo!"

"Nope, it's the mosquito. They are responsible for more deaths in Africa than any other animal."

"That's cheating! They are insects," said Rick with a laugh.

"So, you don't want this?"

Junior held up a can of spray called Mosi Guard, with the letters OLE on it. He explained it stood for "Oil of Lemon." It was a popular insect repellent that was all natural.

Rick snatched the can and covered himself with it before passing it to Jules. They all played the animal name game as they finished their baby cigars. Gary got the yawns, which were contagious, and soon everyone was yawning. Junior said his goodnights and everyone followed him inside to call it a night.

Rick and Jules cuddled in bed, but they were too tired to do anything else; Jules soon fell asleep. Rick lay awake a while longer, staring at the ceiling, thinking of all the times he'd been close to losing Jules before, like when he went over the waterfall, and when she was carjacked in Mississippi, and when she lost their unborn baby. He was thankful to have her close by his side here in Zambia. The constant singing of the crickets eventually got to him, and he drifted off to sleep.

Around three a.m., Rick was jolted awake to the sound of a gunshot. Jules startled beside him with a gasp. He put his arm across her and murmured, "Stay put." She nodded, wide-eyed in the dark.

He grabbed the .45 Junior had loaned him and ran out into the great room. Gary was already standing by the wide-open front door. They both flanked the door, and Rick peered around it to see outside.

Boom!

Another shot rang out in the darkness. The fire from the gun lit up the night, and Rick could make out Junior firing his gun in the air.

"Junior, you okay?!" yelled Rick.

Junior turned around and strolled back to the lodge nonchalantly as if nothing had happened.

"What happened?" asked Rick.

"Elephants!"

"What?"

"Yeah, elephants were getting too close to the cabin. They will destroy my garden. I love them, but I love my maize more. They took off. You can go back to sleep. I'll show you in the morning."

"Phew! You scared the crap out of me."

"I'm sorry, Mr. Rick. It's just another day in Africa."

Rick returned to the bedroom and let Jules know what had happened.

"Thank goodness," she murmured before letting her eyes close again.

He was so amped up now he doubted he'd be able to fall back asleep. He was right. A sliver of morning sun crept through the curtains, and he heard Junior rustling around in the kitchen. He joined Junior quietly, and Jules never moved.

"Good morning, Junior."

"Morning, Mr. Rick."

"Whatcha makin'?"

"Munali coffee. It's made from a mix of crickets and grasshoppers."

The look on Rick's face was priceless, and Junior burst out laughing and quickly covered his mouth so as not to wake the others. He pulled the coffee bag out of the cabinet and passed it to Rick. It was a brand called Munali, known for its citrus-like acidity and excellent, tightly knit body. Junior continued to laugh quietly as Rick carefully took his first sip.

"Wow, it's exquisite."

"Nothing but the best for the great Rick Waters," said Junior as he patted Rick on the back.

Rick still found it hard to believe that he was somewhat of a celebrity here in Zambia, thanks to the media coverage of the Ava case.

"Your joke gives me an idea." Rick poured a quarter cup of coffee into a new cup and stepped onto the porch, found a dead cricket, and waited.

The smell of the delectable coffee wafted through the cabin and soon woke up the slumbering Jules. She joined the boys in the kitchen.

"Coffee, Jules?" asked Rick as he bit his lip, trying not to laugh.

He took the coffee cup he had placed a cricket in, pretended to take a sip, then passed it to Jules.

"It's cricket and grasshopper coffee. Try it."

Jules stood there incredulously, staring at Rick, then looked down into the coffee cup and made a repugnant face. Rick couldn't hold it in anymore and cracked up. Jules shot him an ugly look. She didn't buy it for one second. She was used to Rick messing with her.

"Let's get Gary," said Jules.

Rick's eyes lit up and he gave her a thumbs-up. A couple of minutes later, Gary stumbled into the kitchen, yawning with his hand over his mouth.

"Gary, try this. It's cricket and grasshopper coffee," said Jules as she gave Rick a side glance.

Gary took the cup from her hand, downed it, and started to chew on the cricket.

"Eewwww!" said the group at the same time.

"What? I've been to Thailand," said Gary.

"You gonna fit right in here, Mr. Gary," exclaimed Junior.

Rick winced and quickly poured Gary a fresh cup.

"Here, drink this. It's the real coffee," said Rick.

Gary took a sip. Thought for a second, then said, "I think I like the other one better. Tastes nuttier."

"You're sick!" responded Jules.

CHAPTER TWO

After breakfast, Junior pulled out a large map of the Kafue National Park and placed it on the table while Gary did the dishes. As Rick and Jules stood looking at the map, Junior circled some areas that he wanted to emphasize.

"This is the area where the elephants cross over from the park into public land. It's not illegal to kill an elephant in self-defense and they can be hunted, but only a small number of permits are given out each year. Most of the poaching happens in this area, and even into the boundary of the park. My father was killed here!"

Junior pointed to an area where two roads came together near the park's edge. Rick could see the look in Junior's eyes as he spoke of his father. Initially, it looked like sadness, then it transformed into anger and then into a mixture of the two.

"Come, let me show you."

They put on their hiking gear and sidearms and climbed into Junior's Overland. He drove slowly north on a road adjacent to the Kafue River, and eventually stopped where the dusty dirt road intersected with territorial road M9 by the Hook Bridge. Rick climbed out, did a quick scan of the area where Junior's father was shot, then grabbed a pair of binoculars and looked out over the bridge.

"I'm sorry to ask this, but can you show me the position your father was found in and the direction of the shot?" asked Rick.

Junior walked a few feet away and explained how his father's truck was parked. He lay on the ground in the same position as the crime photos. It put it into a better perspective for Rick. It appeared that the bullet came from across the bridge, from somewhere inside of the park. Rick zoomed in across the bridge and spotted a small building.

"What is that building over there?" Rick pointed at it.

Junior hopped up and dusted off his pants and shirt. "That is the police control point. It's the entrance into the park. It's rarely manned."

"Can we go across the bridge?"

"Of course. The local police found a casing from a 30-06 by the building, and the theory is that it came from the murder weapon. It matched the ballistics of the bullet taken from my dad's back. They don't think it was anyone from law enforcement as the standard issue rifle for the police is an AK-47. The problem is that the 30-06 is by far the most popular rifle in Africa. It's like finding a needle in a haystack. Find that rifle and find the killer."

They all climbed back in, and Junior idled across the small bridge. Along the banks of the river lay several large crocodiles basking in the sun. Suddenly, a small green-bodied, yellow-bellied parrot landed on the hood of Junior's Overland.

"Ooh look, a parrot!" exclaimed Jules.

"That is Mumguay. He is a Senegal parrot. He is very far from home," said Junior.

"Where is Senegal?" asked Rick.

"It's on the west coast of Africa over five thousand kilometers from here."

"What's he doing here?" asked Jules.

"I think he was someone's pet and escaped. He is very friendly. I have been seeing him here since I was a teenager. Come, Mumguay, come," said Junior.

"How do you know his name?"

"You'll see."

The little parrot hopped clumsily across the hood of Junior's Overland then used his beak to climb onto the side mirror beside Junior.

"Phwwwwwhhht Phwoooooh," squawked Mumguay as Jules leaned over for a better look.

"He thinks you're pretty, Miss Jules."

Mumguay turned his head sideways then said, "Mumguay want peanut."

Junior opened his backpack, pulled out a peanut in the shell, and handed it to the bird. Mumguay held it up with his right foot and devoured it. After a few peanuts and phrases, he flew off and disappeared into the bush. A pang of sadness hit Rick's chest. He missed Chief. Chief was an umbrella cockatoo Rick had rescued from a guy in Orlando who was moving overseas for work. Chief was currently in the care of Possum, back in Key West.

Junior's eyes flashed across the bridge as he put the Overland in gear and continued the journey. As usual, no police were at their post where they should be. Once across the bridge, Junior turned left on a dirt road beside the river-bank and headed south. He followed the winding river to a spot with an overlook. Everyone climbed out, and Junior took out a spotting scope and secured it to a tripod. He looked through it, made a few adjustments, and had Rick look through it.

What Rick saw turned his stomach. He counted in his head at least fifteen rotting carcasses of elephants. None had tusks, and it was obvious they were removed with an axe. They all took turns looking through the scope. Jules teared up, quickly looked away, and turned her gaze to the ground. The sight of the mutilated elephants affected everyone.

"That is why my father is dead!" exclaimed Junior.

"We'll get them, Junior. I promise. One way or another, they will take responsibility for what they have done to your father and those poor elephants as well," said Rick.

Rick felt nauseous at the sight of the elephant slaughter grounds. It made him angry and disgusted at the human race. He had never spent much time around elephants but knew they were family oriented and had strong memories. There was just no excuse for such violence toward such beautiful animals. He was more determined than ever to solve the case and make the scumbags pay. As much as he didn't want to, he knew he had to get a closer look and try to find a clue. Hopefully a spent bullet casing or other evidence he could use to track down the guilty.

"Can we go down there?"

"Yes, Mr. Rick. Let's all get back in the truck."

Junior slowly drove them down the hill in four-wheel drive and parked a few yards away from the carnage. The smell was overwhelming; Junior passed out some handkerchiefs so everyone could cover their mouths. The sight of the tragic deaths was too much for Jules, and she quickly returned to the Overland. Rick and Gary searched the ground for shell casings and came up with nothing. Rick noticed a large hole in the skull of several elephants.

"What kind of gun would cause this entry wound?" he asked.

"Probably a Nitro," replied Junior.

"A Nitro?"

"Yes, Mr. Rick. A .577 Nitro Express, commonly known as an elephant gun. They are popular with the poachers. It's a single bore rifle with a bullet this big."

He held out his hands in front of his chest about five inches apart, indicating the size of the bullet.

"The most popular one is made by Westley Richards from the UK. They cost around 60,000 pounds," he continued.

"Poachers can afford that?"

"There is big money in ivory, but last year several of the rifles disappeared from the evidence locker in Lusaka. They were scheduled to be destroyed, but someone on the inside took them."

"Man, I hate to do this. Can I borrow a big knife, Junior?"

He jogged over to the Overland, opened a side hatch, and pulled out a tool kit. Rick tied the handkerchief around his face and used a large screwdriver and hunting knife. He dug around the exit wound, trying to find the bullet. He gagged several times as he poked and prodded in the elephant's brain. He felt something and switched over to a long pair of needle-nose pliers. After several failed attempts that reminded him of the board game *Operation*, he slowly pulled out the projectile.

He grabbed a shop rag from the toolbox and wiped it clean. He could see the telltale markings left by the rifle. That would be the key to finding out who'd shot the elephant.

"I can't believe the local authorities didn't get this. It's detective 101," said Rick.

"Why should they? They already know who killed it. They got paid to keep quiet," responded Junior.

"Well, there's not enough money in the world to shut me up!" exclaimed Rick.

He dug through several more elephant skulls and found two more bullets matching the ones he had already discovered. He would need to do a forensic ballistic test on the bullets. It was clear even with the naked eye that these bullets came from the same gun. The trick would be to find that gun. It would have to be owned by a poacher—no true hunter would have done such a terrible thing to an innocent animal.

After returning to Junior's Overland, the group drove north toward Junior's dad's camp. His dad used to run photo safaris when he wasn't fighting poachers. The poachers had ransacked the camp after his death, looking for any information that might lead them to the tusks his dad had stolen from them to return to the government. Taking them off the black market was the best way to crush the poachers.

"I just realized I never asked you what you do for a living, Junior," said Rick.

"I was following in my father's footsteps and creating another photo safari company in the east end of the park. It was just getting off the ground when my father was shot. So, first I must pivot. I want to restore my father's legacy and help the animals. I know the poachers won't be happy if they find out what I'm doing, but I don't care."

It was clear he was on a mission, determined to help the animals and protect the wildlife and solve his father's murder.

When they arrived at his father's camp, police tape was still up around the property. The case had gone cold and the SAPS had walked away from further investigation. To be safe, they all donned latex gloves and booties from Rick's crime tools bag. The place looked like it had been hit by a tornado. All the furniture was turned over and drawers were pulled out and on the floor. After an hour of searching, it was apparent the police had either found what they were looking for or there was nothing to be found. Junior made a call to the SAPS and asked them if it was okay for him to return to the property and clean it up. They agreed and told him they had just forgotten to remove the crime scene tape. It would be better for them to stay in the camp overnight than make their way back to Junior's place, since it would be dark soon.

Jules took the liberty of picking up the shards of broken glass and utensils scattered all over the kitchen floor. Rick and Gary put all the furniture upright and the drawers back in place, while Junior bagged up all the old linens. There was running water and electricity in the camp, but no washing machine or dryer. He bagged his dirty laundry for a cleaning service he used, and made all the beds with extra linens from the closet.

After a couple hours of diligent work, the place was again livable. Fortunately, all the game wrapped and dated in the chest freezer was still good. It was easy to tell that it hadn't been left open, because there was no sign of melted and refrozen water. There were also lots of cans of beans and other vegetables that were dented from being tossed around but still intact. Junior took out some ostrich filets and fufu, a local starch that could be frozen, thawed, and panfried. Using that along with some canned string beans, he put together a quick comfort food dinner.

Jules passed around a photo album she'd found in Junior's dad's bedroom, which contained many photographs of wildlife. She commented on one photograph in particular—a picture of a huge lion yawning near a watering hole.

"That was one of my father's favorite lions," Junior said, grinning. "He got close to it more than any other male lion. He always carried two things with him when he went into the bush: a Canon with a long lens and a rifle for protection. He never once had to fire his rifle and kill an animal. The closest he ever came was firing in the air once to stop a charging elephant."

"I know you miss him. He seems like he was a great man," said Jules.

"Thank you, Miss Jules," replied Junior.

"Please just call me Jules."

"Okay, okay, I will try."

They all enjoyed dinner and a few local African wines. After dinner, they sat around the table to make a list of all the potential suspects.

The list included both locals and visitors who had been seen in the area recently. Each suspect would be investigated thoroughly, and some of them would have alibis that checked out. The SAPS had hardly looked for evidence and quickly closed the case. Rick was certain that one of the poachers had committed the crime and would be brought to justice.

Junior told them that the local community had been shaken by the events. The local government had claimed they would increase security measures in the area and had held a town meeting to discuss the importance of safety. Everyone in the small town was reminded of the importance of coming together in times of crisis and how, together, they could prevent similar tragedies in the future. In the end, it was nothing more than a PR stunt by local government. Within days, it was back to business as usual for the poachers.

They were all yawning in unison and decided it was time for bed. It had been a long day.

The next morning, they woke up early, ready to get up and at it. They decided to venture out and explore the African landscape. Everywhere they went, they were greeted by locals and quickly learned about the history of the area. Rick was in awe of the beauty of the region and was inspired to learn more. One thing he learned for sure was that the African people were proud of their homeland. The day's excursion gave him and his companions a sense of wonder and appreciation for the people and the culture and animals they encountered.

Once they were back at the camp, Rick called Possum to check on the progress of the repairs on *Nine-Tenths*.

"Hey, Possum, how's it going?"

"Good, Rick. The major fiberglass repairs are all done and the new gelcoat is on. I was just about to email you a sketch I made of a wrap that may work. It has the name on the side with Chief in that photo you took when we landed that big marlin with Carson. I will have it cartoonized if you approve it. I'm actually kinda getting bored here in Key West. I can only do the *Duval Crawl* so many times."

"I know, buddy. I wish you were here with us, especially with your good camera kit. I think I've seen every type of animal in Africa," replied Rick. "Hey, I'm gonna put you on speaker so you can speak to everyone."

"Okay, cool. Hello, y'all. Possum here."

"Hi, Possum," said Jules.

"Hello, Mr. Possum. My name is Junior."

"Mr. Possum?"

"Sorry, I mean Possum," replied Junior.

"Is Gary there?" asked Possum.

"Hey, Possum, yeah I'm here."

"Listen, I got a call from Captain Larry Lane as well as the marina in Annapolis. There's some paperwork you need to sign to get this ship delivered. How do you want to do it? I think we can do some of it online. I'll find out," said Possum.

"I have an idea. I think I'll fly back and take care of the paperwork, then you can come back with me in the jet. I can make sure the ship is taken care of and swing by Destin and make sure we don't have a ten-foot pile of letters at the office. You okay with that, Rick?"

"Whatever y'all decide is fine by me. I actually could use your amazing research skills here, Possum. Plus, you can bring your cameras." Johnie could take over looking after Chief for Possum.

"Okay, it's settled. I'll call Clay and get the jet ready."

"Listen, instead of me taking your new jet back, why don't I just fly commercial? I have a ton of miles that are about to expire. Just tell me the airport code and I'll book it."

"It's Lusaka. The airport code is LUN. What airline are your miles on?" asked Gary.

"American."

"Hold on."

A minute went by as Gary looked up flights on his phone.

"They have a flight right out of Key West with a stop in Miami and Doha, Qatar."

"All right, I'm on it. I'll text you my itinerary soon, Rick. I'm excited! See y'all soon."

"Bye, Possum," said everyone in unison.

Junior decided it was a good time to head back to his camp in the south. He locked up his dad's camp and put the police tape back, hoping it would keep anyone away that had looting on their mind.

Once back at Junior's base camp, they decided to head to Lusaka and rent some rooms near the airport until Gary left. The next day, they would head to the east side of the park in search of a few of the people the police had already interviewed. None were connected to the poachers but knew them.

CHAPTER THREE

Junior dropped Rick and the gang off at the airport hotel. He said he'd meet them the next day. His plan was to take the Overland into a friend's shop and get some custom work done on it.

Rick and Jules settled into their room and planned a little going away dinner for Gary. Junior had suggested an Indian food place close to the airport called The Royal Dil. They all met in the lobby at 6:40 and hopped in a taxi. They decided to go family style and all ordered different dishes. Gary invited his pilot Clay to join them.

"Whatchu drinkin, Clay?"

"I'll start with a double Long Island iced tea and a couple shots of Jaeger," said Clay with a wink.

"Ha-ha, nice try."

It was obvious Clay was just messing around. He knew he had to fly in the morning, and the strongest thing he'd be drinking would be a club soda.

The waiter brought the gang a few rounds of a local beer called Chibuku, a fermented beer made from sorghum. It was a unique experience for everyone, as the beer was served in a calabash, a traditional African gourd. The taste of the beer was different from anything they had tried before, with a hint of citrus and a slightly sour finish. As they sipped their drinks, they began discussing the differences between the traditional beer and the more generic beers they were used to. Everyone agreed that the Chibuku was a more flavorful beer, and the conversation soon turned to plans for the next day's interviews of locals connected to the case.

Rick pulled out his wallet and was getting ready to pay the bill when he heard a ruckus coming from a few tables over. Suddenly, there were gunshots. Three masked men were yelling at the customers. Rick stiffened. He and everyone else hurried to get on the ground with their hands behind their heads. *Dammit, I should've brought a gun*, he thought.

"What are we gonna do, Rick?" whispered Gary.

"I don't know. I'm not holding."

"Me neither."

Jules was shaking beside Rick as tears welled up in her eyes. She sat up on her knees, and Rick waved her to get back down.

"Get on the ground now!" yelled one of the men toward Jules.

"Jules, do what they say," insisted Rick.

"Not today!"

The look in Jules's eyes was unlike any he'd ever seen before. She was trembling and a tear rolled down her cheek, but she had a fierce stare. The man with the shotgun started moving toward her and yelling for her to get down. The other two were rifling through the pockets of the customers near the entrance, snatching gold chains and jewelry from women's necks, and kicking the men in the sides and taking their wallets.

As the man got closer, Rick begged Jules to get down. She was in a zone, as if she couldn't even hear him.

The man got directly in front of Jules and screamed for her to drop. He pulled back the shotgun and was about to slam the stock into Jules's face. As he pulled back, she flung her arms forward, revealing the handgun Junior had given her back at his camp. She pulled the trigger, hitting the man directly in the chest. His body reeled backward almost in slow motion, and he dropped the shotgun.

Rick rolled over, grabbed the shotgun, and fired toward the other two men, hitting one in the arm. His arm fell to the ground with the pistol still in his hand. The other man turned to run, and Jules unloaded her automatic, hitting him several times in the back. He fell face forward over a table, and it crashed to the ground.

Rick knew it would be a matter of minutes until the police showed up. He picked up both shell casings from Jules's automatic pistol, the spent shotgun shells, and his credit card from the guest check holder, scanned the room for surveillance cameras, then ripped Gary up from the floor and grabbed Jules's hand. Clay jumped up and followed them, and they were out the door before any other customers even got up from the floor.

They ran down the street and into an alley. Rick wiped the handgun clean and ditched it in a storm drain. Jules was hyperventilating.

"Calm down, baby. Breathe. In, one, two, three, four, now out, one, two, three, four."

They could hear sirens coming from several directions. Rick peered around the corner, and they ran across the street and into a bar called Chicago's Reloaded. They sat at the corner of the bar with Jules in the middle in front of a big-screen TV. Rick waved a bartender over.

"Hey, buddy, we'll have three pints of Mosi Lager and a club soda."

Rick squeezed Jules's hand and whispered, "It'll be all right." He was in shock himself at what she had done. He didn't even know she'd brought the gun with her. A long line of police cars flew past the bar.

"What's going on?" Rick asked the bartender.

"I'm not sure."

He changed the soccer game on TV to the local news channel. Within a few minutes, a breaking news bulletin scrolled across the bottom of the screen. The anchors switched to a reporter on the ground. A young woman with a microphone stood in front of a CBS News van directly in front of The Royal Dil and began to speak. The bartender turned the TV up.

"Good evening, I'm Michelle Agani reporting live for CBS News. Two masked men were killed tonight and one was severely wounded at a popular restaurant, The Royal Dil. Reports say a woman who was eating at the restaurant just started firing at the men who were wielding weapons. They are believed to be the same men who have shot up several other restaurants over the past three months. I'm with restaurant owner Rashi Khatri. Rashi, can you tell me what happened?"

"It happened so fast I didn't see much. A tan, dark-haired woman and three men ran out as soon as the shooting happened. She is a hero!"

Several locals in the background began cheering when he called Jules a hero. The camera panned over to them and two men in the corner of the screen jumping up and down with their fists in the air.

"We are going to SAPS Sergeant Julius Bertone now. Sergeant, can you add anything?" asked the reporter.

"This obviously just happened and will be an ongoing investigation, so I can't comment too much now. Once we identify the gunmen, we'll have more for you. We have identified a tattoo on one of the men, and it matches a tattoo caught on a camera in another restaurant robbery. We would like to question the woman involved in tonight's shooting. If anyone knows who she is or can identify her, please contact the tips hotline."

"For CBS News, I'm Michelle Agani. Back to you, Zamandi."

Rick looked over at Jules and whispered in her ear, "I think you need to go with Gary, baby. I can hold down the fort here. Possum will be here in a little over a day. It's too dangerous for you here now."

"I don't wanna go, Rick. I wanna be with you."

"I know, Jules, but we already know some of the cops here are corrupt. You can go back to Destin and run the main office. Do some bond retrieval jobs or help Gary with the new ship. I just think it's best if you aren't here after what happened. I must say, I was blown away by how you handled yourself. I was beyond impressed. Please just go with Gary, okay? You can kiss Chief for me. We can Face-time as much as you want."

Jules bit her lip, then sighed. "Okay, I'll go, but you better come back to Florida soon. Don't get your ass in trouble here!"

"Yes, ma'am," replied Rick as he kissed her on the forehead. He turned to Gary's pilot. "How soon can you fly, Clay?"

"I'm not gonna lie, I'm a little shaken up, but I think we can be wheels up in about forty-five minutes."

"Okay, y'all go ahead. I'll settle the tab. I love you, Jules. See you soon."

"I love you too, Rick. Please be careful."

Jules wrapped her arms around Rick and almost squeezed the breath out of him.

"You want me to stay, Rick?" asked Gary.

"No, just take care of Jules. I'm counting on you, buddy."

"You know I will!"

Clay stepped outside and flagged down a taxi. Rick gave Jules a long, loving kiss and walked her to the door. He shook Gary's hand and patted him on the shoulder, turned around, and sat back down at the bar. His mind jumped to Junior. He would have to tell him what had happened, take a leap of faith, and pray he would keep quiet. It was his handgun Jules had used. Besides, he already knew they'd been dining at that Indian restaurant since he'd recommended it.

Rick's phone began to vibrate. It was Junior. *Is he psychic?*

"Are you okay, Rick? I saw the news. What happened?"

"I can't talk now. Can you pick me up at Chicago's Reloaded?"

"Yeah, I'll be there in fifteen minutes. I'm driving my little red Nissan pickup. My Overland will be ready tomorrow."

Rick ordered another beer and paid the tab in cash. As soon as he took his last sip, Junior pulled up to the curb. Rick hopped in, and Junior drove toward the airport hotel.

"What happened, Mr. Rick? Where's Miss Jules?"

"I have to be honest with you, Junior. Jules and Gary are gone. We had just finished dinner and I was about to pay when three guys busted in and started yelling and fired a shot in the air. Little did I know, Jules brought the pistol you gave her to the restaurant. A few months back, she was carjacked in Mississippi. Something changed in her. She took self-defense lessons, got her concealed carry permit, and started working part time as a bounty hunter. The look in her eyes when those guys were yelling kinda freaked me out. She was in a zone and went into action. She shot a guy who was about to cold cock her with the butt of his shotgun. It all just spiraled out of control after that. I ditched the gun. I guess I owe you a new .45."

"Don't worry about it, Rick. None of those guns were registered to me or my dad. We got them at a gun show in Ndola. You got her prints off?"

"One hundred percent. Plus, good luck finding it. It'll be a rusty antique by the time it's found."

"What's the plan now?" asked Junior.

"I lie low for a couple days and wait for Possum. I'd like to interview a few of the people the police already questioned, and some I will do by phone. When will your Overland be finished?"

"Tomorrow afternoon at the latest."

"Okay, just drop me at the hotel and we can rendezvous then. I need to talk to someone in the poachers' group.

Either someone who dislikes the guy running it or someone who isn't part of it anymore. Can you get me a name?"

"I'll work on that. I think I know someone I can talk to for that info. The only problem is, he's in jail right now. He took the rap for Kelvin for an illegal albino rhino killing. The only person he'll talk to is a lawyer."

"That gives me an idea. See you tomorrow."

Junior dropped off Rick at the back of the hotel and left. Rick got to his room and turned on the TV. The news was still reporting on the chaos at the restaurant; they mentioned men who were with the woman who fired the shot. The police still had no idea who they were and without surveillance cameras, they never would. He kicked off his shoes and saw he'd missed a text from Jules en route to the hotel.

> *Rick, we are taking off now. Please be careful I love you, Jules.*

> *XXOO*

He texted her back, knowing she'd see it the next day when they landed.

> *I'm safe, Jules. In hotel. I love you too. Talk soon.*

> *Rick.*

He washed his face and sat on the edge of the bed watching the news. The rush of everything began to wear off and he realized he was completely exhausted. He lay down on the bed and the next thing he knew, it was 8:30 a.m. He hadn't slept that hard in a long time. He'd missed another text from Jules.

> *Rick, we are refueling. All is well. I'll call you from Florida.*

Rick lay back down and dozed off again for an hour. He was awakened by room service. He politely asked them to come back later. He brushed his teeth and there was a knock at the door.

Dammit, I told her to come back later!

Rick opened the door, and standing in front of him were two SAPS officers.

"Mr. Rick Waters?"

"Yes, what can I do for you?"

"You need to come with us. We have some questions. Where is Miss Juliana Castro?"

"She left, won't be back. Can I at least put my damn pants on?"

"Go ahead."

The officers followed Rick into his room with their weapons drawn. Two more officers had opened Gary's adjoining room with the help of the front desk manager.

"Am I getting some kind of award or something?" asked Rick sarcastically.

The officer didn't respond. He was all business and never cracked a smile.

"May I text someone before we leave? I might need bail money."

The meanest-looking one just nodded.

> Possum, heading to jail. You are now playing a lawyer. Don't ask, just bring cash. Time to put your acting hat on again. Call Junior. 011-260-21 555 6465

Rick hit "send," then deleted the message on his side of the phone. He knew Possum would be smart enough to not text back, since the cops would likely take Rick's phone.

They escorted him to the station for questioning in silence. The smell of the inside of the police car reminded Rick of a time he was arrested for impersonating an idiot. Back in college, he was taken in for public intoxication and running his mouth. It wasn't the first, second, or fifth time he'd been in the back of a squad car, but now he knew how to play the game.

At the station, they put him in a room with three chairs and a small metal table. The room was ice cold and he was only wearing a thin t-shirt and jeans. He glanced up at the camera in the corner of the room's ceiling and then gave a polite nod. After about an hour, two detectives entered the room.

"Mr. Rick Waters. I am Detective Boyd Abara and this is Sergeant Damien Tersoo. We'd like to ask you some questions about a shooting that occurred at The Royal Dil last night. We know you were there. You were identified by one of the patrons who recognized you from being on TV for solving the Ava Giovanni murder. I know you think you are some sort of big shot crime detective, but you are in our country now. Two men are dead and one is in critical condition and missing his right arm. They were unable to save it at the hospital."

Rick started laughing and holding his stomach.

"What's so funny, Mr. Waters?"

"This is almost too much. Let me guess, you are the good cop, and your husky friend is the bad cop? Plus, I just had a vision of a guy missing his arm and wondered if he'd take on the moniker Lefty."

"This is a very serious matter, Mr. Waters. I need you to focus and answer our questions. Were you at The Royal Dil last night? We believe you were, as was a woman named…" He flipped through his notes, trying to be professional "… Juliana Castro. We also need to speak with her as well."

Rick put his hand to his chin, pretending to be in deep thought.

"Okay, okay."

He pointed at the husky sergeant.

"Get your notepad out. What I'm about to tell you is of the utmost importance, and you'll want to make sure you get what I say down on paper."

Rick could see the excitement in his eyes as he fumbled for his notepad and pen. They both sat down and put their notepads on the table.

"Okay, you ready?"

They picked up their pens in great anticipation, hanging on every word. Rick rubbed his hands together and paused as if he wanted to make sure he shared the information in the right way. The tick of the clock sitting behind Rick seemed to grow in volume as they held their breath and waited for him to speak. Then he said it.

"Lawyer."

They both dropped their pens in disgust and shook their heads. The interview was over. Rick knew they had nothing and couldn't legally hold him. They might try and pull some stunt or trumped-up charge, but he was prepared to stay if they did. They left the room and slammed the door behind them.

The clock told Rick that Possum would be landing soon. All he had to do was wait. He was actually giddy with excitement to see what outfit and persona Possum would show up as. Possum was a natural-born actor and could have done it for a living, if he hadn't become a professor.

Seconds turned into minutes and minutes into hours as he waited in the cold room. He wasn't officially under arrest and knew he could leave, but they were not returning, no doubt because they hoped he'd eventually get so cold he'd start talking. They also had to arrange for a court-appointed lawyer for Rick, not knowing Possum would be his decoy lawyer shortly. After three hours of waiting, the door finally opened.

"Mr. Waters, your lawyer is here."

Possum strolled in with a grin on his face that could only be described as a possum-eating grin. In what was the most exaggerated Cockney accent, Possum spoke.

"Well, hello, Rickster. You've gotten yourself in another Barney?"

"Barney?"

"Rubble...trouble! Mate."

> Oh my God, he's stealing
> lines from Ocean's Eleven.

"Let's see if we can't loosen up this pokey. Scuze me, mate, what's me client charged wif?" asked Possum to the detective.

"Nothing yet, we need to ask him a few questions."

"Right! That's just rats and mice. I guess me client is as good as an oily rag and we'll be short of a sheet and yet to be."

"Huh?" asked the confused detective.

"We're leaving, mate. Don't you speak English?!"

The detective shook his head and gave Rick and Possum the stank eye, then stepped aside and held the door open. It took everything in Rick's power not to burst out laughing at Possum's performance.

CHAPTER FOUR

"Did you copy that accent from *Ocean's Eleven*?" asked Rick with a laugh.

"Not bad, huh?"

"I'm out, so I guess it worked. I doubt you'll be receiving an Oscar, but you have my vote," said Rick.

As they walked out of the station, Junior pulled up to the curb in the Overland.

"Hey, jailbird, good to see you," said Junior with a chuckle.

"So, what's the plan?" asked Rick.

"I got a call from a guy in the park. He says he knows something about my father's murder but he only wants to talk to you, Rick. The *famous detective Rick Waters*," said Junior.

"Where is he?" asked Rick.

"He lives in Ndola, a suburb of Zambia. We're going there now. It's about a five and a half hour drive due north. Just kick back and relax. Possum and I will get you there.

Oh, he told me how he got his name," said Junior as he cranked up "The Race Is On" by George Jones.

Rick climbed in the back of the Overland and stretched out. He texted Jules but she didn't respond. He grabbed a Wild Dog IPA from the fridge. It was one of the most popular local craft beers made in Zambia.

"This beer has a hint of biscuit flour-dusted mango and orange citrus, and some crème brulee-caramelized, malty sweetness. The bitterness, which bodes more toward a double IPA, IMO, sticks with you the whole way. Finish is just a bit spicy hot with alcohol, sweet, and bitter on the sides of my tongue," said Rick with a grin.

Possum and Junior looked back at Rick in bewilderment.

"Haha, I was just reading the description on the can," said Rick.

Junior had stocked the fridge with several different local beers for them all to try. Rick popped a top and kicked up his feet. He was glad to be out of jail and stoked to be back on the case.

The ride was bumpy and long, and by the time they arrived, it was late, so they pulled off to the road into a rest area to grab some shut-eye. Rick peeked out of the window and could see the reflection of the moon on a slow-running river next to the road.

"Don't get any ideas tonight, Rick, of peeing beside the Overland. That river is full of crocs and other beasts. Just use the head," said Junior.

"Got it!" Rick saluted Junior.

The mattresses Junior had installed in each of the bunks were all closed cell foam, soft, yet firm enough to not cause a backache. Each bunk had its own curtain for privacy, a vent, and a small TV with a DVD player. On the roof was a Starlink in-motion satellite internet flat-dish with Fubo TV. Rick put on some *Forensic Files* and before he knew it, he had fallen asleep.

The smell of fresh coffee woke Rick up. As usual, Possum was the first one up and had started breakfast with Junior's blessing. He was making his famous biscuits and gravy, but he had to go with what Junior had in the fridge. He used bush pig sausage and goat milk for the gravy. The biscuits were made from Ghanaian gari, which was a type of biscuit made from fermented cassava. They tasted different and were super rich but definitely hit bottom.

"Rick, I picked up some things while you were in jail that may come in handy," said Junior as he plopped a large black duffel bag on the table.

He unzipped it and pulled out an automatic 12-gauge assault rifle. Rick dug through the bag and started laying the weapons on the table: four matching Vektor CP1 9-millimeter handguns, and five boxes of ammo. Plus, three night-vision goggles. There was an assortment of other 9mms, including two Berettas and a Springfield XD-M Elite. Rick chose the Springfield, one of his favorite gun manufacturers. He looked closely at it and saw the serial number had been filed off. All the guns had their serial number removed.

"Where'd you get these, Junior?" asked Possum.

"Black market in Lusaka. You can get anything there. I saw lots of ivory. The local police just looked the other way. It makes me so angry. They either don't care or are getting paid off. It truly makes me sick!" replied Junior.

"I'm glad you got these. We hopefully won't need them, but they could also make the difference in life or death," said Rick.

Rick's phone whistled. It was Jules.

> Hi Rick, we made it to Key West.

> That's great, baby. Your little jailbird is out.

> What?!

> Oh, I'll explain later. It's kinda funny actually.

> Okay, Rick. Johnie and Gary are taking me to the new ship in the morning. It's supposed to be in port tomorrow. Gary just got off the phone with Captain Lane.

> That's great, baby. Send me some pics.

> *I will. I love you.*

> *Love you too.*

Suddenly, the entire Overland shook, and Rick nearly fell out of his chair.

Boom!

It shook again and knocked over two coffee cups.

"What the fuck?!" yelled Possum.

"It's a hippo. Look!" shouted Junior.

A huge female hippo was ramming into the side of the Overland. Two of her babies were hiding behind her. Junior ran to the cab and fired up the Overland. The tires barked as he threw it into gear and floored it in reverse. The hippo was coming fast. He whipped the steering wheel hard left and punched it. The hippo just glanced the rear edge of the overland cracking one of the turn signals.

"Damn hippos!" exclaimed Junior.

"I'm so glad I took your advice and didn't pee outside," said Rick.

"Yeah, we have some serious critters here. You just have to keep your head on a swivel."

"I heard that!"

They drove down the road a few miles then pulled over to check the damage to the Overland. Junior had installed extra-thick stainless steel rocker panels on the bottom third of the Overland, and the only damage they could find was the cracked turn signal. Junior applied some red translucent tape to it until he could get a replacement.

They arrived in Ndola just before lunch. Junior called the guy who wanted to talk to them. He gave Junior directions to a camp just outside of Demalisques de Leshwe's west entrance. The camp was primitive and set up in a small clearing surrounded by sickle leafed Albizia trees. The bright pink flowers on the silk trees were stunning. As they slowly pulled up to the camp, Rick instructed Junior to turn around and face the Overland toward the exit just in case. He didn't like the way the area looked and was afraid of an ambush. Something just didn't feel right to him.

"How do you know this guy, Junior?" asked Rick.

"I don't, but I know he tipped off my dad a few times about poachers."

"Okay, you need to walk out first and meet him. We will flank both sides of the Overland to be safe. Take a gun with you. Actually, take two."

Rick handed Junior two of the CP1 9-millimeters and two extra magazines. Rick went to the front of the Overland, while Possum took the passenger's side rear. Junior shook hands with the man as Rick watched his body language carefully. They began to talk and were just out of earshot. Rick noticed him look over Junior's left shoulder toward the trees on the edge of the clearing. Rick grabbed the spotting scope and scanned the area. He saw a bush move and then a reflection of something shiny from the sun. As he zoomed in, he saw it: a scope.

"Get down, Junior!" yelled Rick.

Junior hit the ground just as the man he was talking to ran back into the camp. The ground around Junior exploded as bullets hit all around him. Rick couldn't hear the shots.

"Sniper!"

Junior crawled back to the Overland and hid behind the driver's side door. Both Rick and Possum ran around to the driver's side. Bullets ricocheted off the Overland; one shattered the window. There only seemed to be one shooter. Rick pinpointed his hiding spot, but he was too far away to hit with a handgun. The bullets kept flying.

A bullet whizzed by Rick's ear and hit the hood. It was coming from behind him. He dove to the ground and opened fire toward the camp. The man inside was firing back at him. Junior had crouched down by the front tire and unloaded both guns as fast as he could. One hit the man in the chest, and he fell forward face down on the porch. Junior sprinted toward the camp, dove inside, and slammed the door. Bullets riddled the wooden door.

"On three, cover me!" yelled Rick. "One, two, three!"

Having reloaded both of his pistols, Junior began to fire toward the shooter hiding in the bush. Rick ran in a zigzag to the entrance of the clearing and hid behind a rock. Possum reloaded and waited for Rick's signal. Rick waved at Possum, and he emptied his handgun, then the 12-gauge, toward the sniper. Rick ran around the back of him and suddenly the shooting stopped. Rick stood up.

"I got him!"

Rick grabbed the man and pulled his limp body into the clearing. He scanned the entire area and saw it was clear.

"Who is he?" asked Rick as Junior and Possum jogged up.

Junior dug into the guy's front pocket and pulled out a pack of menthol cigarettes, then went into his back pocket and found his wallet. When he opened it up, he dropped it in shock.

Captain Joshua Apera – SAPS (STF)

"He's a cop!" exclaimed Junior.

"Not just a cop; he's STF, special task force, the equivalent of our S.W.A.T. units stateside," replied Rick.

"We need to get rid of the bodies. Killing a cop, even a dirty cop, won't go well for us," said Junior.

"Where?"

"The Luapula River. It's a couple hours north if we cut through the park."

Together they wrapped the bodies in tarps and tied them to the roof. It was no easy task but the only way they could do it without getting caught. Rick removed all the weapons and IDs and placed them in a sack. He and Possum went inside the camp to look for any clues. He found a cell phone and put it in his pocket. He climbed up to the roof, used the dead informant's fingerprint to open the phone, then changed the password. Now he had access to the phone and all calls and texts.

Rick climbed back down from the roof and found Junior using a brush with some bleach and water to clean the blood off the porch of the camp. He then apparently changed his mind and decided to burn it down. He poured some fuel on the couch and dropped a match. The flames hit the ceiling and as they pulled out of the entrance, the entire camp was engulfed in flames.

Rick scrolled though the phone and saw the last text was from a number in Lusaka with directions to the camp. As he was reading it, the phone pinged and another text came in.

Is it done?

Rick didn't know what to text back. He thought for a minute, then began to type.

They didn't show. I'm aborting. Coming in.

That would give them some time, anyway.
The phone pinged again.

Meet me at the nest.

Which nest?

Stop playing, you know what nest!

Rick opened the Google Maps app and saw the last search, which brought the sniper to the camp. He did a reverse search and it took him to a location near Kitwe. He saved it on the phone and showed Junior.

"That's by the rail station. We can dump the bodies downriver then head there. There's no SAPS office there, so these must be rogue cops."

"Okay, it's time for an old-fashioned stakeout."

They dropped the bodies on the edge of the river, and before they even got back in the Overland, over a dozen crocodiles dragged them into the river and began to rip them apart. There would be nothing left within minutes. Rick felt queasy.

They proceeded to Kitwe. Once there, Rick got an idea.

"I'm gonna try and draw the man to us instead of us trying to find him. I'm gonna text him. Is there a doctor's office close by?"

"Yes, the Carewell Oasis Clinic is a few blocks away," replied Junior.

"Perfect."

Rick took the phone and texted the man again.

Meet me at Carewell Oasis Clinic, I was bit by something.

Okay, be there in twenty.

Junior drove to the back of the clinic.

"What's the plan?"

"We need to get this guy alive. He may be the key to solving this. He's gonna be packing, so it won't be easy."

"Use this," said Junior as he handed Rick a rifle.

It was a tranq gun. He opened a small case and pulled out two yellow darts.

"What is it?" asked Rick.

"It's a lion tranquilizer."

"Won't that kill him?" asked Possum.

"It could, but I have a box of Tolazoline. It reverses the effects of Xylazine, the animal tranquilizer. We just need to get him inside the Overland. If he codes, I'll bring him back. Don't shoot him twice, just don't miss."

Rick took a position behind a dumpster and waited. About fifteen minutes later, a SAPS car pulled up. The man in uniform walked inside the clinic and then texted the phone.

> Where are you?

> I stepped outside, I'm on the side of the building, smoking. I was tired of waiting.

> Mwana wambwa!

The officer walked toward the left side of the building and as soon as he turned the corner, Rick fired. It hit him in the thigh. The guy looked down then reached for his weapon. Before he took another step, he dropped like a ton of bricks.

Junior pulled up next to him, and he and Possum heaved him into the Overland as Rick jogged up.

"Get his keys," said Rick.

Possum grabbed his keys.

"Follow us by Mindola dam," said Junior.

Possum ran to the cruiser and spun it around. He donned the policeman's hat that was sitting on the seat and put it on.

When they arrived near the dam, Junior drove to the east side of the lake and took a stick and placed it against the gas pedal of the police cruiser. He threw it into gear, and the car ran down the bank and into the water. Within minutes, it was gone. The cop's breathing was labored. Rick used his own cuffs to secure him to the bench seat.

"He's not doing well. Grab the Tolazoline!" yelled Rick.

Junior grabbed the Tolazoline needle and injected it into his leg. He gasped for air and came to in a panic. He looked freaked out, and began to yell.

"Shut up!"

The man kept yelling.

Rick closed his fist tight and hit him as hard as he could, knocking him out again.

"Rick!" exclaimed Possum.

"Well, he wouldn't shut up. Gag him!"

Junior checked his pulse and his breathing. "He's fine." He put a sock in his mouth and wrapped it up tight with a handkerchief.

"Let's go. We need to go somewhere off the grid."

Junior drove toward the Kafue Reserve and eventually back to his camp. Once the cop awakened, he started struggling to get loose. Rick took out his pistol and placed the barrel against his forehead.

"Stop moving and be quiet. I don't wanna have to clean up your brains in here. I just mopped the floor. You understand?!"

He nodded in agreement and gave Rick a death stare.

"You can look at me all you want, but if you don't stop moving, I'm gonna fuck you up!"

Rick and Possum helped the cop to his feet and walked him to the camp. Once inside, they tied him to a chair in the center of the kitchen.

Rick whispered to Possum, "Operation Tarantino."

Possum stepped outside and started talking to Junior. They returned a few minutes later with a bag of tools, a 12-volt battery, and jumper cables. The cop's eyes got big.

"Listen up, I'm gonna take the gag out of your mouth. You can yell all you want to. It's just gonna piss me off and no one will hear you. When I'm pissed off, I tend to cause pain. Got it?" asked Rick.

The cop nodded yes.

Rick removed the gag from his mouth and helped him drink some water. He took out the phone from the dead sniper and put it up to his face.

"Who besides you sent the sniper after us?"

"Fuck you."

"Oh, fuck me?"

Rick opened his MacBook, put the song "Stuck In The Middle" on loop, and waved Possum over. He rolled out the tools and knives on the table. Rick began to sharpen the huge buck knife while grinning at the cop. Sweat was rolling off his forehead.

Possum carried the battery over and placed it at his feet. He hooked up the jumper cables and quickly touched them together, causing huge sparks. The cop just about jumped out of his skin. Junior plugged in a grinder, cranked it up a few times, and placed it against a piece of cold steel, creating a nasty, scary sound. The cop tried to look back but couldn't see what he was doing.

"I'm gonna ask you again. Who is your boss? Who planned this?"

"Fuck you!"

"Spark him up!"

Junior took a handheld taser, sat behind the cop, and placed it inches from his back. Possum moved toward the cop and touched his chest with the positive and negative terminals as Junior pushed the button on the taser against his back. His body jolted in the seat and he nearly passed out.

"Okay, okay, stop! I'll tell you."

Rick hit "record" on his iPhone and listened.

"I was contacted by a man who paid me to take you out. I don't know his name."

"How much did he pay you?"

"Five thousand in US funds."

"Five thousand? That's all I'm worth? Spark him up!"

Possum moved closer again with the jumper cables.

"No, no, please! I got his first name. That's all I have, I swear. It's Faraji."

"Where do we find this Faraji?"

"I have no idea."

Rick opened the cop's wallet and looked at his families' photos inside. He pulled out one of the pics of a young boy and girl.

"Maybe I'll pay them a visit and that will clear up your memory."

The cop started shaking.

"Okay, I'll call him. I'll have him meet me."

Rick handed him his phone.

"Put it on speaker. Don't try anything. If you try to call or text anyone other than Faraji, I'll get your kids and feed them to the crocs while you watch. Then you'll be next. Go it?"

The cop just nodded.

CHAPTER FIVE

Ring Ring.

"Faraji, it's Yuusf. We need to talk."

"Where?"

"Meet me at…hold on."

Yuusf looked up at Rick and mouthed the word, "Where?"

Rick typed *Hook Bridge noon tomorrow* on his MacBook.

"Let's meet at noon at Hook Bridge on the M9 tomorrow."

"Okay, I'll be there."

They hung up and Yuusf described the Mercedes G Wagon Faraji would be driving.

Rick and Possum helped Yuusf into the truck after midnight. They hid the Overland behind some bushes and staked out the best vantage points to ambush Faraji. Around ten a.m., Rick climbed into a tree with the tranquilizer gun, and

Possum hid by the bridge with another tranq gun. Junior remained with Yuusf, who was still handcuffed in the Overland. They all wore earpieces and held their position and waited. Around ten minutes to noon, Rick spotted the Mercedes coming down the road toward the bridge.

"It's go-time," said Rick over the radio.

"Possum ready."

"Junior ready."

The Mercedes crossed the bridge and stopped at the end close to Possum's hiding spot. A tall man in fatigues climbed down from the G Wagon. He had a bolt action rifle slung over his shoulder. He looked around and called for Yuusf, then texted him.

As Yuusf's phone vibrated in Rick's pocket, Rick aimed and slowly squeezed the trigger. The dart hit the man in the neck. He reached up and pulled it out and slung his rifle off his shoulder. He fell to one knee and wobbled for a few seconds, then fell face forward in the gravel. Rick climbed down, ran toward the man, and zip-tied his hands behind his back. Possum and Junior ran up to assist Rick.

"Great shot, Rick!" exclaimed Possum.

Rick showed off his buff biceps by proudly polishing his nails against them in a comical manner. Even though Faraji was unconscious, Junior checked his pulse and blood pressure and found that he appeared to be in good health. They raced back to Junior's camp, and Rick kept a watchful eye on the zip-tied scoundrel to make sure he wouldn't try anything fishy.

Upon reaching the camp, Yuusf was left in the Overland while Faraji was placed in a seat located directly in the heart of the kitchen.

"Aaalllrighty!"

Once again, Rick slammed his finger down on "Stuck In The Middle" and *Boom!*—he hit "play" on his MacBook.

"Let the crazy ensue!"

Junior injected Faraji with an anti-tranquilizer. He slowly returned to consciousness in a highly disoriented state without cognizance of his current circumstances. Rick excitedly spun around in front of him with a mischievous glint in his eye, happily sharpening his ridiculously large Buck knife.

"All right, Faraji! Let's chat—what was the dealio with sending somebody to take us down?" asked Rick with a wicked grin.

"Who are you?" Faraji half spat, half mumbled.

"Don't be coy with me. You know exactly who I am! The question is, who are you? Or better yet, who do you work for? I know you had something to do with killing Junior's father. I'm gonna take you and your gang down one way or another. The SAPS don't seem to care and are definitely involved. The upper government may want to bring you in to face justice, but I personally don't care. There are two types of justice, and crocodile justice works just fine with me. Chomp Chomp!" said Rick as he opened and closed his arms together like a snapping crocodile.

Faraji's eyes flitted around anxiously as Junior connected the jumper cables to the car battery and momentarily brought the two ends together, resulting in a loud spark. Faraji jumped and began to sweat. Rick continued to dance comically as he sharpened the knife.

"I can't tell you! They will kill me and my entire family."

Rick pulled out his 9-millimeter, chambered a round right beside Faraji's ear, and set it on the table beside him.

"If you don't talk, I'm gonna splatter your brains all over this kitchen. I just don't care!" yelled Rick an inch from Faraji's face.

Rick waved Junior over with the battery, and he set it up on the floor between Faraji's legs. Out of nowhere, Faraji broke free—he must've been rubbing the zip ties against the chair the entire time—and grabbed the handgun and fired a round right at Rick. The bullet ripped through his shirt, just grazing his arm. Junior tackled him and they fell backward on the floor. He was fighting Faraji for control of the pistol as they rolled on the ground with Faraji's feet still zip-tied to the chair.

Boom!

The gun went off and a silence fell over the group. Both Faraji and Junior were unmoving. Rick's heart slammed against his chest.

Junior slowly rolled off of Faraji, revealing the fatal shot through Faraji's chest. A pool of blood formed around Faraji. He was dead.

"Son of a bitch!" exclaimed Rick.

"What are we gonna do, Rick?" asked Junior.

"Let me think for a minute."

Rick paced back and forth, racking his brain to figure out how to make this work for them.

"Okay, I got it. Bring Yuusf in here. Just play along."

Possum and Junior went to the Overland and walked Yuusf back into the camp. When they opened the door and he saw Faraji's bloody body on the floor, he struggled to get away. Junior punched him hard in the gut and he folded over.

"Sit him down!" yelled Rick.

Junior pulled up another chair and secured him to it with extra zip ties. He made sure to face the chair toward Faraji's body. Yuusf couldn't look away if he tried.

"You killed him? Why?" asked Yuusf.

"Simple. He wouldn't tell me what I needed to hear. That puts you in a tough position. For your sake, you need to tell me who is in charge."

"I've told you everything I know, I swear. You may as well kill me because I don't know anything else," pleaded Yuusf.

"I tell you what. I have a better idea. I'm gonna kill your family. Junior, take the Overland to his home and cut his family's throats. Make sure you take your iPhone. I want him to watch on Facetime."

Junior grabbed his phone and the big Buck knife, then headed out the door. He fired up the Overland and drove off.

"Wait, wait! I'll tell you. Please don't hurt my family. I have worked for the SAPS for over a decade. I was approached by a man named Kelvin Marcus to have you killed. I hired Faraji. I swear that's all I know."

There we go. Now we're getting somewhere.

"What about the ivory?"

"What ivory?"

"The ivory that was stolen from Kelvin. Where is it?" yelled Rick.

"I have no idea, I swear. Kelvin has a long rap sheet for poaching. He has many friends inside of SAPS. We tend to look the other way when it comes to his poaching. Half of my precinct has taken money from him. I have no idea about stolen ivory. He just told me that you and your crew were causing him problems and you needed to be eliminated. So, I hired Faraji and paid him to get it done."

"I thought Faraji hired you?!"

"No, no, no. He was a long-time informant for us and also a drug dealer. I paid him to kill you and he pawned it off on someone else," said Yuusf.

"You're damn right he did. He hired a cop—a sniper. He's in the belly of a croc now. How fucking high does this go?!"

"I can't tell you any more. I don't know any more. Please, you may as well kill me. If they find out I talked to you, I'm dead and so is my entire family anyway. I'm not a bad man. I just got involved in something I shouldn't have. I love my family. If you let me go, I will keep my mouth shut."

"You gotta give me more than that. I already knew most of that. You know what? I'm sick of this. Give me the grinder, Possum."

Possum plugged in the grinder and passed it to Rick. Rick picked it up and turned it on.

"I guess I'll start with your knees."

"Stop! The rumor is it's Colin Mulenga. Leader of the UPND."

"What's the UPND?"

"United Party for National Development," injected Possum.

"The damn government set this plan in motion?" asked Rick.

"That's the talk on the street. He wants to build a big resort development at the edge of the animal reserve. He wants to annex the southern part of the Kafue Reserve and turn it into private land for development. He needs to get the property by Itezhi Tezhi Dam, so the resort can be waterfront on the lake. That is truly all I know. Please, I'm just a police officer. I'm sorry I got involved."

"We need somewhere to hide Yuusf until we can sort this out," Rick said to Possum.

Once Junior came back in from outside—he hadn't driven far before turning back around, since it was just a ploy—Rick told him the same thing. Junior pulled a large colorful rug toward him, revealing a door in the floor. He unlocked the recessed lock and opened it up. It had stairs leading to a room down below. Rick stepped down into and there was a ten-foot-wide cage in the corner of the room.

"What's that for?" asked Rick.

"My father helped me build it. I used it to hold big cats that had been injured. My father had a similar one at his camp," replied Junior.

"If it's good enough for a lion, it's good enough for Yuusf."

Rick and Possum helped Yuusf down the stairs and locked him in the cage. He placed a gallon of fresh water in the cage and a large bucket and toilet paper.

"Home sweet home, Yuusf," said Rick.

Rick locked the massive padlock and hung the key around his neck. It was time to find out what Colin Mulenga was all about.

After conducting some research, Rick was able to ascertain that Colin's office was located in Chirundu. Junior put several weeks' worth of dry rations and bottled water in the cage for Yuusf, and they closed up the hidden door and covered it with the rug.

"He'll be fine. Let's go to Chirundu. It's at the very bottom of the reserve," said Junior.

"I have an idea. Possum, you ready to put your acting hat on again?"

"Hell yeah, hombre! What am I gonna be this time? A reporter, accountant? What?"

"Can you still do that Norwegian accent?

"Nå må du høre på meg, for faen!" replied Possum.

"Let's keep it in English, please. What's that mean anyway?"

"Basically, it means, 'Now you better listen to me.'"

"Possum, you will be an investor from Norway. You name will be Ole Hannsen, a wealthy property guy looking to invest in Zambia. I'll set you up with a business card and a website. You just need to come up with a backstory."

"I'll find some companies and create a similar-sounding name. I can say I come from a long line of investors in Africa. Don't worry, we'll work it out," replied Possum.

"What are we gonna do with Faraji's body?" asked Rick.

"This is Africa. We'll let Africa take care of him. Help me load him onto my ATV," said Junior.

The three of them hauled his body onto the back of the ATV and then drove a mile into the bush. Along the way, they passed several hyenas, a small pride of lions, and some wild dogs. They removed his clothing and laid his body beneath a bush. Once back at the camp, Junior burned his clothes and scattered the ashes in his garden. By morning, Faraji would be just a bad memory.

They started the trek to Chirundu. It would take them about ten hours. Junior had Rick book a room at the Gwabi River Lodge. It was a small base camp with a pool and meal service.

Junior went a little north first and jumped on the A9 directly through Kafue National Park that would take them around the outskirts of Lusaka into Chirundu. About an hour into the trip, they had a blowout on the Overland. Junior changed the tire while Rick and Possum kept a watch for hungry animals or plain bad humans. The A9 had a bad reputation for kidnapping and carjacking. It wouldn't happen on their watch.

Rick was a little nervous to be getting so close to Lusaka after getting arrested, so when they neared it, Junior went off road at Kasula and right through the center of Blue Lagoon National Park. It was dark when they pulled into the park. Instead of driving through the night, they decided to rest. It was a relatively small park compared to Kafue, but it had a large, diverse variety of animals. They decided to build a small fire and grill hot dogs outside for dinner.

Rick placed rocks in a wide circle, and Possum put on his headlamp and went to collect some firewood. He had to make a few trips, and on the third trip, he yelled. He ran back holding his hand. He held it out for Rick to see.

"What bit you?" asked Rick.

"A damn snake."

"Can you describe it?" asked Junior.

"It was bright green. Almost neon green, and it fell out of a tree when I pulled on a dead limb."

Eyes wide, Junior ran over to the Overland and came back with a photo book. He flipped through the pages.

"Was it this?"

"Exactly! Oh my God, it hurts," exclaimed Possum.

"Sit down, Possum. This is gonna hurt even more."

He pulled out his pocket knife. Possum began to get dizzy and his beathing sounded labored.

"Bite down on this," said Junior, handing Possum his wallet.

Rick watched with a racing heart as Possum stuck the wallet into his mouth, and Junior cut the bites open with his pocket knife and began to suck out the venom. He spit continuously. Possum could no longer hold his head up and began to lean. The area around his bite began to show signs of necrosis and turn black. Possum slumped to the ground as Junior continued to work on him.

"He was bit by a green mamba. We have to get him to the hospital. He doesn't have much time. Help me pick him up."

"Holy shit! Let's hurry," exclaimed Rick.

Together they dragged him into the Overland and placed him on the floor. His breathing was very shallow and he was completely unconscious. Junior could barely speak from the numbing effect of the venom on his tongue.

"Mr. Rick, you must drive."

Junior punched in an address on his phone and handed it to Rick.

"I can help Possum breathe."

Rick looked down at Possum and he was turning blue. "Hang on, buddy," he said.

Junior pulled out his first-aid kit, took out an Ambu Bag, and started squeezing air into Possum's lungs. Rick floored the Overland, bound for UTH, the University Teaching Hospital. It was the closest place they could get the antivenom.

Rick looked in the rearview and could see Possum's color coming back. He still wasn't moving as Junior continued to squeeze the pump and occasionally check his pulse. Rick was driving like a madman and praying he wouldn't get another flat tire. He had no desire to go back into Lusaka but would do whatever he had to do to save his best friend. He looked at Junior in the rearview mirror. His face was swollen from the venom he'd sucked out of Possum, but he was still constantly pumping the bag. The ride was rough and stuff was falling out of the cabinets from all the potholes.

The ride seemed like it took forever. Once they were on the highway, five miles from the hospital, a cop pulled up behind them and hit his lights. Rick pulled over and waved the cop over.

"Snake bite! Green mamba! Can you give us an escort?"

The cop looked inside and saw Junior pumping the bag for Possum.

"Follow me."

Rick pulled up to the hospital and jumped out of the Overland. The cop ran inside the hospital, and two people came running out with a gurney. Junior handed Possum off to one of the nurses and she began to pump the bag. She opened his eyelids, held a flashlight to his pupils, and shook her head. They pushed him into the hospital, and he disappeared behind some doors. Rick was beside himself. Junior came in shortly after and had to sit down from the venom.

Rick called over a nurse and she took him inside as well. Rick paced back and forth, asking each nurse what was going on. He couldn't lose Possum. This couldn't be the way his friend would go.

After what seemed like a lifetime, a doctor came out and looked for Rick.

"Hello, are you the family?"

"Yes, how is he?"

"I have to be honest. It's touch and go. We administered the antivenom and it returned his breathing, but he is in a coma. Your other friend will be fine. He didn't require much antivenom. His face is still a little swollen, but his tongue is back to normal. We have someone staying with the first patient all night and we will monitor him continuously. Your other friend will be released soon."

Rick ran his hand through his hair and began to pray.

"I need you to fill out some paperwork. We don't even know his name."

"It's Poss...ahem, Mike Jackson. Of course, I'll fill out whatever you need."

The doctor walked him over to the desk and introduced him to the administrator. Rick filled out all of the paperwork.

"Thank you, sir. There is no charge here. We are a teaching hospital. Where was he bitten?"

"Over by Blue Lagoon National Park. He was collecting firewood," replied Rick.

"He's very lucky. Green mamba bites are extremely dangerous. They deliver a highly potent mixture of rapid-acting presynaptic and postsynaptic neurotoxins, cardiotoxins, and fasciculins."

"English?" asked Rick.

"Oh, I'm sorry. The neurotoxin attacks the nervous system, the cardiotoxins can cause heart palpitations, and the fasciculins can cause paralysis. The nurse told me that she saw lacerations on the bites. Did someone try to remove the venom?"

"Yes, Junior sucked out as much as he could. He's the one with the swollen face. He also pumped the Ambu Bag the whole way here."

"If your friend makes it, you can thank Junior then. Removing that venom and breathing for him may have just saved his life. The doctor will be out again soon for an update."

"Thank you, ma'am. I'll be right here."

Rick sat down in the waiting area. He was a mess and doing his best to hold back the tears. He was praying like never before. Soon after, Junior came out in a wheelchair pushed by a pretty young nurse.

Rick leaped to his feet. "Junior! Are you okay?"

"Yeah, I'll be fine. I guess I don't need lip augmentation anytime soon. Ha-ha. How is Possum?"

Rick wrapped his arms around Junior and squeezed him tight.

"He's in a coma, but the nurse said you may have saved his life."

"He'll make it. I just know it, Mr. Rick."

"Just call me Rick. From now on, I'm Rick. Okay, Junior?"

"Okay Mr... I mean, Rick."

An hour went by and the doctor came back out.

"How is he?"

"He is still in a coma, but we did an MRI and there doesn't seem to be any cardiac damage. He didn't get enough venom to cause internal muscular damage. His hand will survive, but he will have some scarring. We may have to do a couple of grafts. Time will tell. The epidermis on his hand will heal; there was some damage to the subcutaneous layer, but we removed the dead areas. All we can do is wait. You may want to get a hotel nearby."

"Thanks, Doctor, we'll be fine right here unless Junior wants a room."

"I'm good, Rick. If I get too tired, I'll go nap in the Overland."

"Oh crap. I forgot about the Overland. I need to move it."

Rick jogged outside. When he returned, he passed the keys to Junior.

"If it's gonna be a couple of days, I want to put you up in a nice room. It's the least I can do."

"I'm okay, Rick. I wanna be here for Mr. Possum too. I mean Possum."

Rick let out a small laugh and patted Junior on the back.

"Please pray with me."

Rick took Junior's hand and began to pray.

"Dear Lord, please don't take out Possum now. He has so much more to do in life. I'd trade places with him if I could. I ask this in Jesus Christ's name. Amen."

CHAPTER SIX

Captain Larry Lane called the harbormaster in Key West to let him know his ETA. They had prearranged a mooring for him at the seaplane base. There wasn't a marina that could accommodate the length of the explorer vessel. Gary, Jules, and Johnie took a twenty-foot center console Gary had rented out to meet the ship. It would be the first time Johnie and Jules laid eyes on it since Gary purchased it. She was a beauty—a 130-foot steel hull cutter, fully equipped with every possible toy for treasure hunting and exploration money could buy.

"Ahoy, Captain!" yelled Gary as he waved up to the captain on the helm.

He waved back and motioned for them to swing around to the mooring ball. He had made a deal to borrow one of the balls from a rich guy he had captained for before, used for his mega yacht when he was in Key West. They were currently in the Mediterranean, so it was available for quite a long time. Gary passed up the eye of the ball to one of the mates Captain Larry had hired to help with the delivery. Once the vessel was secured, Gary motored the little center console to the stern and side-tied it to the swim platform. Captain Larry came down and assisted Jules up onto the ship. Gary and Johnie soon followed.

"Hello, Captain Larry, this is Jules and Johnie. You spoke on the phone to Johnie several times. Jules is Rick's girlfriend. He is in Africa still."

"Why hello, Johnie, nice to put a face to the voice," said the captain, shaking Johnie's hand.

"Hi Jules, nice to meet you," he said as he gave her a big hug.

"Nice to meet you too," she replied.

"Okay, enough with the formalities. I need a beer. It's been five days of treacherous seas and I am parched."

"But it's only 9:30 a.m.," said Johnie.

"As Jimmy Buffett almost said, 'It's 9:30 p.m. somewhere!'"

Captain Larry popped the top of a Busch Light and gave them the grand tour. Johnie and Gary joined him in drinking his morning beverage of choice, while Jules grabbed a cup of coffee.

"As you can see, she's equipped with everything we'd ever possibly need for treasure hunting. See these pipes? They are basically sea vacuums for filtering sand on the bottom. I had all the hydraulic lines replaced on the crane that is secured to the R.O.V. Speaking of the R.O.V, look inside. I had a new LCD screen installed that will serve as the command center if we do any manned dives. She's designed to be operated from up top like a drone, but she can also accommodate two people. I added a shark cage like you requested, Gary. I doubt we'll need it, but you never know. There are eight full sets of scuba gear and two helmet suits. We have a top-of-the-line air compressor on board—and wait until you see this. Follow me."

They all hung on his every word as he showed them the new toy.

"What is it?" asked Johnie.

"Looks like a dolphin," said Jules.

"It is. Plus, it's a diving speedboat," replied Captain Larry.

He twisted a handle and the top of the dolphin's head opened up, revealing a steering wheel and two seats.

"It's made by a company called Seabreacher. It has a 230hp intercooled high-performance engine and can leap into the air and dive as well. It's totally cool," said Captain Larry.

"But what's it used for, Captain Larry?" asked Johnie.

"Just call me Larry. No need to be formal. It's used for fun!"

Jules starting snapping pictures to send to Rick. He was gonna be so excited.

> Rick, Capt. Larry arrived
> with the new ship. Check out
> this motorized dolphin.

> That's neat Jules, can
> you call me? Something's
> happened. I was just about
> to text you.

"Excuse me, guys. I need to call Rick real quick."

She stepped a few feet away and clicked on Rick's number.

"Hi, Rick, what's going on?"

"Hi, baby. It's Possum. He was bit by a green mamba and is in the ICU."

Her hand flew to her mouth. "What?! Is he gonna be okay?"

"We don't know yet."

"Oh my God. Not Possum," she said as tears began to run down her face.

Johnie poked Gary in the side and motioned for him to look over at Jules, who was now crying. They walked over to her.

"Rick, I'm gonna put you on speaker. Gary and Johnie are here."

"What's wrong, Rick?" asked Gary.

"Hey y'all, Possum was bitten by a green mamba snake and is in the ICU. Luckily, Junior sucked out some of the venom and kept him breathing on the ride to the hospital. Possum is in a coma but breathing on his own. The doctor said he has no heart damage, which is amazing. All we can do now is wait."

"I'm so sorry, Rick. Do you want us to fly there?"

"Naw, y'all just hold down the fort there and I'll keep you posted. The best thing we can do right now is pray for Possum. If and when he comes out of it, y'all will be the first to know."

"Thanks, Rick. I know he's gonna make it. He's gonna love this new ship. So are you, Rick. It's a treasure hunter's dream," said Gary.

"Tell him we all love him when he wakes up," added Johnie.

"Okay guys, let me talk to Jules real quick."

"Bye, buddy," they said in unison.

"Jules, I just don't want you to worry. Possum is a strong guy and I know in my gut that he's gonna pull through. Please don't cry. It makes me wanna cry."

Jules wiped her face and gave a half a laugh. "Okay, Rick. I'll take care of the boys here, and you just keep us abreast of Possum's condition. Is there anything you want me to tell Gary in regards to the ship?"

"It's pretty much his, baby. Let him know that I'll chip in if he wants to keep Captain Larry on the payroll for a while until Johnnie is ready to take the helm or we hire a permanent captain."

"Okay, I'll let him know. All my love to Possum and you too, my love."

"I love you, Jules. Talk soon."

Jules dried her eyes and joined the boys for the rest of the tour.

Two days went by and Possum remained in a coma. Rick had slept on chairs in the waiting room the first night, but Junior talked him into taking a bunk in the Overland the next. He wanted to stay as close to the hospital as possible. He yawned and glanced down at his watch. It was 7:40 a.m. and Junior was milling about in the Overland. Rick rolled out of his bunk and joined Junior for a cup of coffee.

A knock came on the door of the Overland. It was the doctor who was looking after Possum.

"Good morning. I have some good news. Your friend Michael has awakened from his coma. He's disoriented and confused but doesn't seem to have any long-term neurological issues. We are gonna keep him for a few more days for observation, but we do expect a full recovery. His hand is stiff and he will probably need some physical therapy for it. The venom did a number on the muscle that controls his thumb and forefinger, but in time, he should regain full use of it," said Dr. Aadan.

"Thank you, Doctor, you just made my day! When can we visit him?"

"We are gonna run some more tests on him today and if he does well, we'll probably move him out of the ICU this afternoon and you can visit him then. I'm gonna head back in. He is responsive. Is there anything you want me to tell him?"

"Yeah, tell him we want him to get well soon. He needs to ride the new dolphin."

"Huh?"

"Just tell him that. It'll make sense to him when I visit."

"Okie dokie. Will do. I have your cell number and I'll text you when he's available for visitation."

"Thanks, Doc," said Rick as he patted him on the back.

Once the doctor was gone, Rick took a big sip of his coffee and looked up toward the ceiling and mouthed, "Thank you, Lord."

He and Junior decided to go to the hospital cafeteria for breakfast. It was the closest place and neither one of them felt like cooking. The food was actually quite nice. Rick got flapjacks, and Junior got bacon and eggs with a side of avocado toast. They chatted as they ate, mostly talking about Possum. Rick was going stir crazy being stuck at the hospital but was super stoked Possum was going to recover. He decided to do some more research on Colin Mulenga on his MacBook as they ate. Since Possum would be out of commission for a few more days, he figured it would be best to get as much dirt on Colin as he could to help Possum once they did finally meet.

Through his deep dark web searches, Rick found out that Colin owned an apartment in Lusaka, which was his main residence, but he also kept an apartment in Chirundu that he worked out of. It was the middle of the week, so he would most likely be in Chirundu. His wife was a spokesperson for The National Achievement Council, an organization that helped develop properties and businesses for up-and-coming African entrepreneurs. She was giving a speech tonight at seven p.m. for a gala in Lusaka. Rick pulled up the address of their home. It was only seven miles away.

"Junior, you up for a little B&E?"

"B&E?"

"Breaking and entering. We need to case Colin Mulenga's house today and get inside tonight. You in?"

"Hell yeah. If he had anything to do with my father's death, I'm 100 percent in."

"Okay, let's get as close as we can to the property and see if we can case it. This monster Overland sticks out like a sore thumb. Can we rent something more inconspicuous?"

"I have a better idea," said Junior. "One of my good friends owns a twenty-four-hour plumbing service. I can borrow one of his vans."

"Perfect! Look, you know the last place I want to be is in Lusaka since that shooting at the restaurant, but Possum is here and we have to be here, so we better make the best of it. I was brainstorming last night because I couldn't sleep. I was wondering if there could be any clues in your dad's new Defender. Where is it?"

"Last I heard, it was in a police compound. I doubt they will ever release it. My dad didn't make a will and instead of going to probate, they will probably auction it off at some point or keep it for themselves. Damn corrupt sons of bitches."

"Or we could steal it back?" said Rick with a wicked look in his eye.

"Are you crazy?"

"Some people think so. I guess we'll find out. First things first. Let's case Colin's place."

Junior got on the phone and arranged to have the plumber's van dropped off by The Cross Park, a nice little family park on the outskirts of Lusaka on Leopards Hill Road. There, they switched vehicles and put on the company vests that his friend had hung in the back of the van.

A short while later, they pulled up across the street from Colin's house. Rick climbed in the back and grabbed his binoculars. He counted five cameras on the outside of the home. There was no way to take them out without cutting the power to the entire home. The best thing they could do was disguise their faces. The bigger problem was, the front door had a coded lock on it. Almost impossible to crack. He'd have to get in another way. He scanned the roof and saw a skylight.

Bingo.

The van was equipped with a ladder on the roof, so scaling the home would be no problem. He spotted movement inside and focused his binoculars on the large window on the right side of the house. He counted three people. One had to be Mrs. Mulenga, and the other two were probably maids. An older model Chevy was parked in the driveway, which probably belonged to the maids, and the garage door was closed. Mrs. Mulenga's car was most likely inside there.

It was time to get what they'd need to get inside. Junior took Rick to a hardware store and they bought heavy-duty wire cutters, gloves, and overalls. They then went to a costume store, where Rick purchased a beard and mustache kit and non-prescription clear glasses. He got Junior a Fu Manchu mustache and a big fake nose attached to glasses. Under the cover of night, they would put the plan into action.

They left and decided to case the police impound lot. It was a junky lot with a small office and an automatic gate.

"We'll need the gate code to get your dad's car out," said Rick.

"I'm on it," said Junior.

Junior walked up to the gate and a door buzzed, letting him walk in beside the large gate. "Hello, ma'am," he said to the lady in the office. "I'm looking for a car that was stolen and might be on the lot."

As he spoke with the woman, he saw the keys to all the cars hanging on the wall behind her. He spotted his dad's keys right away. They were the only ones with a small elephant attached to the key ring.

A call came in over the radio as a wrecker approached the main gate, towing a car. The woman reached over to a keypad beside her desk, and Junior focused hard to memorize the numbers she typed in.

Four, Three, Six, One, Enter.

"Sorry, sir, I don't think we have the car you're looking for," said the woman. Of course, he'd made up the stolen car in the first place, so it obviously wasn't on the lot.

"Well, thank you anyway," he said.

As he walked out, he saw his dad's Defender backed in three rows in the back against the fence. He strolled out of the lot and around the corner to where Rick was parked.

"Did you get it?" asked Rick.

"You betcha," said Junior. He quickly repeated the code for Rick, who scribbled it down so they would remember it. "The keys are inside the office. I didn't see any cameras on the office, but there may be some outside of the gate. We'll just have to deal with them I guess."

"Yeah, with these disguises they'll be looking for the black and white Cheech and Chong. Ha-ha!" said Rick.

"There is a cyclone door beside the gate, and she let me in with a buzzer. I'm not sure how we'll get inside."

"How tall is the fence?"

"I'd say eight feet and it has razor wire on top. So, climbing it is out of the question."

"I guess we'll have to jump it."

Junior frowned. "Jump it?"

"You'll see. Is there a high school nearby?"

"Yeah, Lusaka High is about three miles from here. Why?"

"Do they have a track team?"

"Of course."

"Then leave it to me. I was quite an athlete in school. You'll never guess what my main event in track and field was."

"Pole vaulting?"

Rick grinned. "Why, you little genius, you!"

They grabbed some fast food and waited for the sun to disappear on the African horizon. Soon it was time for a little fun at Colin Mulenga's house. Junior parked the van a few houses down as Rick looked through binoculars.

After an hour, the garage door opened and a black Mercedes SL 300 backed out. When the driver turned the corner, Rick recognized her as the same woman from inside the house earlier—Mrs. Mulenga. He looked at his watch. It was 5:39 p.m.; she was on her way to her speech. As soon as she rounded the corner out of sight, Junior backed the van into the driveway. They had already donned their disguises. Junior rolled out a long suction hose and proceeded to hook it to the PVC septic vent pipe on the side of the house.

Rick pulled the ladder down from the truck and ran around to the back of the house. It had an eight-foot-tall wooden fence all around the backyard, so he was out of view from the neighbors. He climbed the ladder and approached the skylight. It was directly above the kitchen island. He pried it open and stuck his head in. He could see a keypad by the front door. Luckily, there was no sensor on the skylight.

"It's go-time," said Rick through the walkie-talkie.

"10-4, standing by," replied Junior.

Rick positioned himself above the island, dropped his duffel bag, and lowered himself down. He had about a three-foot drop. There was no way he was going back out the way he came in.

There were no cameras inside the house, as far as he could tell after a quick sweep. With his gloves on, he started looking through drawers for anything that could help him find out who Colin Mulenga really was.

After an exhaustive search of the bedroom, he moved to the office. An iMac was sitting on the desk. He pulled out his MacBook from his backpack, synced it to the iMac, and cloned the hard drive. It was a five-hundred-gig hard drive, and he used a program called Acronis to clone it. It would take around twenty minutes.

Inside the desk was a file drawer. He scrolled though it and found a file called Mulenga Resort. Inside were plans to build a three-hundred-room resort and casino with an attached waterpark that sat right on the lake beside Itezhi Tezhi Dam, on Kafue National Park property. He snapped dozens of photos while he waited for the hard drive to copy. There was a to-do list on the desk, and when he took a photo of it, he saw a name he recognized: Kelvin Marcus.

His MacBook dinged, letting him know the clone was complete. He put everything back in the duffel bag, made his way to the front door, and picked up the walkie-talkie.

"Cut the power!"

Junior had already opened the electrical panel on the side of the house. He grabbed the main breaker and turned it off. That initiated the backup battery. He immediately cut the main lead with the wire cutters.

Inside, the keyboard lights went off. Rick opened the front door and strolled out. They quickly rolled up the suction hose and high-tailed out of there. They left the ladder in the back. The Mulengas would know they'd been robbed; there was no hiding it.

As they approached the Overland and changed vehicles, Junior called his friend and told him to report the plumber's van as stolen. They made their way to the high school.

Rick ran onto the field and found a stack of pole-vaulting poles by a large mat next to the track. He picked out one he liked and strapped it to the side of the Overland. Once they arrived at the impound lot, Rick removed the pole and walked around to the back of the property. He probably only had one shot at this. He looked for the best place to land and prayed he wouldn't sprain his ankle or worse. He stuck his lock-picking kit inside the front of his pants and dug a small hole by the fence.

Junior was positioned by the front gate door on lookout. He gave Rick the thumbs-up, and Rick stepped back ten feet. He took a deep breath and exhaled. It was now or never. He ran toward the fence and planted the pole in the ground. The pole bent as he was raised into the air. He cleared the fence and fell to the ground with a roll.

Phew!

As he stood up and dusted himself off, he saw a black shadow coming toward him fast. As it got closer, he heard the growling. It was a rottweiler guard dog.

"Son of a bitch!" he said out loud.

The dog was sprinting toward Rick at full speed. Rick ran as fast as he could toward an old Ford van and climbed on top. The dog hit the van with a loud tug and started clawing and scratching to get to Rick. He was barking and growling as foam spewed from his mouth. Rick grabbed the radio.

"Junior! Dog! Tranq it! Hurry!" he exclaimed out of breath.

He waited with baited breath for Junior to run to the Overland and come back with his tranq gun. After a minute or so, the dog let out a loud yelp. Thirty seconds later, it went down and flopped over. It was out cold.

Rick jumped down from the van and ran over to the office. In under a minute, he had picked the lock and was inside. He raced around the counter and pushed the button to open the side door on the fence. Junior ran in and grabbed his dad's key fob from the wall. He ran to the Defender and fired it up. Rick typed in the code for the gate. Nothing. He tried it again slower. Still nothing.

"Junior, are you sure that's the right code?"

"Yes!" replied Junior on the walkie-talkie.

Rick tried it again. It was a no-go.

Fuck it, we gotta get out of here.

He ran around to the passenger's side of the Defender.

"Let's go!" yelled Rick.

"What about the gate?"

"It's a cyclone fence gate. Just ram it. We have no choice."

Junior threw the Defender into gear and floored it. He hit the gate and sparks flew. The entire gate flew into the center of the street, and the Defender bounced when it hit the uneven part of the road. He turned left, away from where the Overland was parked. As he turned the corner, blue lights appeared in the distance.

"They're coming!" yelled Junior.

A cop car was closing in on them.

"I saw an alarm on the door at the office. The place was so run-down, I assumed it was broken. I guess not," said Rick.

Junior floored the Defender once more and took a right on a cross street with the cruiser right on his tail. "We have to lose this guy or we are both going down."

The car pulled up behind the Defender in an attempt to try a pit maneuver. Junior veered right just in time and turned up an alley. The cop blew past the alley and hit reverse, and was soon close behind them again. They were closing in on a construction site. Rick pointed at a pile of dirt with cones around it.

"Move over and let him get close," said Rick.

The cop car was approaching the driver's side again, getting in position for the pit maneuver. As he got within two feet of the SUV's rear, Junior slammed on the brakes then ripped the steering wheel left, slamming into the passenger's side of the cop car, sending it directly into the dirt mound. The car hit the dirt and flew through the air, spinning as steel and dirt were flung in every direction. The car smashed into the road upside down and spun around into a utility pole. The Defender came to a stop.

Rick jumped out to see if the cop was okay. He was hanging by the seatbelt cursing. Rick saluted him and jumped back into the Defender.

"We have to hide this thing fast!" said Rick.

"I know exactly where to go!"

Junior drove the speed limit and kept to surface streets. He approached a storage unit area and keyed in the code. The gate opened and he pulled up to a unit, jumped out, and unlocked the combination lock. Rick jumped over to the passenger's side and quickly pulled inside, killed the engine, and grabbed his duffel bag. They pulled off their disguises and coveralls and put them in the Defender, then locked up the storage unit. In street clothes, they made it to a side street and Junior called for an Uber.

Within minutes, they were back at the Overland and could see police lights a few blocks up at the impound lot. They both climbed up front and let out a huge sigh.

"I'm hungry. You?" asked Rick.

"I could eat."

CHAPTER SEVEN

Rick took a huge bite of his Big Boss chicken sandwich from Hungry Lion. He and Junior sat in a booth at the popular fast-food joint. Junior got the Big One fried chicken platter. As they ate, they reminisced about the night's adventure. Not only had they pulled off one extortionary snatch-and-grab, but also grand theft auto, which were both major offences in Zambia. But they weren't worried about it. It had to be done in the name of justice. Sometimes it took bending the law a little to get the right result.

After dinner, they drove back to the hospital to check on Possum. There had been no change and he was to be moved in the next day or so into a regular room, so instead of sleeping on the mats inside the Overland, Rick offered to spring for a hotel near the hospital. The Neelkanth Sarovar Premiere Hotel was only ten minutes from the hospital and right next to the Manda Hill shopping mall. It would be a nice place for Possum to recuperate once he was released.

It was the only five-star hotel in Lusaka. Rick got adjoining rooms, said goodnight to Junior, and settled in for the night.

He wanted to get out of Lusaka as soon as humanly possible, since the police probably still wanted to question him about the shootings at the Indian restaurant. It was a clear case of self-defense. The cops knew it, the district attorney knew it, but he still felt uneasy being there. They hadn't brought charges against him yet, but the shoe could drop at any moment. The last thing he wanted to do was spend time in a Zambian prison. It had been a few days, and nothing had happened, but he knew how the criminal in-justice system worked and it was a slow process. He wanted to solve Junior's father's murder and get the hell out of Africa.

Hmmm—out of Africa, like the movie. Funny

Rick was awakened by his phone vibrating on the night-stand. It was the hospital.

"Hello, this is Rick Waters."

"Mr. Waters, this is Nurse Jacini. I wanted to let you know we are moving your friend Mr. Michael Jackson to a private room in fifteen minutes. He can have visitors up until eight o'clock tonight."

"Thank you so much for calling. We'll be down after breakfast."

"My pleasure, Mr. Waters. Goodbye."

"Bye!" Once he hung up, Rick yelled, "Woo-hoo!"

He was so stoked Possum was going to recover from his nasty green mamba bite. He texted Jules, not thinking about the time. He glanced at his watch and realized it was a little after three a.m. in Key West. He had already hit "send" and couldn't stop the text now.

Jules, Possum is gonna make it!

A few minutes passed and Rick hoped he hadn't awakened Jules. Then his phone whistled.

That's great news! When will you see him?

I guess she's up, thought Rick.

We're gonna go after breakfast. I'll swing by again later at a better time for y'all and maybe we can do a Facetime with Possum and show him the ship? It might lift his spirits.

That would be awesome. Just text me when you're ready. I'm gonna catch a few more winks and then head to the ship around 7 a.m. and do some cleaning and organizing.

Okay baby, sorry I woke you. Get some sleep.

> No worries, Rick. You can
> wake me anytime. I miss you
> so much.

Rick put his phone back on the nightstand and accidentally bumped it, knocking over the lamp. The noise caught Junior's attention, and through the adjoining door he said, "You up, Rick?"

"Yeah, give me a minute."

Rick used the bathroom and brushed his teeth, then opened the adjoining room door. He strolled in with two cups of coffee.

"Where'd you get the coffee?" asked Rick.

"I couldn't sleep and ordered a pot from room service. It's real smooth! Try it."

Rick took a big sip and before he could swallow, Junior said, "It's monkey poop coffee."

Rick spit it out and peppered the wall with java spatter. "What?"

"Its actual name is monkey spit coffee, but it actually comes from the feces of civets. They are a mammal. The partially digested beans are handpicked, cleaned, then roasted."

Rick immediately put a fresh breakfast pod in his Keurig and dumped out the monkey-poop coffee. Junior was bent over laughing as he showed Rick the receipt from room service: *One Pot—Arabica Coffee—$217.33 ZMW/$11.99 US*

"I'm sorry, Rick. I couldn't help it. I knew you'd spit it out. It does exist though. It's made by a company in Indonesia. It's known as kopi luwak. I like you, Rick, but it costs eighty dollars a cup. I don't like you that much. Ha-ha-ha-ha."

"Well, I've heard of a crappy cup of coffee, but that would beat it."

"Good one, Rick. What's the plan today?"

"I just got a call from the hospital. Possum is being moved to a private room, so we can go visit soon. After that, I'd like to go to your storage unit and see if we can get any clues from your dad's Defender."

"Can we go through every inch of it and then clean it? I have a friend who deals in, how can I say it, secondhand cars. He will repair it, paint it, and change the VIN number. Those damn cops will just eventually auction it off or keep it for themselves. They ain't ever getting it back. My dad paid for it and it stays in the family."

"That's fair. If we head over there after we visit Possum, it shouldn't take too long to go through it. It was brand new, right?"

"Oh yeah, it only has about nine hundred miles on it. It's mint except for the scrapes from where I sideswiped that cop car."

"That was money!" exclaimed Rick.

"Yeah, looked like a scene from *Hot Pursuit*."

Rick and Junior walked down to the Copper Pot restaurant located in the lobby and sat down for some local breakfast cuisine. After breakfast, they headed to the hospital.

"I'm here to visit Possu—I mean, Mr. Jackson."

"He's in room 1023, just sign in here. Only two at a time please."

"Perfect. There's just two of us."

Rick considered picking up a plastic green snake to mess with Possum but thought twice about it and changed his mind. It might give Possum a heart attack.

"Possum! You're alive!" exclaimed Rick as soon as he walked through the door.

"I wasn't passed out. I was playing me."

"Ha-ha, very funny. Playing Possum."

"In all seriousness, I need to thank you, Junior. The doctor and nurses told me what you did. I am eternally grateful. They told me your lips, tongue, and face got all swollen from sucking out the poison."

"Just be glad it didn't bite you on the crotch. You'd be dead."

They all busted out laughing at Junior's joke. It was an oldie but a goodie.

"I truly owe you one, Junior. Anything."

"Hmmm, let me think. How about a million dollars?" he said jokingly.

"Done!" said Possum in a serious tone.

"Just get well, that's all I ask."

"I'm working on it," replied Possum.

After their short visit, Rick and Junior made their way to the storage unit. Luckily, Junior's unit was in the rear of the property and opened to a fence. The place was a ghost town, so they had no issues taking their time and going through the Defender. Rick checked under the seats, in the rear storage area, and then in all the seat pockets. It was clean as a whistle. The only things in the SUV were a mounted radar detector on the front window, an empty can of Coke, and a map of Kafue Park. Rick opened the map on the hood. There was no writing or highlights on it.

Frustrated, he sat back in the driver seat and slammed his palm down on the center console. It popped open and he closed it, since it was empty. Then he noticed it had two compartments. Instinctively, he checked the upper compartment that he needed to push a button to open. Inside, he found a small yellow pad and a pen.

"Junior, do you have a pencil?"

He jogged over to his Overland and brought back a brand-new sharpened pencil. Rick stepped out and laid the notepad on the hood. He turned the pencil sideways and started rubbing the lead in a pattern softly. He got through the entire pad and kept holding it up to the light. On the last half of the paper, words began to appear. Rick grabbed a flashlight and laid it under the first page, revealing the words even better.

Junior,
I stashed the ivory near the cave of bats. Follow road
from Majuaneti to the

The rest of the words were off the page.

"Does this look familiar?"

"Yes, those are the words my father had written on the map. Where are the rest of them?"

"It looks like he laid the map in the pad, but the writing continued beyond the edge of the pad. It's all we have!? What are Majuaneti and the cave of bats?"

"The only cave with bats I know is close to the park, and Majuaneti is a small town on RD491. The Bat Caves are a pretty big tourist draw. I can't believe he'd hide the ivory in those caves."

"Read it again. It says *near* the cave of bats. Can you remember anything else written on the map?"

"I literally looked at it once, folded it up, and stuck it in my glove box. I vaguely remember it saying what you just read."

"Have you ever been hypnotized?"

"No, but if it will help, I'm game."

"I know a guy in Houston named TC LeNormand who does hypnotic transgression therapy. I've used him in other cases and it can help someone remember things hidden in their past memories. He usually does it in person, but flying him to Africa is probably a no-go. Maybe he can do something over the phone or computer. I'll call him."

"Is there anything else you wanna search for in the Defender, or can I clean it up and let my friend know he can come get it? I'm thinking of having it painted camo for my future photo safaris."

"Yeah, go ahead. I got what I needed. At least part of it," replied Rick.

Junior unplugged the radar detector and put it in a plastic bag. He threw out the coke can and a couple of old lollipop sticks, which brought a little tear to his eye. His dad always had a lollipop in his mouth. He remembered making fun of his dad and calling him the black Kojak, since he was bald and loved lollipops. He wiped away the tear and tossed the trash in the dumpster. He planned to mount the radar detector in his new Overland eventually, but stuck it in the console for now.

Junior called his buddy, and he arrived a half hour later with an enclosed trailer. Rick and Junior helped him load the Defender inside and secure it to the floor. Once he left, they decided to head back to the hospital.

"Let's Facetime with Possum and Jules in Florida," said Rick. "I'm sure Possum will be happy to see them."

Rick snuck a beer into the hospital and handed it to Possum, which made his eyes light up. He cracked the top and took a huge swig.

"Ahhh that's nice!"

"I'm gonna call Jules now. She was so worried about you. I told her we could Facetime, so you could see the new treasure-hunting ship. Take sort of a virtual tour. Cool?"

"Awesome, let's do it."

Jules's phone rang twice before she picked up.

"Hi, baby, I'm with Possum."

"Caw, caw," rang out on the phone as Chief heard Rick's voice and mimicked a crow. It was one of his favorite sounds.

"Hi, Chief. I miss you, buddy!" said Rick as he looked into the phone and saw Chief flapping his wings on Jules's shoulder.

Rick moved to the bed and turned the phone so Possum could see.

"Hi, Jules. Hi, Chief. So good to see y'all."

"Hi, Possum. You gave us quite a scare! Don't play with snakes anymore, okay?" said Jules.

"Don't worry. I'd kiss a bat's rabid ass before I go near another damn green mamba."

"Funny you say that. You might just get to do that soon," interjected Rick.

"Huh?"

"Never mind, I'll tell you later. Two words: road trip!"

Possum nodded with a huge smile on his face.

Jules gave Possum the grand tour of the new ship. All the boys were in town getting supplies, and she was the only one on board. She promised to let them know how well Possum looked and was recovering. After the tour, they all said their goodbyes and Rick ended the call.

"Okay, tell me more about kissing a bat's ass!" said Possum.

"You must be psychic, dude. We located part of the writing that Junior's father wrote on the original map that burned up in his Toyota. Anyway, the note referred to an area near the cave of bats. We're going there as soon as you're released. Have you gotten any indication from the doctor?"

"He's supposed to be back at four p.m. and I'll find out then. I'll have him contact you as soon as he lets me know. Maybe later y'all can bring me something good to eat. I'm tired of this bland hospital food."

"I'll scrounge something up for ya, buddy."

Rick smirked, knowing what he was gonna do to Possum with a plastic snake now that he was feeling so much better.

Rick and Junior left and drove into town to buy a map for the Bat Cave area. That along with the Google Earth search revealed several caves in the vicinity, plus a few more outside of the tourist area. They'd start there. At 4:30, Rick's phone whistled. It was a text from Possum's doctor.

Mr. Jackson will be released at six o'clock.

Thanks, Doc. You did a great job!

A thumbs-up emoji popped up on Rick's phone.

"We have an hour and a half before Possum is released. I'm gonna call TC in Houston. You ready?" he asked Junior.

"Ready as I'll ever be."

Rick called the number TC gave him from the last case. He picked up on the third ring.

"Rick, how goes it?"

"Hey TC, all good. I have a quick question. Can you do that hypnosis thing you do over the phone or computer? I have a friend trying to remember something."

"I've gotten some good results over Zoom. When did you want to do it?"

"Now if you can."

"Ummm, yeah, I can do that. My next appointment is thirty minutes out."

"Okay, let me set the scene for you. My friend here is Junior. His father was murdered after he hid a large stash of illegal elephant ivory. He gave Junior a map with some directions written on it. That map has been destroyed. Junior only looked at the map once, and we are trying to finish the sentence that we recovered from a notepad where he wrote down the directions. The sentence I was able to pull says—*Junior, I stashed the ivory near the cave of bats. Follow road from Majuaneti to the...* That's all we have."

"Okay, give me a couple of minutes to set up the Zoom call and I'll text you a password. Just place Junior in front of your laptop and take notes."

"Gotcha. Standing by."

They hung up, and Rick pulled out his MacBook while Junior pulled over to a parking lot and climbed to the back of the Overland. Shortly thereafter, Rick's phone whistled with a password for the Zoom meeting. Rick typed it in, grabbed a notepad, and lowered the lights, as Junior introduced himself to TC.

"Okay, Junior. I want you to watch this pencil. I'm going to move it back and forth. Follow it with your eyes but don't move your head."

Junior followed it closely as TC moved it slowly back and forth.

"Now, close your eyes and go back to the last time you saw the map. On the count of three, you will be back there at that exact time. One, two, three..."

Junior closed his eyes.

"I'm going to read the note to you," said TC. "Finish the sentence: *Junior, I stashed the ivory near the cave of bats. Follow road from Majuaneti to the...*"

Junior took a deep breath and said, "Bat Cave, go five kilometers north and map the sausage rock arrow. The route of the ivory is under the left shiny tree island in the river border of Z's."

"Is there any more, Junior?"

"No."

"Okay, on the count of three you will return from your sleep. One, two, three…"

Junior opened his eyes.

"Dammit, it didn't work. I couldn't remember a thing!"

Rick turned the notepad toward Junior. His eyes widened.

"I said that?"

"You did. It makes no sense. What the hell is a sausage rock? Maybe it's a tree that has shiny bark?"

"I have no idea. Anyway, thank you, TC. I appreciate you."

"My pleasure. If I can help in any way, don't hesitate to give me a call."

"Thanks, TC," interjected Rick before he closed his MacBook.

"Let's grab Possum some comfort food and break him out of that hospital. I need to stop by a toy store first."

"Okay, I know one by the hotel."

Rick ran into the gift shop and returned with a long green plastic snake.

"Oh no, you're not!"

Rick grinned. "Oh yes, I am. He'll get me back, I'm sure. We've been pulling shit like this for years."

They stopped at the Hungry Lion and got Possum a Big Boss chicken sandwich combo. Rick rolled up the green plastic snake and stuck it inside the bag just beneath the sandwich box. When they arrived at the hospital, Rick opened his video camera on his phone and handed it to Junior.

"Make sure you get his reaction."

"I will!"

"You're getting out of here, buddy! I'm sure you're starved. I got you this killer chicken sandwich. Here ya go," said Rick as he passed the bag to Possum and placed the drink beside his bed.

Possum reached into the bag and pulled out the sandwich, then looked into the bag to grab the fries.

"Son of a bitch!" he yelled as he tossed the bag.

He damn near fell off of the bed.

"Paybacks are a bitch, Rick!"

"I know. I know. But you are gonna go viral!"

CHAPTER EIGHT

The doctor signed the release papers for Possum, and the nurse pushed him to the exit in a wheelchair. Considering he had just been bitten by a green mamba, one of Africa's most venomous snakes, he was feeling better than he had in months. His only issue was his hand. It was stiff and would take time to improve with therapy. He was given a list of exercises from the onsite therapist and planned to do them on his own until he got back to Florida.

Rick let Possum ride up front with Junior as they made their way to Majuaneti. It was about a two-hour drive southeast from the hospital. They got there late in the evening and decided to dry camp for the night. Junior had topped off all of the water tanks before they left, and they could stay in the Overland for up to seven days off the grid. Junior made chip beef sandwiches he had picked up at the market before Possum's release.

After dinner, Rick showed Possum what he had deciphered from the note and what TC had pulled from Junior's memory. He read it aloud.

> *Junior,*
> *I stashed the ivory near the cave of bats. Follow road from Majuaneti to the Bat Cave, go five kilometers north and map the sausage rock arrow. The route of the ivory is under the left shiny tree island in the river border of Z's.*

"What do you think? It doesn't make a lot of sense to me," said Rick.

Possum read it again and again.

"What the hell is a sausage rock?"

"No clue," replied Junior.

"What part of the sentence did you get from you Zoom session?"

Junior leaned over and drew a pencil line between the words *the* and *Bat*.

"Everything from Bat Cave forward came from our session," said Junior.

"You know, I remember talking to TC a few times about his hypnosis sessions. He said words and phrases can something be backward in a session. Let's play around with the words a little."

Possum circled the words that didn't make sense and began to rearrange them. *Sausage, shiny, map, arrow.* He changed the sentence a few times.

"How about this?"

I stashed the ivory near the cave of bats. Follow the sausage road from Majuaneti to the Bat Cave, go five kilometers north and left to the shiny rock arrow. The map of the ivory is under the tree island in the river border of Z's.

Junior looked again. "Still doesn't make sense. Try again." Possum moved the words around again and then slid it to Junior.

I stashed the ivory near the cave of bats. Follow road on the map from Majuaneti to Bat Cave, go five kilometers north to the sausage tree. The route of the ivory is under the shiny rock arrow to river island in the border of Z's.

Junior stared at it. Then as if a lightbulb went off, he said, "That's it! *Sausage tree.* Now that makes sense."

"Sausage tree makes sense? What the hell is a sausage tree?"

"They are large trees that have a sausage shape fruit that weigh up to ten pounds. They are known to grow in this area.

"What about shiny rock?" asked Possum.

"Not sure about that one. Maybe it's a rock near a tree that's shiny? Or...maybe it's referring to a hematite or amethyst. I read that they are common down here," said Rick.

"We may be on to something. The part that doesn't make sense is the part about river island and border of Z's," said Possum.

"Sometimes Zambia and Zimbabwe are referred to as Z's, as in *World War Z*, that movie. There is no river near Majuaneti though. So, island river leaves me clueless," said Junior, scratching his head.

"In the morning, we'll continue past the Bat Caves and see if we can find this sausage tree and shiny rock," said Rick. "It's all we got so far."

They called it a night and all went to their bunks.

Jules had spent a lot of time organizing and cleaning the new explorer ship. She was getting bored and missing Rick and trying to keep busy doing anything to keep her mind off the situation. It was the first time in a long time that she and Rick had been apart this long, and she was hating it.

She noticed that the dinghy registration had expired. She decided to take care of it for Gary. He gave her the paperwork and his credit card, and she took one of the scooters down Truman Avenue to the Monroe County Tax Collector's Office to pay for it. As she stood in line, there was a TV in the corner of the room that kept scrolling with images of wanted people. She watched it in boredom, waiting for her number to be called. Several of the people on the wanted video had broken their probation or were wanted for failure to appear. She wrote down a few names. It had been a while since she'd played bounty hunter and she needed something to do.

Ever since she had been carjacked in Mississippi a few months back, she'd vowed to never let anyone get the jump on her again or take advantage of her. After many therapy sessions, she'd decided to take control if her life and had started a little side business as a bounty hunter. She had taken down countless fugitives and every single time, it got her blood flowing. She had no idea how long Rick would in Africa, and they didn't have a firm date on when they'd try to retrieve the Mayan gold they had dumped off of the stern of *Nine-Tenths*. So, she figured now was as good a time as any to take on another job.

She hopped onto her scooter and drove up Truman to US1 over to Stock Island and parked at Key West Bail Bonds.

"Good afternoon, I'm Juliana Castro. I'm a licensed bail enforcement agent from up in Destin. Do you ever need any help? I mean, do you hire outside contractors?"

"Hello, Miss Castro. I'm Albert, I own the place. We can use all the help we can get. What is your specialty?"

"I'm up for whatever. I just need to work a few cases to stay busy. You have anything hot you need help with?"

Albert thought for a minute then slid a folder toward her.

"Take your pick. We pay first come first serve here."

She opened it up and thumbed through the printouts. She picked two of them and asked Albert to make copies for her. One was a young Dominican girl with a probation violation. The other was a more serious case that paid well. It was a known drug dealer with three felony counts for trafficking. He'd been released on bond and had failed to appear for his court date. She'd dust off her skills with the young Dominican girl first then try to tackle the drug dealer. She decided to keep it from Rick. Not because she was being sneaky; she just didn't want him to worry. He had enough on his plate. After all, he knew she would do whatever she wanted as far as bond recovery went and he supported her. She did, however, speak to Gary about it back at the ship.

"When do you think we'll shove off to recover the gold?" asked Jules.

"I'm not sure, Jules. It ain't going anywhere and we need to do a shakedown cruise first. Maybe over to the Bahama banks. Why?"

"I'm bored," she said as she slid the two photocopies of the fugitives over to Gary.

He picked them up and raised his right eyebrow.

"Wanna have some fun and make some cash?" asked Jules.

"Sure, I'm in the mood to crack a head or two. You can keep the cash. Call it my bounty hunter lesson."

"It's actually referred to as 'bail enforcement agent'," she said.

"See, I'm learning already."

They both laughed and agreed to work together. It would be at least a couple of weeks until the repairs on *Nine-Tenths* were completed. Then they'd have to deliver the yacht back to Destin, circle back, and focus on the gold recovery. They all hoped Rick would be back by then.

Jules pulled out her laptop and did a Lexis Nexus search for the Dominican girl. Rick had given her the password for his Lexis Nexus account, a detailed website for everything from background checks to work history. She typed in the woman's name and last-known address: *Dahiana Peña— 5537 College Rd, Key West, FL 33040*

A cross check revealed that the address was a homeless shelter assistance business and her last-known employer was the Blue Marlin Motel. Jules would start there. Gary would come along as a backup in case anything went sideways. He had rented a Chevy Suburban and had been using it to get supplies for the new ship.

When they arrived, Gary parked across the street from the Blue Marlin, and Jules crossed over. She stopped by the office and asked if Dahiana worked there anymore, saying she was a friend. The man behind the counter told her to speak with one of the maids. Jules found her cart and got her attention.

"Excuse me, I'm looking for Dahiana, is she here? I owe her some money."

"Is you a cop?!"

"No, no, nothing like that. We are friends and she was gonna help me get a job here and loaned me sixty dollars. I just wanna pay her back."

"Oh okay, she's working at the Southwinds. She died her hair red. You know, after she got in trouble."

"Gotcha."

"I can give her the money if you want. I see her a lot."

"Sure, I'd appreciate that. Just let her know I stopped by."

Jules handed her the sixty dollars and quickly walked around the corner back toward the Suburban.

"Miss, miss, I didn't get your name…"

Jules was around the corner and gone before the woman could get her attention. She figured the sixty was a finder's fee. She'd get well over six hundred dollars for returning Dahiana to custody.

"Let's roll. She's at the Southwinds."

Gary plugged the address into his GPS, and they stopped a block away from the motel. Jules hid behind some palm fronds while Gary went around the back. She waited and watched.

There was a maid's cart sitting in front of room six toward the back. The door was closed and there didn't seem to be any movement. After fifteen minutes, the door opened and a dark woman with bright red hair stepped out of the room with a cleaning bin in her right hand. She placed it on the cart and began to push the cart to the next room. Jules slowly walked up behind her.

When she got a few feet from her, she said, "Excuse me, Dahiana Peña?"

The woman slammed the cart into the wall and began to run to the back of the building with Jules in hot pursuit. As the woman turned the corner, she ran right into Gary's chest and it stopped her in her tracks. She spun around to face Jules's 9mm right in her face.

"Don't move!"

Jules tossed the handcuffs to Gary, and he snapped them into place with her arms behind her back. Dahiana was defeated. She didn't even struggle any longer. They walked her to the Suburban, and Jules sat in the rear seat behind her as Gary drove toward the M.C.S.O. Admissions and Release building. After filling out the intake form, they returned to the Suburban.

"One down, one to go," said Jules with a wink.

"Who's next?" asked Gary.

"This guy. He's much more dangerous and the bounty is ten thousand."

Gary read aloud:

Elijah James:
Felony Possession with Intent to Sell or Distribute
Felony Trafficking
Failure To Appear

She had printed out his rap sheet, and it was as long as her arm and included arrests for battery, armed robbery, and kidnapping. He was an extremely dangerous criminal and wouldn't be easy to find. Jules searched his Facebook profile, but it hadn't been active for some time. She scrolled down and looked at his check-ins. A few months back, he had checked into a strip club in Ft. Lauderdale and another one in Miami. He sure loved the ladies. His last-known address was just off of Brickell in downtown Miami.

"Wanna go to Miami?" asked Jules.

"Everybody's got a cousin in Miami," replied Gary.

They made the three-hour trip and got adjoining rooms at the W hotel. After dinner, they drove over to the Scarlett's Caberet. Jules waited in the Suburban while Gary went in alone.

Gary approached the bartender and slid a photo of Elijah across the bar.

"You know this guy?"

Without even looking at it, he slid it back to Gary.

"Never seen him before."

Gary placed a hundred-dollar bill on the photo and slid it back.

"How about now?"

He glanced down at it, snatched the hundred-dollar bill, and slid the photo back.

"He's been in here before. Whatcha drinking?"

"Club soda. Will this cover it?"

Gary slid two more hundred-dollar bills across the bar.

"He comes in on Tuesdays. It's bottle night. He usually gets that corner table."

Gary nodded and walked out.

"What's the deal?" asked Jules.

"Okay, you owe me three hundred dollars. Ha-ha. The bartender said he usually comes in on Tuesdays. That's tomorrow. Maybe you can get a job as a stripper?"

Jules playfully slapped Gary. "Not in a million years! But I will be a cocktail waitress."

"That's even better, Jules. Go inside and see if they will hire you. We can come back tomorrow night and nail that son of a bitch."

"Done!"

Jules put on fresh lipstick and some striking blue eyeshadow. She strolled in and walked back out ten minutes later carrying a skinny black skirt and a top on a hanger, and hopped in the front seat.

"You're looking at Scarlett's Cabaret's newest cocktail waitress. They wanted me to dance, but I told them I can make them more money as a waitress. I start at six tomorrow."

"Perfect. I'll wear my finest suit and slick back my hair. It was so dark in there and with this baseball cap on, the bartender will never even recognize me."

They made their way back to the W hotel and went over the plan for the next night as Gary ordered room service.

"You know Rick's gonna kick my ass for letting you do this."

"Rick and I have an agreement. He knows I like to do skip tracing and he supports me."

"I know, but this guy is dangerous. I'm a little concerned."

"We'll be fine. You know you catch a lot more bees with honey than vinegar. I'm gonna charm the crap out of this guy if he shows. He won't know what hit him."

"Okay, Jules, it's your show."

The parking lot was packed when Gary dropped off Jules at the strip club. He drove up the street and took a spot in a paid lot. He waited twenty minutes then headed to the cabaret. They were early and the corner table had a "Reserved" sign on it. Gary sat down and enjoyed some of the dancers.

Jules came around a few times and took his order, always delivering club soda. Gary had gone through all of his single bills by nine p.m. when Elijah stepped inside. Several dancers rushed up to him and rubbed on his chest. He tipped them all and had a huge wad of hondos.

He had an entourage with him. Some rather large guys. They needed to separate him from his muscle. He was sure that if anyone could do it, Jules could.

"Good evening, what can I get you fine gentlemen tonight?"

"The usual," replied Elijah.

She went to the bar, and the bartender had already placed a new bottle of Cîroc with set-ups. She delivered it to him and made sure he saw her cleavage as she bent over and placed it on the table.

"You're new here, ain't you?" he said, eyeing her up and down.

"Yep, first night. They wanted me to dance, but I wanna try my hand at cocktail waitressing first."

"Why don't you come dance for me? I'll take care of you."

"Enjoy your Cîroc, sir," she said as she turned and walked away.

He watched her walk back to the bar and Gary noticed. It was on.

Jules worked the room and checked back with Elijah's table often. Every time she went by, he tried to touch her and she pushed his hand away.

"How much you gonna make here tonight?" asked Elijah.

"The bartender said I can make up to three hundred if we have a good night."

"I'll pay you a thousand dollars if you'll give me a private dance." Elijah motioned to a back room with his head.

He slid a stack of hundred-dollar bills across the table toward her. She had him exactly where she wanted him. She pretended to think about it, picked up the cash, stuck it in her bra, then said, "Okay, fifteen minutes only, no touching. Deal?"

"Deal!"

She put down her tray and gave Gary a look, then she took Elijah's hand and led him to the private room. She sat him in a chair in the middle of the room and turned on Def Leppard's "Pour Some Sugar On Me." She started to slowly dance in front of him as he took her clothes off with his eyes. She moved around and behind him, tracing his arm with her fingers. She put her fingers in his hair and slowly pulled out her taser. As he melted into the chair from her rubbing his head, she placed the taser against his neck and pushed the button.

He yelped loudly and fell to the floor. She pulled her cuffs out of her purse and put his hands behind his back. The goons outside heard him yell and ran to the private room. Gary was right behind them. As they shoved the door open, one of them pulled out his pistol.

"Don't move, scumbag!" yelled Gary as he took aim at the man's back. All three of them put their hands in the air. The music on the main dance floor was so loud, no one even noticed what was going on.

"Come around here, Jules," said Gary. To the men, he snapped, "Don't move a muscle and lose the gun."

The man in the middle slowly lowered his right arm and placed the gun on the floor.

"Kick it away," demanded Gary.

He did as he was told. Jules stood behind the guy on the left, and Gary was behind the guy on the right. He nodded and Jules tased the guy in front of her. He fell to the floor, as did the other guy. Before the middle guy could turn around, they both tased him and he violently shook and fell to his knees, then straight down on his face. Gary put oversized zip ties on them all and dug through their pockets. Each one of them had an eight ball of coke in their pockets.

Jules and Gary grabbed Elijah, put his arms around their necks, and slowly walked out of the room and locked the door behind them. He looked like a rag doll as they helped him out toward the exit door. Jules was relieved to be getting out of there. She despised places like that and the people who frequented them. All she could think about was taking a shower and burning her clothes.

"He's wasted. I'm gonna get him home," said Gary to no one in particular as the girls looked on.

Once they were back in the Suburban, Jules handcuffed Elijah to the door handle. Gary drove off with his iPhone against his ear.

"911, what's your emergency?"

"Some guys with guns at Scarlett's Cabaret busted up a private room and have drugs on them."

"We'll send a unit there now. Who am I speaking with?"

"Never mind, just go get 'em."

He hung up and they drove toward the Miami Dade Police Department on 2nd Avenue. They handed Elijah over to one of the officers and filled out the necessary paperwork. On the way back to the Suburban, they slapped a high-five in the air.

"Easy money!" said Gary.

"Plus, that idiot paid me a thousand dollars to dance, which lasted all of thirty seconds. Counting that plus my tips, I made a bonus of $1167. Drinks are on me!" exclaimed Jules.

"Ha-ha, clink, clink," replied Gary.

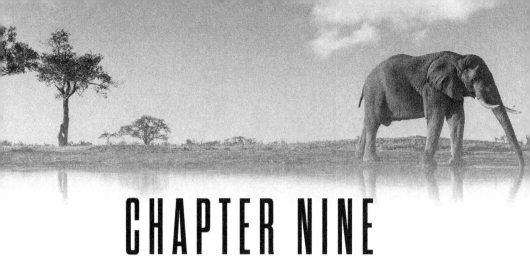

CHAPTER NINE

There was a line of cars turning into the parking area off of the dirt two-track road for the Bat Caves.

"Look, that is a sausage tree. Actually, all five of those are," said Junior as he pointed at a group of trees.

They turned due north on the dirt road when they reached the sausage trees. The road ran out and they were on rough terrain now. The Overland could handle almost any terrain and they steadily made progress. Once they were about five kilometers north, they starting scanning the area for more sausage trees. Another kilometer ahead was a ridge, and just on the other side of the ridge stood a tall, lone sausage tree. Junior said it was rare to only see one sausage tree, as their fruit was popular with many animals that would excrete the seeds all over the area.

Once they got closer, they realized why there was a single one standing here. The entire area near the tree had been cleared for cultivation. Squatting farmers would plant areas off the beaten path with khat bushes. It was obvious that the area had just recently been tilled. Off in the distance, Rick spotted a large burn pile that was still smoldering. Looking through his binoculars, it was clear where all the other sausage trees had ended up. The problem was now, which tree was Junior's dad referring to?

"How the hell are we gonna find it?" asked Rick in frustration.

They scanned the entire area and realized there were no shiny rocks anywhere in the area.

"This makes no sense. Remember that sausage tree on the main road before we turned north?" asked Possum.

"Yeah, why?"

"Maybe I still have the words out of order. How about try this."

Possum pulled the note out of his pocket and reread it.

I stashed the ivory near the cave of bats. Follow road on the map from Majuaneti to Bat Cave, go five kilometers north to the sausage tree. The route of the ivory is under the shiny rock arrow to left river island in the border of Z's.

"Now let's move the word 'left' after the second 'ivory'. 'Left river' never really made sense to me."

I stashed the ivory near the cave of bats. Follow road on the map from Majuaneti to Bat Cave, go five kilometers north to the sausage tree. The route of the ivory is left under the shiny rock arrow to river island in the border of Z's.

"That would mean we turn left at the sausage trees," said Rick. "Isn't the Kafue River about five kilometers south of here? Maybe we're looking for an arrowhead made from a shiny rock."

"Yeah, but look at this."

Possum pulled out his iPad with a Google Earth view of the river five kilometers from the first sausage tree cluster. There were two little islands. One on the north side of the river and one on the south.

"That's it!" exclaimed Junior. "It just came back to me. He was referring to the north island. I used to have a hunting blind there, and my dad and I would hide there and video the mass wildebeest migration. Just move the word 'north' in front of the word 'island'."

I stashed the ivory near the cave of bats. Follow road on the map from Majuaneti to Bat Cave, go five kilometers to the sausage tree arrow. The route of the ivory is left under the shiny rock arrow to north river island in the border of Z's.

Junior slapped his knee in excitement. "That has to be it! The Kafue River is divided in the middle between the north and the south island. The north side is Zambia and the south side Zimbabwe. *The border of Z's.*"

Rick let out a "whoop!" followed by, "Let's boogie!"

Junior threw the Overland into gear and whipped it around. When they got to the group of sausage trees on the main road, he crossed it and found another dirt road heading south. He made note of his odometer and continued driving.

At the 4.9 kilometer mark, the Kafue River came into view. Rick pulled out his binoculars and scanned the closest island to them, which would be the north one. On the far-left edge, something shiny reflected in the sun. He zoomed in closer and saw it. It was a large, flat piece of amethyst.

Junior pulled over to the river's edge and opened one of the storage areas. He rolled out an inflatable boat, and they took turns pumping it up. Rick put some digging tools in the boat. The river was slow-flowing, so they carried the inflatable upstream from the island and put it in. They'd let the slow current do most of the work to get over to the little sand island. Once they arrived on the river, they pulled the little inflatable up onto the bank of the island and made haste to the shiny rock. It was about four feet by six feet wide and was extremely heavy. Junior took out the shovel and was about to begin digging when Rick stopped him.

"Wait, wait," said Rick. "We'd need a backhoe to get this rock out. I seriously doubt your dad took a backhoe over the river to lift this rock and bury the bounty. Let's think about this. Let's look on the island and see if we can find an arrowhead."

They all walked around, scanning the ground for an arrowhead. They were fairly common near rivers, so it made perfect sense. But they searched and searched and never found one.

"The river rises and falls. Wouldn't an arrowhead get washed away when the river rises?" asked Junior.

"You're right, unless it weighed a lot," replied Rick as he noticed Possum digging the sand from around the rectangular rock.

As he dug, he revealed more of the rock, and soon the far-left side of the rock came to a point. When Rick squinted and looked at it with one eye closed, it looked like a giant arrowhead. He and Junior ran over to try and lift it. It wouldn't budge. Rick walked around the back side of the rock and aimed his arm in the direction the arrow was pointing. It pointed exactly toward a sausage tree at the far west end of the island.

The three of them walked over to the tree. At the base of the tree was a flat, almost chrome-looking rock that looked like it had no business being there. Rick grabbed the edge of it and lifted it. Underneath was an aluminum cigar box. They all looked at each other in anxious wonder. Rick slowly lifted open the box and revealed a Ziploc baggie with a note inside. He pulled it out and read aloud.

Junior,

If you found this note then you know I am dead. I've had many threats against me since I swiped the ivory. For the sake of the elephants, please destroy the ivory except for one piece. You'll know the one. My killer will be revealed on the carved ivory. Follow the Apple with the Detector to the location.

I love you, son,
Dad

Junior's eyes were welling up.

Rick put a hand on his shoulder. "I'm sorry, Junior. We're gonna find the person responsible for killing your dad and make them pay. I promise."

"I'm more confused than when we started," said Possum, twisting his mouth.

"Me too. What does 'follow the Apple' mean? There aren't apple trees around here," replied Rick.

"Maybe he meant an Apple product. Like an iPhone or computer," interjected Junior.

"Did your dad have an iPhone?

"No, actually, he had a Samsung," replied Junior.

"What does 'the detector' mean?" asked Rick.

"I don't know. Metal detector? My dad had several of those. They are in his storage unit."

"The one where the Defender was hidden?"

"No, he had a small ten-by-ten he kept his Safari gear in over in Livingstone, close to Victoria Falls. He used to start some safari tours with an excursion to the falls and then go up to his base camp for the animals. He also did gold-hunting excursions on the Zimbabwe side. That's why he bought all the metal detectors. I think he had like ten of them."

They climbed back into the inflatable canoe and got back on the river. Rick looked like he'd just won the lotto. All he could think of was finding gold, but he snapped out of it. That wasn't why they were here. They paddled the inflatable back to the bank, then Junior jogged upstream and drove the Overland back to them. They rolled up the inflatable, bound for Victoria Falls.

"We still need to find out more about Colin Mulenga," said Rick. "We are actually a lot closer to Chirundu than Livingstone. You ready to put on your acting hat, Possum?"

"Oh, yeah. I was practicing my Norwegian accent quite a bit while in the hospital."

"Okay, let's head to Chirundu and get you a suit. I'll try and arrange a meeting with Colin."

Junior started driving east to Chirundu, and Rick pulled out his MacBook and found the email address for Colin. He had his official government email address and another one attached to his land development holdings website: Zulinda International. Rick created a fake email address for Possum as Ole Hannsen and fired off a short, to-the-point request.

Mr. Mulenga,

My name is Ole Hannsen from Oslo. I am an angel investor and property developer. I will be in town for two days only, meeting with potential matches. Your name came up in a meeting I had in Lusaka and I am interested in your casino resort project. Can we meet? I'll be in Chirundu tomorrow and Thursday. Please call my cell or respond to this email as soon as you can.

Sincerely,
Ole Hannsen
+47 90 55 41 38

Rick fired off the email, then created the Norway number using the Google Phone app and forwarded the number to ring on Possum's cell phone.

"Now change your message to be Ole," requested Rick.

Possum pulled his phone out of his backpack and was about to record a new outgoing message when the phone started vibrating. It was a Zambian number.

"Answer it—hurry, before it goes to voicemail."

"Hei, dette er Ole." Possum put the speaker on so Rick and Junior could listen in.

"Hello, is this Mr. Hannsen?"

"Ja, Ole Hannsen. Who is calling?"

"Hi, I'm Colin Mulenga. I just received an email from you regarding a visit to Chirundu."

"Ah, ya, that was fast. I just sent that."

"Yes, well, I'd love to meet with you. Are you free tomorrow?"

"Hold please, let me check my calendar."

Possum held his hand over the phone for half a minute then returned to the line.

"Ya, I have a ten a.m. meeting. I can meet you 'fore or after lunch."

"Most excellent, Mr. Hannsen. Do you know where the Nando's restaurant is? I can meet you there at noon, if that works for you?"

"That is agreeable. I'll see you at noon. Ha det bra, I mean goodbye for now."

"Very impressive, Possum. Throwing in a few Norwegian words really put the icing on the cake," said Rick.

"Well, let's find me something impressive to wear. Dress to impress, as they say," said Possum.

"I have a friend who owns a funeral home in Chirundu. He will have what you need," said Junior.

"I ain't wearing no dead guy's suit!" exclaimed Possum.

"Calm down, Ole. He has brand-new suits he sells at a huge discount for people who want an open casket but don't have a suit. He gets them from France. His daughter goes to school there and she has them shipped to him. Everyone gets their suits from him. His wife is also a tailor, so she can make you look like a million bucks," replied Junior.

Junior put the Overland in four-wheel drive and climbed up the steep bank on the river's edge. Once on blacktop, he put it in two-wheel drive and drove east, bound for Chirundu.

The funeral home didn't even look like a funeral home. It looked just like a normal ranch-style house in a normal sub-urban neighborhood. Rick noticed that many businesses around here looked like that. One house might be a tire shop and another a bakery. Unless you knew any better, you'd just think it was someone's home. There were no business signs anywhere to speak of. Once inside, that all changed. The entire area that would be considered a great room was actually a showroom of caskets.

"Good afternoon, Junior. What brings you here?" asked Paul.

"Paul, these are my friends from America. This guy would like to get one of your custom-tailored suits for a big meeting he's having tomorrow. Can you squeeze him in?" asked Junior as he patted Possum on the shoulder.

"Hold on. Mincy, can you tailor a suit today?" he yelled toward the back of the house.

A petite curly-haired woman strolled in from the back carrying a notepad and a soft measuring tape.

"Yes, I can. I just finished sewing the bottom of a pair of slacks. She wrapped the tape around Possum and up and down his legs and said, "Pick a 44 long. Come with me."

"Have fun," said Rick as Possum walked away with the woman.

She led Possum into one of the converted bedrooms with racks and racks of suits. He pulled out a couple then chose a dark-gray pinstriped suit and black wingtips.

"How fancy is this meeting? I'm sorry, I didn't get your name."

"Oh, it's Poss...uhem... Call me MJ."

"Okay, MJ. How fancy?"

"I need to make a great impression."

"In that case, you'll want cufflinks as well. We just got a new shipment of them in. Also, a matching handkerchief. Here, look at this one."

Possum picked up the silk handkerchief and gave it back to her with a nod. He put on the suit and she made a few marks with tailor's chalk.

"You can pick it up at four-thirty. Paul will take care of the money part."

Possum put his street clothes back on and met the guys in the great room.

Mincy handed Paul a note, and he did some quick calculating. "That will be 4,338.42 kwacha. Or...$240 US."

Rick pulled out three hundred-dollar bills and passed them to Paul. "Keep the change. Make him look amazing."

Paul thanked Rick for his generosity and walked them outside.

"That's quite the Overland you have there, Junior."

"Yeah, it's damn near brand new. It had no scratches on it until we came across an angry hippo," said Junior, pointing at the cracked turn signal.

"You better get that fixed. They'll write you up for it."

"Yeah, I ordered a new light assembly."

They all shook hands, and Junior backed out of the driveway.

"Where to?" asked Junior.

"Let's get some rooms. I'm tired of being cramped in the Overland. No offense," said Rick.

"None taken. There aren't really any hotels here. Only hunting lodges. The nicest one is the Charangwe Hurungwe Safari Lodge. It sits on the bank of the Zambezi River and has amazing sunsets."

"Sounds like a winner!"

Junior drove to the lodge, which was only about six miles outside of Chirundu. It was just as he'd described it. The back deck overlooked the Zambezi, and the outdoor furniture was all hand-carved. Rick rented two luxury doubles. He and Possum would share one and Junior would take the other.

After they all took showers, they met on the deck for some local cuisine and drinks. The service was five star and Rick tried the Maheu, a traditional beverage made from finger millet. It was a drink as old as the people of Zambia. It wasn't to his liking, though, and he decided to stick with beer after that.

After a few hours of ha-ha, clink, clink, they settled in their rooms. It was almost midnight and only five p.m. back in Florida, so Rick stepped onto the terrace to give Jules a call.

"Hey, baby, how's it going? Anything new?" asked Rick.

"Don't be mad, Rick, but I got bored, so Gary and I did a couple of skip traces. They went smooth and we already delivered the perps to the jail."

"You are something else, Jules. I wish you wouldn't do stuff so dangerous, but I'm not about to tell you no."

"I know, Rick. That's why I love you. You let me be me. How's Possum and the case?"

"Possum's doing great. He's gonna put on his acting hat tomorrow and become Ole Hannsen. He's got it down pat."

"Ha-ha, I always said he should be an actor."

"Is Chief there?"

"No, we are actually driving south on A1A now. We'll be back in Key West in three hours. You want me to call you back?"

"Naw, I'll catch him tomorrow or the next day. I'll be long into dreamland by then. Give him a kiss on the beak for me and say hi to Gary and Johnie."

"Gary's right here. He just waved hi. What about my kiss?!"

Rick put his lips to the phone and made an exaggerated kissing sound in the mouthpiece.

"That's better, mister."

Jules did the same back and said goodbye.

Rick climbed into his double bed and covered his head with a pillow to block out Possum's snoring on the bed next to his. He fell asleep within minutes.

Around 3:30 a.m., Rick was awakened by a loud crashing sound. Powerful flashlights blinded him.

"Don't move. Put your hands behind your head!" yelled one of the men.

"Which is it? Don't move or put my hands behind my head?" said Rick sarcastically.

"Get on the ground and put your hands behind your head. Cross your ankles."

Rick reluctantly did as he was told, as Possum sat there with his hands in the air.

"What's this about?!"

"You are wanted for questioning about a shooting in Lusaka."

"Where are you taking me?"

"Lusaka Central Correctional Facility. You will have a first appearance in the morning with Judge Malonic."

"What am I charged with?"

"Second-degree murder and unlawful use of a firearm."

"Possum, go ahead with the planned meeting and call Gary."

"Okay, Rick. We'll get you out ASAP."

The two officers picked Rick up and dragged him out of the door, then threw him into the back of a van and disappeared into the black night.

By now, everyone in the lodge was awake and outside to see what was going on, including Junior.

"They took Rick!" Possum hollered at him.

"Where?"

"Lusaka Central Correctional Facility."

"Oh crap, that place is a hell hole. He won't last long there. It's probably a shakedown."

Possum ran back into his room and called Gary.

"Gary, it's Possum. The local police just busted in here and dragged Rick down to the jail. He is being arraigned in the morning. Junior thinks it's about money. Please monitor your phone. We may need to wire some money to get him out."

"Okay, I'll fly there if need be. Just keep me posted. I'll keep this between us. I don't want Jules to freak out."

"Good idea. I'll call you tomorrow after his first appearance."

Possum looked at the clock and it was almost four a.m. He was way too wired to go back to sleep, so he and Junior made some coffee and discussed what to do next.

"Rick wants me to go ahead with the meeting. I think we need to head to the prison instead."

"How about I go to the hearing and you stay here and do the meeting? They have a lodge car you can use. I'll leave shortly. First appearance is usually at eight a.m. I'll see if I can talk to the judge," said Junior.

"I guess that's what we have to do. How bad is that prison?"

"Have you seen the movie *Midnight Express*?"

"Yeah, that bad?"

"*Midnight Express* is a Hilton compared to Lusaka Central Correctional Facility. Plus, he's white and American. It won't go well for him."

"Rick is one of the toughest sons of bitches I've ever known. If anyone can survive it, he can."

"I hope you're right. I'll be praying."

CHAPTER TEN

Rick was lying face down on the floor of the van as one of the cops leaned over and whispered in his ear.

"You are gonna be popular where you're going. Fresh meat!"

"Fuck you!" said Rick, which earned him a quick kick to his ribcage.

"Ugggh!" he moaned.

Once he was fingerprinted and photographed at the jail, he was placed in a holding cell to await his appearance before the judge. There were five other locals in the small room with metal benches. The toilet looked like it hadn't been cleaned since the place opened. Flies and roaches outnumbered the inmates a hundred to one.

When the door locked behind Rick, he turned around to see a huge man with a cut above his eye. The man looked at Rick, and a huge grin came over his face. He stepped toward Rick.

Rick knew he had to make an example of the man right way or he was gonna have a bad experience on the inside.

When the man was about two feet away, Rick looked down at the man's shoes, which made the man glance down, too. Rick closed his fist and swung harder than he ever had with an uppercut just under the man's chin. Rick's hand writhed in pain from connecting to the bone.

The man just stood there for a brief second, then like a hewn tree falling in the forest, he toppled face down on the concrete with his hands still by his side. He was knocked out cold before his face hit the ground. When he faceplanted, his nose exploded and blood splattered all over the stainless-steel toilet.

"Who's next!?" asked Rick as he waved two other men over.

They all had stood up, but at the sight of the giant man lying there like a bag of potatoes, they sat back down and made a motion toward Rick to stay away. Rick took a spot at the end of the bench, and the men closest to him moved farther away. He had made the impression he needed to make before being put into general population.

Possum parked the loaner car a few blocks from Nando's and arrived fifteen minutes before noon. He had picked up a magazine at a local stand and ordered a coffee while he waited for Colin to arrive. In his suit and designer reading glasses, he looked the part of a wealthy businessman. Colin arrived promptly at noon and waved at Possum, who was the only white man in the restaurant.

"You must be Mr. Hannsen?" said Colin.

"Please call me Ole."

The two men shook hands and Colin ordered a Munkoyo, a local Zambian drink made from maize.

"So, tell me about your project, Colin. I don't have a lot of time, but I am interested in your proposal."

"It has been a pet project of mine for some time. The plan is to build a three-hundred room resort and casino on the banks of the Kafue River. It will be the only five-star resort for hundreds of miles. Its location is ideal for attracting hunters and their families due to its proximity to safari land. The waterpark alone will draw thousands. Here is a copy of the plans."

Before Colin could roll out the plans, Possum said in his best Norwegian accent, "En utfordring."

"Excuse me?"

"It means, you have a big problem," replied Possum as he pointed at the northern edge of the plans.

"You've done your homework. I'm impressed," said Colin.

"How do you plan to build part of the resort on Kafue National Park land?"

Colin leaned in and winked at Possum. "As I'm sure you already know, I am in the government. I have a few less than scrupulous, shall we say, men on the inside, who have taken care of my main obstacle."

"What's the main obstacle?"

"Not what, who. Never mind. It's been handled. I have a proposal with the land commissioner to annex part of the park to be used for the resort. I just need a little thank you money to get the ball rolling."

Possum frowned. "I'm not getting involved in anything illegal."

"No, no, Mr. Hannsen, you misunderstand. In Africa, it's the way things are done. One scratches another back here, if you catch my drift."

"So, you are referring to bribe money."

"We call it campaign contributions. I'm sure you're familiar with it in your monarchy," said Colin.

"I see. How much are you seeking for...this campaign money, as you call it?" asked Possum.

"We need seven hundred and fifty thousand US dollars in seed money before we can move forward. I have two other main investors all at a 15 percent cut. You would be the third. I will retain 55 percent of the holdings. The problem is my other investors are with the opposition government and don't want anything to do with the rezoning. They are good to go with the main investment but fear their reputations being ruined if they donate to the opposing party. Do you understand? Each of the main investments is $10 million US. What do you think?"

Possum thought for a minute and studied the resort plans then said, "I am willing to invest ten million plus the $750,000 campaign contribution on one condition."

"What is it?"

"I want 18 percent of the company and two seats on the board. It's nonnegotiable."

Colin leaned back in his seat and stroked his chin.

"How soon can you get the funds? The $750k needs to be in cash."

"I can have it wired in a day or so. Do we have a deal?"

"We do, Mr. Hannsen. We do."

They shook hands and Colin walked out of the restaurant. He almost skipped out, it looked like to Possum. His Norwegian act had worked perfectly.

"All rise! The Judiciary Court is now in session. The Honorable Judge Malonic is presiding," said the bailiff.

Junior stood up from his seat in the courtroom. He'd arrived early to make sure he didn't miss the session.

In shackles and an orange jumpsuit, Rick rose to his feet at the front of the room, then sat back down once the judge was seated. The judge set bond amounts for several men and sentenced one to thirty days without a trial before he got to Rick's docket.

"Mr. Waters, I understand you have been appointed council. How do you plead?"

"Not guilty, Your Honor."

Silence fell over the courtroom as the judge read over the charges against Rick. Junior tapped Rick's court-appointed attorney on the shoulder and whispered something inaudible in his ear.

The lawyer nodded and stood up to go to the judge. "Your Honor, may we meet in your chambers?"

"As you wish."

"Mr. Waters has no family in Zambia, but his field guide Junior would like to address you, if that is agreeable."

"Let him come back."

The judge exited through a side door, and the bailiff escorted Junior and the lawyer to his chambers.

"What is it you wish to discuss, young man?" asked the judge.

"Well, Your Honor, if you look at the initial police report, the men who were shot by Mr. Waters and Miss Castro, who is no longer in the country, were bad men. They had committed several similar armed robberies in the Lusaka area over the past few months. You and I both know it was self-defense."

"I know nothing of the matter and I am offended that you would think I'd make such a judgment without all the facts."

"My apologies. I did not mean to insult you, Your Honor. I was merely stating what the facts are in case this goes to trial. There are several eyewitnesses to the incident, and I feel the state would be embarrassed in the end and lose this case, which would be highly publicized. In my opinion, Mr. Waters and Miss Castro did Lusaka a great favor. Instead of incarceration, they should get an accommodation."

The judge scanned through the police reports silently and then laid the entire folder down on the desk.

"What do you propose I do?"

"Mr. Waters is a man of great means. I propose a large fine and the case be dismissed and expunged from the records. Including Miss Castro's."

The judge put his hands together, crossed his fingers, and placed his chin on them. A few minutes passed by and then he said, "One hundred thousand US dollars and thirty days in the correctional facility. Upon completion of his time served, I will expunge both his and Miss Castro's case. That is my only offer," said the judge.

"But Your Honor, he won't make it in there. It's far too dangerous."

"That's not my problem. Take it or we go to trial."

"He'll never make it thirty days, Your Honor, and you won't get the money."

The judge thought for a minute.

"Okay, he will remain inside the Lusaka Central Correctional Facility until the money is transferred."

"That's fair," replied Junior.

The judge refastened the top button on his robe, and they all proceeded back into the courtroom.

"All rise," said the bailiff.

"Mr. Waters, you are to be remanded in the Lusaka Central Correctional Facility until the time of your trial."

Rick looked shocked. He glanced back at Junior, and Junior winked at him. Before the bailiff whisked Rick away, his lawyer whispered in his ear about the deal that had been made.

Junior immediately called Possum.

"Possum, we need a hundred thousand U.S. dollars to get Rick out. The judge has agreed to expunge both cases if we pay him."

"Damn, and I thought the US justice system was corrupt. I'll call Gary. Where should I have the money wired?"

"You can send it to my escrow account I have in the Bank of Zambia. I'll text you the routing and account number."

"Okay, don't be shocked when you see the account total. I also need to have another $750,000 wired as well. It's for the deal with Colin. The meeting went great!"

"Okay, sounds good. Why don't you take the lodge car back and have them put you on the bus to Lusaka. It will be faster than me coming to get you. I'll get us rooms at that same hotel we stayed in by the airport," said Junior.

Whistles and cat calls rang out as Rick was escorted through general population in the prison. The man he had knocked out cold was sitting in a cell and gave Rick the stank eye. Luckily for Rick, the word had already gotten out that he knew how to fight and wasn't afraid to take on all comers. He knew someone would make a try for him, so he got mentally prepared for what lay ahead. He was placed in a cell with his bedsheet and a personal cup. The bottom bunk was taken by an elderly man who he didn't even look up when Rick entered the cell.

The smell of urine and feces overwhelmed his senses, and he did his best to remain calm. His first order of business was to secure a weapon.

"Hey there, buddy. I'm Rick Waters. What's your name?"

The old man barely lifted his head and softly replied, "Name's Mateo Kimbro, but they calls me Zebra." He partially opened his shirt, revealing his vitiligo—a condition that occurred when pigment-producing cells died or stopped producing melatonin, causing him to have white patches all over his chest and arms.

"Whatcha in for, old timer?"

"Life."

"Life? For what crime?"

"Being poor. I was originally arrested on suspicion of burglary. That was twenty-seven years ago. I didn't have the money to pay the bribe to get off, so I'm here for good."

"Oh my God. That's horrible. I'm so sorry. I gotta ask. Did you do it?"

"I'm innocent. We're all innocent in here. Just ask anyone," he said with a raspy laugh that turned into a cough.

"You seem fine. They don't mess with you here?" asked Rick.

"They respect the elderly. Not when I first got here, though. Some big Zimbabwe man tried to rape me. I shanked him and they left me alone ever since. I can get things, you know. You want cigarettes or a shank?"

"I could definitely use a weapon."

"You'll be fine in the cell, but once you are in the yard, they's gonna be coming for ya."

"Thanks for the warning, Zebra. I'll keep my head on a swivel."

"The shank's gonna cost you two packs of smokes."

"Where do I get them?"

"See Chiumbo. You'll owe him and you don't wanna owe him for long."

"Chiumbo? What kinda name is that?"

"It means tiny, which is funny because he's the biggest guy in here. You can't miss him. He's about eleven feet tall and hangs out by the north fence in the yard," replied Zebra sarcastically.

"Got it," said Rick. "I appreciate your help."

Rick barely slept all night. The sounds of men singing African songs and the whimpering from the new inmates kept him on edge. For once in his life, he was glad to be inside a locked cage.

At sunup, the guards brought breakfast, unlocked and opened the jail doors. The slop on the plate made dog food look appealing. Rick smelled it and gave his portion to

Zebra. He was far too upset to eat. Let alone garbage like that. He hoped lunch would be better.

After breakfast, the doors stayed open and inmates milled around the yard. Some playing basketball. Others talking in small groups. Rick had to get to Chiumbo, and the only way was right through the center of the yard. He knew the danger, but he needed those cigarettes or his days alive would be numbered.

Halfway across the yard, two men started making their way toward him. Everyone in the yard stopped what they were doing and you could hear a pin drop. The tallest one blocked Rick's path and asked, "Wie dink jy is jy Yankee?"

Rick had no idea what he'd said, but he knew Yankee was what many people called people from the states.

"I ain't no Yankee, fuck face. I'm from the south!"

The man looked shocked at Rick's response, and he swung at Rick. In one move, Rick stepped to the right and grabbed his arm as he swung, moved him forward, and flipped him over his shoulder, knocking the man's breath out. Before he could get up, Rick raised his leg and stomped his face and busted his nose wide open. He kicked him several times in the ribs and he curled up like a baby. Cheers erupted in the yard, and a circle surrounded Rick and the other man, who lunged at Rick.

Rick turned sideways and kicked the man in the gut, folding him over. With the man bent over, Rick kneed him in the face then flung him sideways. He rolled to a dead stop. Rick took his fighting position and faced the crowd, waving them over with a crazed look in eyes.

"No takers?!" he yelled.

The men got silent and no one moved toward him.

"That's what I fucking thought," he murmured. He walked toward Chiumbo, and the crowd opened up like when Moses parted the Red Sea.

"Zebra sent me. I need a shank. He said I need two cartons of cigarettes."

"Follow me."

Rick followed the guy toward one of the cells. Chiumbo stepped inside and back out again with two cartons of menthol cigarettes.

"You owe me four cartons. You have two days."

"And if I can't get them?"

"One finger per carton. You understand?"

"Loud and clear."

Rick strolled back to his cell and handed the cigarettes to Zebra.

"Where's my shank?"

"Day after tomorrow. You read?" asked Zebra.

"Yeah, some," replied Rick.

"Check-out the book *Don Quixote* from the book cart. It's been set aside for you at the bottom of the stack. The middle of the book is the most exciting," Zebra winked.

Rick spent the rest of the day in his cell with Zebra, even though the door was wide open. It took some time, but Zebra finally opened up about his arrest when he was a much younger man. It had happened in 1994. He was minding his own business and walking home from work. A cop car pulled up to him and handcuffed him. He was put in a lineup and picked out by a white woman who owned a restaurant in Lusaka. He had never even been in that restaurant before. The judge sentenced him to ten years without a trial. His lawyer said if he could come up with ten thousand dollars, he would be released without a record.

Sounds familiar.

"How are you in for life then?" Rick asked him.

"The guy I killed on the inside who tried to rape me was tied to the Zambian crime syndicate. The judge changed my sentence to life. That was it. My life was over."

"Do you still wanna get out?"

"Yes, I'd give anything to see my grandbabies and great grandbabies. My daughter was pregnant when I was first arrested. I've never met the boy. He's a man now. Here's the last photo I got before the guards started throwing away my mail. I haven't received a letter or a visitor in here in over fifteen years."

As Rick looked at the tattered old photo of Zebra's young grandson, he felt his eyes welling up and squashed that immediately. This was not a place for crying. He was so infuriated and moved at the same time.

"I vow to get you out of here, come hell or highwater!" said Rick.

"Thanks, Rick," said Zebra with eyes that led Rick to think he didn't have faith he'd ever get out.

The one thing he had lost since being on the inside was hope. Hope was gone.

CHAPTER ELEVEN

Gary's private jet touched down at Kenneth Kaunda International Airport. Jules was still in the dark about Rick's incarceration. She was happy to be back in Africa, and all Gary told her was that all charges against her would be dropped once Gary paid some sort of fine. Wiring that kind of money would get the attention of the IRS, SEC, and other government busybodies. So, Gary had flown to Grand Cayman, where he kept an offshore account, and withdrawn $200,000 in big bills to take care of Rick and the scheme Possum was cooking up against Colin Mulenga.

At the airport in Zambia, he and Clay the pilot checked in with customs and immigration and paid off the agent to let Chief in without the proper veterinary paperwork. Once they were cleared, they all climbed into a car Gary had pre-arranged to pick them up.

Everything in Africa was run by money. Even checking in with immigration. Gary had placed a hundred-dollar bill inside of Jules's passport. The agent opened it up, slid the Benjamin in his pocket, and stamped the passport. Gary didn't wanna take any chances of Jules being flagged and possibly arrested, since he hadn't made the payment to the judge yet.

It had been four days since Rick was sent to prison. Every day seemed like a year to Rick. He had to hold on and pray that Gary would get to the judge before someone got to him inside the prison.

That morning, the prison librarian rolled his cart up to Rick's cell. Sitting on top was *Don Quixote*. Rick took the book and nodded at the librarian as he slid a pack of cigarettes to him.

Back on his bunk, he opened the hollowed-out book. Inside was a beauty of a shank. It was made from a plastic ladle and sharpened to a fine point on both sides. Rick hoped he wouldn't have to use it but was thrilled to have it. He tucked it into his waistband and stepped into the yard.

As usual, a couple of inmates sized him up. He did what he always did. Took his fighting stance and waved them over. He had already been in ten fights on the inside. His face looked like a warzone, but it was better than the other guys. Rick had bested them all. None had weapons so far, and he hoped that trend would continue.

At lunchtime, he and Zebra made their way to the mess hall. As much as Rick hated the food, he fought his way through it because he couldn't take a chance of getting sick or weak. The cuisine was exceptional that day. Some sort of stew, but it was green. Rick thought maybe they used iguanas for the meat. He started to take a bite when he was hit in the back of the head by a biscuit. He spun around and saw it was Chiumbo.

"Where's my cigs!?" yelled Chiumbo.

Rick stood up and turned toward him. He had gotten a message to Possum to bring four cartons, but he hadn't arrived yet. He wasn't sure if Possum got the message or if a guard had destroyed it.

"They're coming soon!" said Rick.

"When?! I said two days. It's been four days. Time to pay up."

"Look, I have them coming. I can't pay today. You can't get blood out of a turnip."

It was obvious Chiumbo had no idea what Rick meant by that, but his eyes narrowed with fury. He started walking toward Rick and flashed a pair of side-cutting pliers for him to see. He was coming for one of Rick's fingers. Over the years, Rick had grown accustomed to having all of his digits and had no intention of losing any today. He moved toward Chiumbo and held out his left hand as if offering a finger to him. Chiumbo was flanked by two large men meant to hold Rick down. He had to play this right and only had one chance.

He held out his pinky and said, "Take this one, I rarely use it."

Chiumbo turned his head sideways like a dog trying to figure something out. He reached for Rick with his left hand. He started to move the side cutters toward Rick's finger, and Rick ripped the shank out of his waistband. With lightning speed, he connected it to the left side of Chiumbo's neck and all the way across.

Chiumbo stood there for a second in disbelief as the wound opened up and blood spewed all over the cafeteria floor.

He dropped the side cutters, reached up, and grabbed his neck. A large puddle of blood had already formed at his feet. He wobbled then fell to one knee, then fell face forward. The alarm sounded and inmates started running in all directions.

Rick shoved the shank back into his waistband and returned to his cell. He had dug out a piece of the mortar between two of the cinder blocks on the wall, and now he shoved the weapon inside. He ran some water onto a handful of dirt and patched the crack. In the oppressive heat, it dried quickly and looked like the rest of the wall.

Within minutes, guards busted into Rick's cell and began to rip it apart looking for the shank. One of them threw Rick onto the floor, stood on his back, and frisked him. Afterward, Rick just lay there on his bunk until they finished ransacking his room. No one had ratted him out. He knew even in Africa, snitches get stitches, but even the guards had seen the beginning of the standoff in the mess hall.

"How's Chiumbo?" asked Rick with a smirk on his face.

"He's in the infirmary. If you did this, you ain't ever getting out."

"Cool, I'm kinda liking it here. The food is amazing," replied Rick.

The guards left, and Zebra and Rick began to put the cell back together. Rick was glad he had already tossed the *Don Quixote* book in a trashcan by the mess hall.

"If they find that shank, Rick, you gonna pay," said Zebra.

"They'll never find it. Plus, I ain't gonna be here too much longer."

"I used to think that twenty-seven years ago. Don't think so positive. It will only come back to haunt you."

"Listen, Zebra, I know you feel like you're gonna die inside here, but I won't and I swear to you, neither will you. You have to trust me."

Zebra just grunted under his breath and continued to straighten up the cell.

Gary had the driver take him straight to the hotel where Possum and Junior were staying. Jules carried Chief inside her blouse to avoid questions from the hotel staff. They knocked on Possum's door and were greeted with huge hugs. They were all so happy to be together again.

"Where's Rick, Possum?" asked Jules.

Possum gave Gary an odd look, unaware that Gary hadn't told Jules about Rick's arrest.

"Jules, why don't you sit down," said Gary.

A look of dread filled her eyes. "Is he hurt?! Tell me. Tell me now!"

"No, Jules, he's not hurt. He's in prison. I didn't want you to worry, so I kept it to myself until we got here."

"Prison?! Where?"

"Calm down, it's not as bad as it sounds. He's in the Lusaka Central Correctional Facility. Junior met with the judge at his bogus trial. The judge has agreed to release him and drop all charges against you and Rick and expunge the case if we pay him the fine, aka bribe, of $100,000. That's why we stopped in Grand Cayman," said Gary as he patted the briefcase he was carrying.

Since it was Sunday, there was no court today, but it was a visitation day at the prison.

"Let's go see Rick. He'll be mad at me for bringing you here, but he'll get over it."

A small smile crept over Jules's face as she wiped away a tear.

Possum drove Jules and Gary to the prison, while Junior stayed behind with Clay to guard the money. The peeling paint of the dinghy green walls of the prison and its rusty tin roof were just a prelude of how bad it was inside. Jules's stomach flipped when she saw it. The conditions were abysmal. The prison had a maximum capacity of 1,200 inmates but was busting at the seams with close to 4,000.

Jules, Possum, and Gary made their way through security to the visitation room. They were all frisked; even Jules was felt up by one of the guards. She dared not slap him but gave him a death stare and pulled away from him. Once inside, they waited behind the glass for Rick to appear.

As soon as he reached the glass, Jules couldn't hide the shock on her face at Rick's appearance. He had two black eyes, several cuts on his cheeks, and he had lost a lot of weight in the short time he was inside.

"Oh, Rick," said Jules as she gazed upon him.

She stuck her palm up to the glass and picked up the phone.

"Rick, you look terrible. Are you okay?"

"I'm great. This place is better than Club Med. I have a one-bedroom suite with bunk beds I share with a zebra," said Rick with a wink.

"Huh, a zebra?"

"I'm just kidding. My cellmate is nicknamed Zebra. You'll understand once you meet him. Speaking of which, Possum and Gary, can y'all hear me?"

"Yeah, we can hear," replied Possum as he and Gary leaned in closer to the phone with Jules.

"I need you to speak with the judge. Write this name down: Mateo Kimbro. He was falsely arrested and convicted in 1994 for a crime he was nowhere nearby. His lawyer made a deal with the court to pay a ten-thousand dollar fine, but he had no money, so he's been in here ever since. He saved my life. He's a good man. Let's get him out of here. He deserves his freedom and a place to live. He has a loving family, but they were terrorized over the years and stopped visiting him. Let's make it right."

"I'm all over it, Rick. We meet with the judge in the morning. My goal is to get you and your cellmate out of here and be eating lunch by noon!"

"Oh my God, that would be a dream come true. I'm so sick of eating green stew. I won't say anything to Zebra. I don't wanna get his hopes up. He's all but given up any chance of ever being released," said Rick.

"Time's up!" shouted one of the guards.

"I love you, Rick. Please be careful. I wish I could hold you," said Jules.

"I love you too, Jules," said Rick as the guard ripped the phone out of his hand.

Rick was escorted back to his cell. Zebra looked like he was giddy when Rick was unlocked and shoved inside.

"Rick, Chiumbo survived. The word in the yard is that he will never speak again. When you slashed him, you destroyed his vocal cords. They are saying you are the new leier," said Zebra.

"Leier?"

"Boss, boss of the yard."

"Oh great, that's all I need."

Several inmates approached Rick's cell and handed him a carton of cigarettes with a nod.

I guess it's good to be the king. Too bad I don't smoke.

Rick collected several more cartons as inmates stopped by to pledge their support for him as new leader of the yard. He had to play along. He stacked all the cigarettes under Zebra's bunk. Cigarettes on the inside were the same as cash, or even more valuable.

Junior and Gary stepped into the courthouse, and Junior had the bailiff get the judge's attention. After a short recess, they were led into his chambers.

"Judge Malonic, we are here to settle Rick Water's fine."

Gary opened the briefcase and placed several stacks of hundreds on the judge's desk. He calmly put them in a safe behind his chair.

"Your Honor, if I may, there is a man inside named Mateo Kimbro. In 1994, he was convicted and sentenced to thirty days and a ten-thousand dollar fine. With my utmost respect, I ask that his sentence be commuted and we pay his fine for his release," said Junior.

The judge opened his computer and did a search for Mateo. After a few minutes, he moved closer to the screen and squinted.

"Yes, he was fined $10,000 originally, but shortly after his incarceration, he killed an inmate on the inside," said the judge.

"Can we come to an agreement? He's a good man and has spent nearly twenty-eight years of a thirty-day sentence. It hardly seems fair," replied Junior.

"Don't tell me what is fair and not fair! He's a convicted murderer now."

"My apologies, Your Honor. I meant no offense."

The judge took a deep breath and thought for a minute.

"I supposed I could accept a plea and call it time served for $50,000. What say you?"

Junior looked over at Gary, and he took out another $50,000 and placed it on the judge's desk. The judge picked up the phone and called the prison. After a few minutes, he called over his secretary. She printed out release papers and an expungement document for Rick and Jules. Once the judge signed it, she stamped it and he slid it over to Junior. Junior thanked the judge, and they left the chambers to share the good news with Jules and Possum.

"Let's go get our Rick!"

Jules couldn't hold back her tears of joy, and they were contagious. The only one in the car not crying was Chief, who just bounced up and down and raised his crest, which gave them all a little smile.

Once at the prison, Gary handed the paperwork to the warden. He also wanted some grease, so Gary slid him a bundle of hundreds. After he filed the paperwork, he called the guards to release Rick.

"Waters, grab your mat. You're free," said the guard.

Rick hopped down from the top bunk, looked over at Zebra, and hugged him as he sat on his own bunk.

"Kimbro, stand up," said the guard.

"Oh no, sir, please, I don't wanna change cells. I've been here for eighteen years. Can't you just get me a new cell-mate?"

"Grab your mat. You've been released as well."

The look on Zebra's face melted Rick. The disbelief, the happiness on his face couldn't be described by a poet. Only a masterpiece by Leonardo da Vinci on canvas could've conveyed the feeling expressed by Zebra's eyes.

"I'm free?" asked Zebra, as if he needed to hear it again to believe it.

"Yes, now hurry up before the warden changes his mind."

Zebra shuffled behind Rick toward the exit gate of the prison. He looked over his shoulder as the entire yard raised one fist in the air. Cheers erupted as Rick put his arm around Zebra and helped him walk toward freedom. For the first time since Rick was incarcerated, he saw hope in Zebra's eyes. It moved him.

The guards returned Rick's street clothes that were taken from him when he arrived. Zebra's belongings had long since deteriorated, but they gave him a blue jumpsuit that was used for trustees on work release. When he took off the orange jumper, he threw it to the ground and spit on it.

The gate guard opened the heavy steel door, and Rick and Zebra stepped outside to freedom.

Jules had been pacing by the car and biting her lip, waiting for Rick to emerge. As soon as she saw him, she ran and jumped up on him, wrapping her arms and legs around him, nearly knocking him down. She could feel how thin he was as her fingers felt his ribcage.

"Oh, Rick. I'm so happy you're okay."

"Me too. Let's get the hell out of here."

Zebra just stood there, not really knowing what to do. He had no ride, and no one in his family even knew he was released.

Jules walked over to him, wrapped her arms around him, and thanked him for taking care of Rick on the inside.

"Come on, Zebra, you're coming with us."

Gary called ahead and booked another room for Zebra at the hotel where they were staying. Once at the hotel, he got Zebra's measurements and told him he'd be back with some street clothes. Gary and Possum took the car to the mall and gave Rick and Jules some privacy.

Rick had a loving reunion with Chief as Jules got the shower ready for him. She let him take a long shower. She had Junior show her to Rick's suitcase in the Overland, and she got him a fresh change of clothes. She also borrowed Junior's first-aid kit.

Back in the room, she doted on Rick. Several of the lacerations on his face and chest appeared infected. She carefully, lovingly cleaned his cuts with antiseptic, then covered then with triple antibiotic-coated Band-Aids. He was moving slow and now that he was out, his guard came down and all the injuries were allowed to surface. He groaned old man pains as she worked on him.

"Does that feel better?" said Jules as she lightly patted the new dressings.

"Much better! You take such good care of me. I don't know what I'd do without you."

"And you will never have to know that." Jules kissed his forehead.

Gary and Possum returned with new blue jeans, underwear, and several nice t-shirts and button-downs for Zebra. They also picked him up an overnight bag with a toothbrush, comb, and other bathroom niceties.

Zebra was beyond grateful and still a little in disbelief about what had taken place so quickly. Possum could tell he was guarded. Twenty-seven years in prison would put anyone on edge.

"Mateo, here are your clothes," said Possum.

"Wow, I ain't been called Mateo in nearly three decades. It's nice to hear."

"In that case, we shall call you Mateo from now on. We can put Zebra to rest for good."

Mateo smiled big, revealing the gap in his teeth.

"If you're hungry, we are going to get lunch after Rick's changed. You want to join us?"

"Yes, and can I ask a favor?"

"Of course."

"I haven't slept in a room by myself since I was arrested. Can someone bunk with me?"

"Sure, Mateo. Let me grab my stuff. I'll take the other bed," replied Possum.

At 11:30 a.m., Gary knocked on Possum and Mateo's door. "Y'all ready for lunch?"

"Ready and hangry!" replied Possum.

"We're going to The Marlin. I reserved a private room for us. I hope you like steak, Mateo."

He was left speechless and just followed Possum out of the door.

At the restaurant, Gary ordered a couple bottles of wine for the table as they all sat down.

"Is there anything special you'd like, Mateo?"

"Naw, I'm good. But to be honest, I haven't had a beer since 1994."

Gary ordered a round of Wild Dog Lagers for the table. Mateo just stared at the glass of frosty foam as if he was still dreaming. They all keyed in on him; to Possum, Mateo looked as if he was afraid to pick up the glass and wake up from his dream.

Rick picked up his glass and stood to make a toast. "Here's to Mateo. If it wasn't for him. I wouldn't be here today," said Rick as he raised his pint.

They all clinked glasses, and everyone watched Mateo as he took a slow sip. His eyes closed and he looked as if he'd just stepped into heaven. They all enjoyed the perfectly grilled steaks, and the crew caught Rick up on the case. Suddenly, Mateo stood up.

"I'm a man of few words, but I just want to thank you for this incredible surprise."

"I have one more surprise for you, Mateo. I made a call and I just got a text back. Excuse me for a minute," said Possum.

Possum stepped out of the room and closed the door behind him. After a couple of minutes, he returned and slowly opened the door.

A woman and man stepped inside. Mateo rubbed his eyes, looking at them for a second, and then recognition flooded his face. It was his daughter and the man was his grandson. The same one he still had a tattered picture of that he'd received so many years before. They rushed to him, and he stood up as they all embraced. There wasn't a dry eye in the house.

"Thank you, thank you for doing this. I don't know what to say," said Mateo.

"You are more than welcome. We're all glad you are free now. Your future looks bright," said Gary.

"I guess I best gets me a job. I don't know who will hire a convicted felon at my age, but I gots to try. I also need to find a place to live," replied Mateo.

"You can stay with us, pops. It's a small place, but you are welcome to stay until you find your own place," said Mateo's grandson.

"That gives me an idea," said Gary.

Everyone could see the hamsters in Gary's head spinning round and round on a squeaky wheel. Possum grinned, knowing full well what Gary was up to.

"Would y'all excuse me, I need to find a real estate agent."

"Oh boy, here he goes again," said Rick with a laugh.

CHAPTER TWELVE

Rick and the crew took a rental from Lusaka to Chirundu. Junior took his Overland to check on Yuusf back at his camp. He knew he couldn't keep him in the cage under his camp forever but also knew he was too dangerous to release. He needed to get him arrested somehow so the government could deal with him. Yuusf was a bad man; he should've been in prison years ago for illegal poaching and attempted murder, if not actual murder. He was certainly capable of it.

The strictest crime in Africa was drug trafficking. A person could get more time in jail for drugs than murder or kidnapping. Rumor on the street was that Yuusf loved cocaine. So, Junior came up with a plan. He would tranquilize Yuusf, then plant some cocaine on him, then put him behind the wheel of his car and park in an area where he would definitely get detained. He knew it wasn't ethical, but Yuusf had never paid for his crimes in the past and was involved in his father's death. Getting him off the street would do everyone a favor, including the animals of Kafue Reserve.

He stopped by one of the dealers he knew and bought two eight balls of coke. All he had to do was get to Yuusf without getting caught with the drugs on himself. He stopped at a head shop and bought some plastic baggies and a small scale.

"Let me out!" yelled Yuusf.

"Today is the day. Your info paid off. I'm gonna drop you in Lusaka by your house. I need to blindfold you, though, and handcuff you for the trip," replied Junior.

Junior handed Yuusf a pad and pen.

"Write down your address and we can leave soon."

Yuusf wrote it down and passed it through the cage. Junior had him turn around and put his hands behind his back. He opened the cage, handcuffed him, and blindfolded him. Once his blindfold was on, Junior took a syringe and plunged it into his neck. Yuusf jumped in shock then crumpled to the ground. Junior dragged him outside to the Overland and put his address in the GPS.

Once at his home, he pushed the fob on Yusuf's keychain. An older model 340Z's lights blinked. Junior put Yuusf in the passenger seat, the baggies and scale in the trunk, and drove toward the center of the city and parked in front of a hydrant by a roundabout. It was black as coal that night with no moon. Traffic was all but nonexistent. He waited for a lonely car to pass, then quickly took the handcuffs and blindfold off of Yuusf, checked his watch, and moved him to the driver's seat. He jogged over to the mall and called 911 on a payphone.

"911, what's your emergency?"

"There's a guy on Independence Avenue driving erratically. He almost ran me off the road. I think he's drunk. He just pulled over and is parked in front of the Yalelo Kanele Mall by the Kafue roundabout. I'm afraid he's gonna kill someone or himself if he's not taken off the road."

"What's your name, sir?"

"Uh, Frank Hill. I'm at the mall now."

"Hold please, Mr. Hill."

After a moment, the dispatcher said, "Okay, we have a unit en route now. Please wait there in case they need a statement. Do you want to remain on the line?"

"No, that's okay. I'll hang here then proceed to the police when they arrive."

"Thank you, Mr. Hill."

Junior hung up, walked across Independence, and waited at a bus stop.

After fifteen minutes, two cruisers pulled up behind the 340Z. The cops opened the driver's side door and pulled Yuusf out. One of them handcuffed him then used smelling salts and Yussf came to. He was dazed and confused as the police bent him over the hood and emptied his pockets. They placed a large baggie on the hood and took Yuusf to one of the cars and drove off. A wrecker showed up a few minutes later and began to get Yuusf's car ready to be towed. Junior's work was done.

He Uber'd back to his Overland and began the two-and-a-half-hour journey to Chirundu. Rick and the gang were already asleep in the lodge when he arrived. He grabbed his key that Rick had arranged ahead of time and went to his room. He was still wired and couldn't sleep, so he grabbed a few beers from his Overland and sat on the couch on the back deck overlooking the Zambezi River. The river lazily flowed by and reminded him of his father when he would take Junior fishing. He was feeling sad and called it a night. He said a small prayer before settling in his room.

"Dear God, please give me the strength to find my father's killer. Don't let me stray from the task and bring all the people to justice for this heinous crime. Amen."

The sun rose over the Zambezi as hippos and crocs mingled together. The chirps of birds and sounds of other African wildlife were enchanting to Jules's ears as she gazed out of the terrace. Chief tried to mimic a Goliath Heron but sounded more like he was coughing than squawking, which made Jules laugh out loud. Rick stepped onto the terrace and hugged Jules and kissed Chief on the beak.

"I'm so happy to be free. Having you and Chief here, Jules, is icing on the cake."

"I'm even more happy to be here with you, Rick," she replied and kissed him.

"Let's see what Possum's doing."

Possum was on his laptop when Jules and Rick knocked on the door.

"Come on in, it's unlocked. Check this out."

Rick and Jules gathered around Possum's laptop, and he opened a page on the Zambian government's Freedom of Information website. He scrolled down to Colin Mulenga's name and clicked it. He scrolled down again and pointed at the info on the screen.

"Before he was elected, he worked for a safari outfit out of Mumbwa."

Possum opened another tab, clicked on Wikipedia, and typed in the name of the safari company. He scrolled down to the page of the now defunct business and ran his cursor around the names on the bottom. The founders were Colin Mulenga and Kelvin Marcus.

"Didn't Yuusf say he was approached by Kelvin Marcus to kill Junior's father?"

"Yeah, he did. Let's get Junior over here."

Rick called Junior on the house phone and he came right over.

"Did you know Kelvin Marcus was cofounder of a safari outfit in Mumbwa?" asked Rick.

"What's the name?"

"It's out of business now, but it was called Mumbwa Safari International."

"I've heard of them. They were shut down for alleged poaching on photo safaris. It was on the news, but I had no idea Kelvin Marcus was involved."

"It just says he was cofounder; he could've left the company. But what truly interests me is that Colin Mulenga was the other cofounder."

"Reallllllllyy," replied Junior in an exaggerated impression of Jim Carrey in *Pet Detective*.

"Possum, when are you supposed to meet with Colin again?" asked Rick.

"I just need to text him. I think if we can show him some earnest money, I can convince him to open up more about the project. I'll text him and meet him with $50,000. You can wire me up and we can get him on the record. It might be what we need to break the case open. I just need to let him know I am willing to invest the additional $700,000 in cash plus ten million, and I'm not concerned about how it gets done. If I can gain his interest, he might open up to me."

"Have y'all followed up on checking those metal detectors over at your dad's place by Victoria Falls?"

"Not yet. Your arrest kinda screwed up that idea."

"How about you, Jules, and I go to your father's camp by the falls, and Possum and Gary can meet with Colin."

"I like it," said Possum.

Gary had just walked in and heard what they were saying. "Let me guess, I'm gonna play Ole's lawyer."

"That's right, barrister!" said Rick.

The sound of the falls was deafening as Junior drove Rick and Jules toward his dad's southern safari camp on the T1 to Livingstone. He took the first road to a spot his dad used to take him to. The sun was just setting and the mist coming off the falls looked like fog over the bayou, on a cool spring morning. The massive falls also reminded Rick of the time he went over one of the highest falls in the world and somehow survived. It gave him a chill.

They pulled into Junior's father's camp, and Junior unlocked the sliding door of the huge metal Quonset hut. Hanging on the wall were several different types of metal detectors. Rick pulled out a copy of the note Junior's dad had left for him and read it aloud.

Junior,

If you found this note then you know I am dead. I've had many threats against me since I swiped the ivory. For the sake of the elephants, please destroy the ivory

except for one piece. You'll know the one. My killer
will be revealed on the carved ivory. Follow the Apple
with the Detector to the location.

I love you, son,
Dad

They each took a metal detector off of the wall and opened them up, looking behind the battery enclosures and inside the hollow tube handles. After an hour of exhaustive searching, they came up with absolutely nothing. It was a dead end. Rick read the note aloud a few more times.

"It just doesn't make sense. Your dad only had a Samsung phone, right? What about his computer?" asked Rick.

"As far as I know, he had a Microsoft Surface. I actually have it. It's in the bottom cabinet of the Overland."

"Can you go get it?"

"Sure."

Junior ran out of the Quonset hut then returned with his dad's laptop. Rick fired it up.

"It's password protected," said Rick.

"Try elephants12."

Rick typed it in and it opened up. He searched all the documents for anything related to ivory, detectors, Apple. Nothing came up. He checked the recent browser history— lots of photography sites and Facebook. Bandile's Facebook page didn't reveal anything either. Rick closed the screen in frustration just as his phone whistled. It was from Possum.

> Meeting with Colin 10:00 a.m.
> tomorrow.

10–4, do us proud.

Possum texted a thumbs-up emoji.

Junior locked up the Quonset hut, and they began the overnight drive back to Chirundu. It was a slow-going trip as there were no fences alongside the T1, and they had to keep an eye out for loose cattle and other animals. Rick was itching to drive the Overland. He vowed to get one when he got back to Florida.

After a while, Junior pulled over and switched places with Rick. Rick kept it under fifty and ran all the fog lights and the overhead light bar. It lit up the highway like a nighttime game at Florida State. Junior's phone pinged and he checked the text. He gave Rick an odd look and then made a call.

"It's my little sister. I haven't spoken to her in five years."

Junior talked and the conversation seemed heated, but Rick couldn't understand a single word, as Junior spoke in his native tongue the entire time. Once the call ended, a huge smile crept across his face.

"What happened? Why haven't you spoken to her in five years? I'm sorry, that's rude of me. It's none of my business," said Rick.

"It's okay. I don't mind. My sister and the entire family sort of had a falling out five years ago. She was always the most strong-willed in our family. I also had an older brother, but he was killed in a safari accident in 2003."

"I'm so sorry," replied Rick.

"It's okay. Time heals all wound, right? Apparently, it also heals fallouts. My sister had been working in the capital as a lobbyist for years. She became opposed to expanding the Kafue National Park, which would have protected another large herd of elephants and other animals. Instead of being on the park's side, she rallied behind the opposition and it was voted down in legislation. My dad was furious with her and they both said things they regretted. I took my dad's side and she felt betrayed. She vowed to never speak to either of us again. She just returned from a trip to Kenya and found out about my dad's death. She had no idea. She wants to get together and bury the hatchet. She's coming to Chirundu tomorrow. I'm thrilled to see her again and make things right."

"That's great, Junior. Family is important," said Rick.

"The most important," added Jules.

Rick drove the rest of the way, and both Jules and Junior fell asleep in their seats. They arrived back at the lodge at sunup, and Rick went straight to bed. He had Jules set an alarm for him for ten in the morning.

When Rick woke up, Possum and Gary had already left for the meeting with Colin. He made some coffee and joined Jules on the terrace. She was talking to Junior and another woman.

"Good morning, sleepy head. Just kidding. I appreciate you driving all night. This is my sister, Jacinda," said Junior.

Jacinda was tall and lanky with jet-black long hair in a ponytail. She had a tight build like that of a swimmer or a cyclist. She offered her hand for Rick to shake. "Nice to meet you, Rick. You have a lovely wife; you better hang on to her."

"Wife? We got married, Jules?" said Rick with a laugh.

"Oh, I'm sorry, I assumed you were married. You're wearing the same rings."

"Don't be. We got these rings in Mexico. I know it's kinda childish, but we call them our promise rings. Like back in high school. Maybe we'll get married one day. Huh, Jules?"

"Perhaps," replied Jules sarcastically, then grinned.

"I wonder how Possum's meeting is going," said Rick to no one in particular.

"I spoke to Gary and Possum before they left, and they said they'll be back sometime after lunch. I was thinking we could go the firing range and shoot some targets. Jacinda is now lobbying for the Civilian Gun Registration; it's basically Zambia's version of the NRA. She gets lots of perks. She was just given a dozen new rifles and a boatload of ammo to be auctioned in Lusaka for her expenses. It's a workaround for campaign donations. You wanna check them out?"

"Does a hippo shit in the water?!" exclaimed Rick.

Jacinda escorted the group over to her Tacoma. There was a large wooden crate sitting in the back. She pried it open, revealing a dozen or more brand-new rifles. The other box was full of ammo. Rick picked up the first gun and admired it then passed it to Jules. It was almost as big as she was.

"Is this an elephant gun?" asked Jules.

"Yes. My father spent his life protecting the elephants, and I too am opposed to elephant poaching, but the reality is there are a number of legal permits issued each year and the industry is the main income for some extremely poor communities. It's a fine balance, and I'm doing my part to sustain jobs as well as prosecute poachers. Poachers are the problem. If we could eliminate them, we wouldn't have an elephant population issue," said Jacinda.

"All right, everyone, pick out a gun. We're going shooting. We can take the Overland," said Junior.

"That's quite the ride you got there, big brother."

They all grabbed a gun and Rick took two. He selected a Holland & Holland 700 Nitro Express double barrel and a Blaser R8 Big Game rifle. Both Jules and Junior grabbed matching .404 Jeffery bolt action rifles.

"Aren't you gonna choose one, Jacinda?" asked Jules.

"No, I'm using my own gun. It's the only rifle I've ever shot."

"Fair enough. I love my handgun and never wanna shoot another," replied Jules.

The gun range was only ten miles from the lodge. They all lined up and took a full box of ammo. When Rick fired the elephant gun, the boom shook the ground. The recoil on the gun was significant. Jules dared Rick to fire both sides at the same time.

"Naw, I better not."

"I double dog dare you!" said Jules.

"Oh no you di'ent!"

Rick pulled the gun tight against his shoulder and spread his legs with his right leg behind him a little for bracing.

Kaboom!

The gun slammed into his shoulder and moved him back a foot.

"Holy shit! I ain't doing that again."

They all enjoyed the range and at the end, Jacinda started picking up all her shell casings. Rick followed suit.

"Oh, you don't have to pick those up, Rick. I am a reloader. I've been reloading my 30-06 shells for years."

"Oh, cool. Rick stepped over to Jacinda's lane and helped her gather up all the casings. They returned to the lodge a few minutes before Possum and Gary came back. Jacinda had to head back to the capital but promised to return soon and take some time off to reconnect with her big brother. They hugged for a long time, and it put a smile on Jules's face. They said their goodbyes, and Possum waved Rick and the gang over to his room to listen to the recording he'd made of the meeting with Colin.

CHAPTER THIRTEEN

Colin Mulenga: *Nice to see you again, Mr. Hannsen.*

Ole Hannsen: *Ya, you as well, Mr. Mulenga. I have some earnest money for you. I still need to do more due diligence, but this should show my intentions are legitimate.*

Colin Mulenga: *I see. What questions do you have for me?*

A shuffling of papers could be heard on the recording. Possum coughed then continued in his Norwegian accent.

Ole Hannsen: *Ahh, what guarantee do I have that you will indeed be able to annex the portion of Kafue Park that you plan to use to build the water park resort?*

Colin Mulenga: *I have men on the inside working with the local government to ensure that happens in a timely matter.*

Ole Hannsen: *Can you elaborate?*

Colin Mulenga: *I'd prefer not to. My contacts are confidential, but I can assure you it will happen.*

Ole Hannsen: *Can I infer that you are bending the law?*

Colin Mulenga: *Wouldn't you prefer to have plausible deniability, Mr. Hannsen?*

There was a long silence on the recording. Then Possum continued.

Ole Hannsen: *Since you can't or won't tell me your contacts, can you tell me what strategies you are imposing?*

Colin Mulenga: *We are using any means necessary. I will leave it at that.*

There was another twenty minutes of back-and-forth small talk over financial details and lots of revelry about the resort Colin planned to build. Then another pause as Possum tried a different tactic and dropped a bombshell on Colin to see how he reacted.

Ole Hannsen: *I know there has been some violence in the park recently between poachers and some folks who protect the wildlife. Were your men involved in any way with the death of Bandile Dlamini?*

Silence again came over the recording.

Colin Mulenga: *The police have determined that was an accident. All I have to say is that while the death of Mr. Dlamini was tragic and untimely, it did create a runway for our project to move forward. I have the deepest sympathies for his family.*

Some shuffling of papers followed, and the two men said goodbye. Possum told Rick and the others that he'd given Colin a briefcase with the $50,000. What Colin didn't know was it was no ordinary briefcase. It had a tracking device planted inside.

"So, what was the expression on his face when you asked about Bandile Dlamini?" asked Rick.

"His eyes widened and he took a pause. I believe he was stunned that I even knew his name. If he was hooked up to a lie detector at the time, I'm positive he would've failed miserably. His body language changed quite abruptly near the end when we were discussing that. When he said the police determined it was an accident, I almost thought for a second he was gonna wink at me," replied Possum.

"Wow! Great job, hombre. That tracker will come in handy. Maybe we can use it to find out who he's gonna give the money to."

"Not only does it have a tracker, but I installed a recording device into the case itself. It uses a highly sensitive micro-electromechanical microphone. It only records when it picks up certain frequencies. I programmed it to pick up 85HZ to 155HZ, which is the dynamic range of both male and female speaking voices. It will not record low range such as road noise and other rumbling sounds, or high-pitched sounds above 155HZ, such as wind noise or birds, etc. Even still, we'll only get about four days' worth of recording due to the battery life. Then we'll have to track down the case to get the recording off of it. That's why I used an inexpensive gawdy briefcase. I hope once the exchange is made, it will be tossed. Then we can pick it up."

"Dang, man, you're turning into some sort of MI6 double agent. Or maybe I should call you Q!"

"Ha-ha, I've been called worse."

"Well, that was a great idea, Possum. I hope it pans out. Let's keep an eye on it and see where it ends up."

Rick called the cleaning service to have some clothes laundered. He went through all of his pockets to make sure he didn't have any money or receipts in them. He found a couple of receipts and some coins and a shell casing from the shooting range when he had started to help Jacinda clean up on the range. He placed it all on his nightstand and put the clothes in a large cotton bag.

As he gazed at his reflection in the mirror, he noticed his black eyes had faded to an off-yellow color. Some of his weight had come back and his ribs were feeling better. He gave God a quick little thank you for getting him out of that nasty Zambian prison.

The crew gathered in the great room of the lodge to go over everything they had so far in the case. Possum decided to take the lead.

"Okay, let's discuss what we have and what we don't have. One, we have the first note and map your dad left for you."

He pushed it across the table so the others could see it.

> I stashed the ivory near the cave of bats. Follow road on the map from Majuaneti to Bat Cave, go five kilometers to the sausage tree arrow. The route of the ivory is left under the shiny rock arrow to north river island in the border of Z's.

"Two, we have the second note."

Junior,

If you found this note then you know I am dead. I've had many threats against me since I swiped the ivory. For the sake of the elephants, please destroy the ivory except for one piece. You'll know the one. My killer will be revealed on the carved ivory. Follow the Apple with the Detector to the location.

I love you, son,
Dad

"Three, we think Colin Mulenga is somehow involved and it may go up higher in the government. What else can anyone add?"

"Can we go back to the second note?" asked Rick. "What bothers me and what's been on my mind is that the words 'Apple' and 'Detector' are capitalized. Do you think that is referring to an Apple product or not?"

"Like I said before, as far as I know, my dad had a Samsung phone and a Microsoft Surface laptop," replied Junior. "Nothing by Apple, so I think it was just a fluke that he capitalized it."

"Plus, we already searched all your dad's metal detectors and found zero clues," interjected Jules.

"What if it's not a metal detector? It only says, 'Detector'."

"Holy shit!" Junior turned and sprinted out the door toward his Overland.

He came back a few minutes later carrying a little baggie. "Whatcha got there?" asked Possum.

"It's my dad's radar detector," said Junior as he handed it to Possum.

"A radar detector? How can we follow that?" asked Rick.

Possum looked at it and flipped it upside down and sideways, looking for any sort of clue. Then he shook it like a kid would shake a present under a Christmas tree to try and figure out what's inside. Something rattled inside of it.

"Quick, grab me a Phillips screwdriver!" exclaimed Possum.

Junior jumped up and ran to his Overland again and quickly returned with a couple of them. Possum picked the appropriate one and began to remove screws. Once he got the final screw out of the bottom plate, he opened it. Something fell out, hit the ground, and rolled under the table. Jules bent down and picked it up.

"It's an Apple AirTag!" said Jules excitedly.

"Holy crap. That's the Apple he was referring to. But he doesn't have an iPhone or a MacBook. There's no way to track it," repeated Junior.

"Maybe he had an iPad we don't know about. Lots of people have iPads but use PCs and android phones. Where else could he have hidden an iPad?" asked Rick.

"I honestly have no idea."

Rick held the AirTag in his palm, staring at it as if he was trying to conjure a way for it to speak to him. He was convinced that if he could get this info from the AirTag, he could find the ivory and the killer of Junior's dad.

Possum raised his hand like he was a student in school wanting to ask a question. "Rick, I did a deep dive into how AirTags work on the Apple site and according to them, AirTags are encrypted daily and there is no way to track history. It's too bad because those little Tiles that I use to find my keys will show history for thirty days. Basically, it's a dead end. Right now, it's in your hand, and even if we had the iPad or MacBook to see it on the app, that's all we would know. It's a waste of time."

Rick closed his fist around it and felt like throwing it across the room. He stopped himself and just set it on the table.

"Why the hell would he have an Apple AirTag inside of his radar detector and not own any other Apple product to utilize how it works? It just doesn't make sense," said Rick as he slammed his fist on the table, startling everyone in the room.

Possum patted Rick on the shoulder and said, "It'll be all right, hombre. Let's just take a deep breath and go in a different direction."

Possum laid the second handwritten note on the table and asked Junior if he had a magnifying glass. He checked in his Overland and didn't have one, so Possum just took a photo of the messy handwritten note, so he could zoom in on each word and make sure they hadn't missed anything. He wrote out each word on a separate piece of paper, and when he got to the word "Detector," he stopped and looked up at Rick as if he had seen a ghost.

Rick leaned closer to watch him and then he wrote the word *Defender* instead of Detector. Even at a second glance of the original note, it looked like Detector, but when it was zoomed in, there was no doubt the word was *Defender*.

"Oh my God!" exclaimed Rick.

He leaned over and kissed Possum on the cheek with an exaggerated kissing sound.

"You freaking genius! That's it. The clue to finding the ivory is in the Defender. Where is it now, Junior?"

"It's at my buddy's place still, remember? I'm having it repainted and getting the VIN changed."

"Call him immediately. Tell him to make sure he doesn't disconnect the battery under any circumstances. We have to get to that Defender. I think I know what your dad meant by that note," said Rick confidently.

Junior stepped outside to call his buddy then came back inside quickly and gave Rick a thumbs-up.

"Well, do tell, Sherlock!" said Possum.

"I remember that on the dash of the Defender was a large curved glass media screen. It's an integrated audio control, info data, and most importantly, built-in GPS. If that GPS has memory, which I assume it does, it will show where your dad hid the ivory. It's most likely going to be in the history and in an off-the-beaten-path place that shows him stopped for an extended period of time."

"Well, what about the AirTag and the fact that he capitalized 'Apple'?" asked Possum.

"I can't figure that part out yet, but we will. I'm not sure the radar detector had anything to do with the note. Did your dad buy the radar detector new or used? Maybe, if it's used, the person he bought it from had the AirTag stuck inside and just forgot about it. Maybe it's just a fluke and has nothing to do with it whatsoever."

"My dad rarely bought used stuff. He always said buying used is just buying other people's problems. That's why he ordered the brand-new Defender instead of buying a used one. I can look in his computer. He used a program called Neat that scanned all of his receipts and kept track of his expenses. He loved that app and even turned me onto it. It really helps with taxes. If he bought it new or used, I should be able to find it inside the program. I'll get on that now," said Junior.

Junior plugged in his dad's computer and opened the Neat program. He scrolled back in the history all the way back to before his dad had purchased the new Defender. He slowly scrolled through each purchase and expense, and after a few minutes found the radar detector. To the right side of it, all it said was *Gift*.

"Dammit! It says gift. He didn't buy it from anyone. Someone gave it to him," exclaimed Junior in frustration.

"Wait, a gift? That changes everything. You know what this means, don't you?" asked Rick.

Junior just shrugged his shoulders, looking confused.

"It means that whoever gave him the radar detector also put the AirTag inside of it, which also means your dad wasn't using the AirTag to keep track of his Defender; it was someone keeping track of your dad. My theory is, whoever gave your dad that radar detector is involved in his murder. I'd bet my last dollar on it."

"Where is the Defender exactly?" asked Possum.

"It's at my buddy Jamire's shop in Chongwe, just east of Lusaka," replied Junior.

"Let's go now!" said Rick.

Everyone went to their rooms and gathered up their things. Once everything was packed back into the Overland, they headed north toward Lusaka. The drive took a little less than three hours.

When they arrived at Junior's buddy's shop, they were greeted by two huge rottweilers at the tall cyclone gate to the property. It had razor wire all around it. The shop was toward the back of the yard, and they could see light coming from under the double doors. It was apparent someone was welding. Junior texted his friend, and out of a side door of the building strolled Jamire. He whistled at the overly excited guard dogs and tied them up to their doghouses with large chains, then jogged over and opened the gate so Junior could drive in. He instructed him to park behind the building and then invited them inside the shop.

"Hey, Junior, y'all, come in. The Defender is coming along nicely. Come, come," said Jamire as he waved for them to follow.

Inside the shop in the corner was the Defender. The hood had been removed and was sitting on a bench. Jamire had been welding a new air induction vent to change the look of the vehicle. The entire SUV had been sanded down to bare metal and was ready for primer. Jamire had just started taping the windows.

"Can we start the Defender? We need to review the GPS dash screen," said Rick.

"Yeah, no problem, let me grab the keys," replied Jamire.

He opened a drawer under a work bench, pulled out the keys, and tossed them to Rick. Junior and Rick climbed in the front seat with Jules and Possum in the back, and Gary leaned over Jules's shoulder to see. Rick fired up the Defender. As the navigation screen came on, Rick clicked on the GPS and scrolled through the most recent trips. He clicked on the trip before the date that Junior's father had been murdered.

The screen changed, and a collective gasp came from the gang as the screen revealed the vehicle on the road. Junior's father had changed the arrow icon on the map to an apple. They all looked at each other without saying a word. *This* apple was the apple Junior's dad had to be referring to in the note. Rick felt confident that if they followed the trip route, they would find the hiding place of the ivory stash. The problem was, they would have to drive the Defender, as there were no addresses in the GPS, only routes. There was a location on the GPS map that Junior's father had visited several times.

"How soon can we take the Defender?" asked Junior.

Jamire thought for a second then said, "I can focus on it and no other jobs and have it all done in three days. I mean, you could drive it now once I reinstall the hood, but I haven't gotten the new VIN yet. If you get pulled over in this, you will be going to jail. I can get the new VIN in a couple of days. If I finish the hood tonight, I can get it in the paint room in the morning. I suggest you just wait for the VIN. If I work through the night, I might be able to get it all done in two days."

"Okay, we'll wait. Is there anywhere we can stay nearby?"

Jamire started laughing. "In Chongwe?" he asked, still laughing. "You can camp on my property, but I suggest y'all drive into Lusaka and grab a hotel."

Junior pulled out his phone to find the closest hotel to the shop on the suburbs of Lusaka, and then decided to call Jacinda and see what hotel she would recommend. He stepped out of the shop to speak to her and came back in a few minutes later.

"My sister said we can stay at her place. She has a five-bedroom home near the University of Lusaka. It's only thirty minutes from here. I guess she's doing well as a lob-byist," said Junior.

"Okay, it's all decided. We will stay at your sister's and hopefully wrap this up in a few days," said Rick, knowing full well it was more wishful thinking than reality, because they still needed to prove who had actually committed the murder, and that answer was tied to the ivory.

"It will be good to catch up more with your sister too. Family is important," said Jules.

"I was thinking the same thing," replied Junior.

CHAPTER FOURTEEN

The heavy iron double gates opened as Junior pulled up to Jacinda's house. She had cameras everywhere. As a lobbyist for the Civilian Gun Registration, she had many enemies both inside and outside the government. She walked a fine line between protecting the park and protecting the rights of legal gun owners.

"Welcome, welcome," said Jacinda as Junior parked the Overland behind her Tacoma on the circular driveway.

On the straight pad beside her driveway, under a carport, was a newer model Audi R8. A car that could fetch around $175,000 brand new. Rick noticed the double garage and wondered what she had parked in there. Her house was more of a mansion than a house. She had armed guards and bars on her windows. The entire estate was fenced in with an eight-foot brick wall.

Junior whistled, impressed. "Dayum, little sister, you're doing well!"

"What can I say, being a lobbyist has been very good to me," she said as she hugged Junior.

They all grabbed their overnight bags and followed Jacinda into her home. The huge front door led to an expansive great room. On the walls were several heads of African animals. Rick stepped up to a large mount of a greater kudu. On a gold, engraved nameplate read, *Jacinda Dlamini, Zimbabwe 2014.*

"Wow, you shot all these?" asked Rick.

"Yep, I'm an avid hunter. Most of my hunts took place in Zambia and Zimbabwe, but I've also hunted in Kenya and Tanzania. I learned hunting from our dad, just like Junior. We had a bit of a difference of opinion about the parks, but that's in the past. I have taken much more big game. There's a bunch of photos on my iPad over there. You can check them out after dinner if you want." She pointed to an iPad sitting on the coffee table.

"That would be great," said Rick.

Jacinda had an entire staff—a butler, a maid, and cooking staff. They all lived on the property behind the mansion in a separate detached guesthouse. She showed them all to their rooms and they freshened up for dinner. Everything in her house was top-of-the-line. Zambia was a poor country and her house rivaled mansions in Beverly Hills.

After Rick showered, Jules hopped in and he decided to call Johnie to see how everything back in Florida was going. He looked at his watch and it was almost six p.m. He did a little math in his head and realized it was almost eleven a.m. in the Keys. He pulled up Johnie's name and hit send.

"Hi, Rick, what's up?"

"Hi, Johnie, we are in a beautiful home in Zambia. I wanted to see how *Nine-Tenths* is coming along and find out what's up with the new ship."

"I'm glad you called. I was thinking of calling you. *Nine-Tenths* is almost done and will be by tomorrow or the next day. I wanted to do a few upgrades on it, though, but need to run 'em by you first."

"Okay, I'm listening."

"There is a new type of real-type sonar called Panoptix side-scanning sonar. It can see the bait or lure placement, 180 degrees around the boat. It's like having surveillance cameras in the water. The ship has two of them. They are incredibly impressive."

"How much?"

"The entire system runs around $13,000 plus the cost of installation. We'll save a little money since the boat is already in the yard. I have a few more things I'd like to do that will help with our charters. I just need the go-ahead."

"I tell you what. Go ahead with the new sonar thing, and if there's other stuff you think will help the business, go ahead while we're still in the yard. If any other things cost over $20,000, text me. I trust your judgment."

"Thanks, Rick. I just spoke to Captain Lane and he wants to do a shakedown cruise of the ship. It will be just me, Captain Lane, and a boat hand I met in Key West. Is that cool? I want to go back to the spot where y'all dropped the Mayan gold and use the ship's side-scanning sonar and see if we can see it and find out the depth."

"That sounds great. Please keep me posted."

"Okay, Rick. Y'all be safe. Any idea when y'all will return?"

"Hopefully within a week. I'll know more in a couple of days."

"Sounds good. Talk to you soon."

Jules stepped out of the shower carrying Chief. He looked like a drowned rat.

"Awe, Chief! You lucky bird. You got to shower with Jules. I'm jealous."

Jules laughed as she set Chief on top of his travel cage, and he shook like a wet dog to dry off some. She grabbed a towel and patted him until he was mostly dry. Rick had already gotten dressed, and Jules threw on some shorts and a microfiber shirt.

"Dinner time," hollered Junior from the hallway.

They all gathered around a huge, circular, hand-carved mahogany table. The staff poured wine for everyone and prepared the multi-course dinner.

"Can you catch me up on my dad's murder investigation?" asked Jacinda.

Rick looked over at Junior and he nodded in approval.

"Well, so far, we have found an Apple AirTag planted inside of a radar detector. We are confident it wasn't your dad's, since he had no Apple devices. He used mostly Samsung and Microsoft stuff. We believe the answer to who killed him is tied to a huge stash of ivory."

"Oh, ivory, huh? I can relate to the phone thing. I started with an iPhone and tried to switch to a Samsung Note and it was like trying to learn a new language." Jacinda chuckled. "I returned it quickly and went back to an iPhone. I think it kinda depends on what you start with and are familiar with. I remember my dad bragging about his laptop and I jokingly laughed at him because I use an iMac. I'm Apple all the way. I love the way they all sync to each other."

"That's true. I'm all Apple too. I love my iPhone," said Rick.

"So, what else?" asked Jacinda.

"This is huge. We found a note from your dad indicating the location was on his GPS. We plan to take his Defender in a few days to the location where we think he stashed the ivory."

"Can I go?" asked Jacinda.

Rick again looked over at Junior, who nodded yes.

"I've gotta be honest. It could be extremely dangerous. We have no idea what we will encounter. I will drive the Defender with Jules. Gary, Junior, and Possum can follow in the Overland."

"I'm not afraid. I'll bring Old Faithful."

"Old Faithful?"

"My 30-06 rifle. As a matter of fact, if you want more firepower, we can bring my private security men with us. They are on salary, so we may as well use them. I travel alone sometimes, but anytime I'm doing any lobbyist work, they are always there. I hired some of the finest snipers and security men money can buy. Plus, I have more weapons and ammo than most gun stores. You're all welcome to use whatever you want."

"Thanks, Jacinda. We could use someone to watch our six," replied Rick.

The next couple of days seemed to drag. All Rick wanted to do was get the Defender and head out to try and find the ivory. He was chomping at the bit. The one good thing about staying at Jacinda's place was that she and Junior reconnected and rebounded. It was a great thing to witness. They hung out, laughed and cried, and relived old times when they were kids. They were once again brother and sister in every respect. Junior seemed gung-ho to have Jacinda go on the mission with them.

They went over the details of what they'd do once they found the evidence they needed. They couldn't trust the local authorities, so Rick reached out to Carson, his friend from the FBI, to see if he could find a top cop on the inside they could trust. Rick was fully expecting that the evidence would lead to the takedown of some highly respected people in the government, including Colin Mulenga. It was beginning to feel like a conspiracy. Rick sent Carson a text and he called him right back.

"Hey, Rick, what's shaking?"

"Hi, Carson, thanks for getting back to me so fast."

"No worries, what can I do you for?"

"In the next day or so, I feel confident that I will find out who the killer or killers were on the case I'm working on. My problem is, I don't know who I can trust in law enforcement here. Corruption goes high up in Zambia, and I think this will shake up some government officials. I don't want to see this thing buried, or worse, us buried. Who can I trust? Does Zambia have an organization like the FBI here? Who would you report to if you were me?

There was a long pause on the phone, then Carson said, "Your best bet is Interpol. I have a contact for Interpol in Italy. I worked on a profile for him for a case in the UK. I think he's done some work in Africa somewhere. If he's not your guy, he'll tell me who is. Let me make some calls and I'll get back to you as soon as I can. Probably by the end of the day. My day, not yours. What is it, like 8:45 p.m. where you are?"

"That's right," replied Rick.

"Okay, hold tight and I'll call you back."

"Thanks, Carson. I'll be standing by."

Rick kept Carson's call close to the vest. He trusted his crew explicitly, but he wasn't sure if Junior or his sister might say something accidentally to the wrong person. It wasn't that he didn't trust them, he just knew loose lips sank ships. If they were gonna take down whoever did this, the local po-po could not get any wind of it. Jacinda knew too many people in the government. She might tell someone she thought she could trust, and it might backfire. For now, he would keep it to himself.

Once he was off the phone with Carson, he joined the others in the great room. Jacinda was off somewhere else.

"Rick, I just got off of the phone with my buddy and the Defender will be ready tomorrow afternoon," said Junior.

Damn, I need that contact from Carson first.

"Okay, so let's plan to leave in the morning, day after tomorrow, around six a.m. Let's spend the day packing your Overland and staging the weapons for the Defender."

"Great idea, Rick. Have you thought of what you want to do with the ivory once we find it?" asked Junior.

"As a matter of fact, I have. We're gonna blow it up. If Jacinda is cool with it. Maybe Possum can build an IED out of the gunpowder she uses for reloading. I'll gladly pay for it. I've had him researching the best style of bomb, and he might be able to make a simple pipe bomb-type device with a timer. There's no way I'm letting that ivory hit the black market."

"My dad would be so happy to hear that. I'll ask Jacinda if Possum can start that. She has a shop in the little out-building beside the guesthouse where she reloads."

"Perfect. Hey, Possum, come here," yelled Rick.

"What's up, hombre?"

"You ready to build that IED?"

"Yeah, I have the design written in my notepad. I was hoping I could use gunpowder, but it's a low explosive level compared to what we need. We're gonna need C-4 or old-fashioned dynamite. C-4 is optimal because it uses blasting caps and it's much safer than lighting a damn fuse and running."

"Damn, we have all the gunpowder we need already. Where are we gonna get C-4? And we need it fast," said Rick.

"You do know where you are, don't you, Rick?" asked Junior.

"Yeah, why?"

"Man, come on. It's Zambia. Anything you want is available on the black market. Possum, give me a list of what you need, and I'll have it by midnight. Better yet, come with me."

"Hell yeah, road trip!" said Possum. "I'm ready when you are."

"Well, let's go now."

"Should I go too?" asked Rick.

"Naw, the less the better. No offense but y'all are white. One of y'alls is enough" said Junior with a laugh.

"You're gonna need this," interjected Gary as he handed Possum a fat stack of bills.

"Thanks," said Possum. "By the way, Rick, I have an update on the briefcase we gave Colin. I tracked it from his office and then it went all over Chirundu. It made stops, then it continued up and down streets. I finally figured it out after it stopped. It must've been in a garbage truck for some time. I mapped it and it ended up in a massive land-fill according to my map. The chances of finding it in the landfill would be nearly impossible. Plus, the battery still had 30 percent charge when it stopped suddenly. I think it was crushed at the landfill. Even if we found it, I think it would be useless."

"Damn, okay. It was a good idea and worth a try anyway."

Possum gathered his notes and a backpack, and he and Junior left. They borrowed Jacinda's Tacoma.

Junior parked next to an alley in Lusaka. At the end of the alley was a large metal door with a sliding speakeasy door grill. Possum handed Junior one of the stacks of bills, like they had discussed on the ride over, and he knocked on the door. After a few seconds, someone slid the metal viewer open, and Junior waved the bills for the man to see. He unlocked the door and swung it open.

"Who you want to see?" said the man in a gravelly voice.

"I don't know. I'm looking for some explosives. C-4 in particular."

"Follow me."

They both followed the man a few yards to another room, and he went in ahead of them and returned to his door watch duties. A good-looking athletic Asian girl approached them.

"How much you looking for?"

Junior looked over at Possum inquisitively.

"Eight to ten pounds or around nine M112 demolition blocks will do just fine."

"That's 95,000 kwacha."

Possum did a little math in his head. "Will you take US currency?"

"Yes," she said quickly.

"We'll also need some blasting caps. Here's five thousand dollars," said Possum as he handed her a stack.

She took the money and exited the room through a black curtain in the rear. Within five minutes, she returned with two small bags. One had the C-4 in it and one had blasting caps.

"Is this military grade?" asked Possum.

She didn't answer, just gave him a look as if she was upset that he even had to ask. He took the hint.

They returned to the Tacoma and began the trip back to Jacinda's. Possum glanced at his watch, and it wasn't even ten o'clock yet.

"Hey, Junior, did you know back in the day, some guys in Vietnam used to heat their rations with C-4? It burns clean with no visible smoke and is highly stable. It's detonated by a shock wave. That's what blasting caps do."

"That's interesting. Let's not try it."

"Ha-ha, I agree."

By the time they arrived at Jacinda's house, Rick, Jules, and Gary had already finished packing the Overland. They decided that Jacinda could follow them in her Tacoma to the site with her security detail close behind. Jacinda showed them to the reload room.

"Nice poster," said Rick as he pointed at the movie poster of Clint Eastwood as Dirty Harry, pointing his famous 44 magnum.

"It was my favorite movie as a kid," remarked Jacinda.

The back wall was plain white drywall, and on one side of the room was the room-length bench and all the reload items needed: dyes, bullets, primers, cases, powder, and shell holder and more.

Possum laid his tools on the bench and began to assemble the IED. He wasn't super comfortable working so close to all that gunpowder, but he wasn't planning on soldering anything and would use wire crimps. He used two four-inch steel pipes with caps and a simple digital timer to set off the blasting caps. He would place the pipes inside of an extra-large ammo box for ease of carrying.

He moved far away from the gunpowder barrel and carefully drilled two small holes in the metal ammo box to run the wires through. Once the packing was complete and the timer mounted on the outside, he placed the tightly packed pipes inside the box. The only thing left to do was wire up the blasting caps with crimps inside the box, seal it shut, and set the timer. They had one shot at this. For safety purposes, he would set the timer for ten minutes and secure the box with a master lock so no one could try and defuse it once the timer was set. Trying to defuse it could cause an explosion, and the risk was too high. So, it was a set-and-forget device. He sure hoped it would do the trick.

Rick joined Possum with Chief on his shoulder. Jacinda's reload room was impressive, but all that gunpowder and boxes and boxes of empty shell casings made him feel uneasy. Not to mention the massive C-4 IED sitting on the workbench.

Rick's phone vibrated and startled him. He stepped outside to take the call. It was Carson.

"Rick, I have a contact for you. His name is Renato Bianchi. He works with a unit of Interpol near Zimbabwe. They will rendezvous with you in Lusaka once you have the evidence. He completely understands your situation and was already aware of the murder of Bandile Dlamini. The crime was on his radar, and he is eager to get involved. Give him a call in the morning and y'all can make arrangements on when to meet. He understands the nature of the case and will be incredibly discreet."

"Thanks so much, Carson. You just made my day."

"No worries. Hey, when are we going fishing again?"

"Soon, my friend, soon. I can't wait to get out of Africa and back to Florida. Get it, out of Africa? Like the movie?"

"Ha-ha, very funny."

"Wait till you see my new toy," added Rick.

"You got a new boat?"

"Nope, a ship."

"Damn, man. I look forward to it. I'll hang up now and text you Renato's info. He speaks perfect English, but his Italian accent is thick. He's a great guy and y'all will hit it off."

"Thanks, Carson. Talk soon."

Rick stepped back into the workshop to see Possum's finished work. His IED was complete, and he just stood there with his arms crossed, admiring his creation.

"How big of an explosion will this thing make?" asked Rick.

"Let's put it this way. There's probably not a demand for ivory dust on the black market."

CHAPTER FIFTEEN

The next day couldn't come soon enough for Rick. He was climbing the walls in his head to get started. He woke up before his alarm went off. Everyone assumed the plan was to get the Defender that afternoon, then leave early the next morning and follow the last-known route on the built-in GPS. Rick had learned a long time ago never to stick to a schedule that was too easy to track. He planned to go with Junior in the Overland, pick up the Defender, and head straight to the site. That way if anyone had tapped their phones, they couldn't get there ahead of them and set up for an ambush. He wouldn't even let Jacinda know until after they picked up the Defender in case one of her security guys was involved that she was unaware of. He knew he needed their protection but also knew not to trust anyone completely. This way they could get to the site, let Jacinda and her detail know, and have a major jumpstart on them. He just needed a way to get his entire crew with them without arousing suspicion.

Junior got the call that the Defender was ready a few minutes before three o'clock. Rick put his plan into motion.

"Jacinda, Junior and I are going to get the Defender and return. Since we have a little time to kill, I thought I'd take my crew into town for dinner after. Can you suggest a good place? You're welcome to go."

Rick knew she wouldn't join them because he had overheard her say that she had a four o'clock Zoom call that day for work the night before.

"I would go, but I have work. Ummm, why don't you take them to The Marlin? They are known for their pepper steak."

"Sounds good. You sure you can't join us?"

"I appreciate the offer, but I have to take this Zoom call. Work never ends when you are a lobbyist."

"I understand. We'll see you after dinner."

Rick motioned with his head for Possum to follow him. He whispered in Possum's ear, "Put the bomb and all your stuff in the Overland. Do it nonchalantly and tell Gary to do the same. Just do it. I'll explain later."

The night before, after everyone had gone to sleep, Rick had put all his gear in the Overland along with most of Jules's things. She was the only one who knew what was going down, as he trusted her completely. He trusted Possum and Gary the same but didn't want them to act any different, and not knowing was the easiest way.

Once Jacinda went onto her office, Possum and Gary discreetly loaded all their stuff into the Overland. Possum gave Rick the go sign.

"All right y'all, let's all go get the Defender in the Overland and I'm gonna take y'all to dinner for your hard work.

We need to blow off a little steam before tomorrow morning's trek."

They all climbed into the Overland with Junior at the wheel and Rick riding shotgun. Jules sat in the very back with Chief in his travel cage, and Possum and Gary sat across from each other on the dinette. As they pulled out of the driveway, the little AirTag chimed several times. It had never done that before. It was so quiet only Rick heard it because it was in his backpack between his legs on the floorboard.

He pulled out his iPhone and did a search for why AirTags chime and found out it could be for a few reasons. It could mean that someone was tracking them or that lost mode had been initiated, or because it had left its home base. Any of those reasons was enough for Rick to ditch it.

It took no time to get to the shop where the Defender waited. Gary paid Junior's friend for the work against his wishes. While everyone admired the Defender, Rick took the AirTag out of his backpack and placed it behind a set of tires behind the Defender. He had placed it inside of a Ziploc baggie, and when no one was looking, he shoved it under a crack in the wall behind the tires in case he needed to retrieve it.

It was go-time. Rick fired up the Defender, and the big screen in the center of the dash lit up. He scrolled to locations and found the route Junior's dad had taken several times before his death. Jules climbed into the front seat and placed Chief on the back seat in the middle. Rick pulled out of the shop as Gary and Possum joined Junior in the Overland. He followed Rick to what he thought was going to be the dinner spot. Rick stopped, put his flashers on, and stepped up to the window of the Overland.

"Change of plans, Junior. We are going to the site now. Don't tell Jacinda until I text you. We need a head start in case there's a mole working with her detail crew."

"Gotcha. I'll follow you. Let's roll."

Rick climbed back into the Overland. Their destination was about two hundred kilometers away on the outskirts of the town of Lunda, just east of Kafue National Park on Route D181.

When they were about an hour out, Rick was about to text Junior, only his own phone whistled.

> Jacinda just texted me. She's upset. She went to my buddy's shop to meet us for dinner, but we had already left. Her Zoom call canceled.

Rick thought for a minute, then texted back.

> Tell her to meet us in Lunda. We can wait there.

He had no intention of meeting her there. It was for her safety and theirs. They had a two-hour jump on them. They would arrive at the site before any snipers could be set up. That way, they could determine if the ivory was there before they arrived in case there was a mole after all. Once they were there, he would just have Junior text her the GPS coordinates.

As they followed the route in the Defender's GPS, they drove past Lunda and drove a few more miles until they came to a dirt road not on any map. Rick turned onto the road as Junior continued to follow. They came to the end of the route and Rick stopped. He turned off the engine of the Defender and looked around. There was nothing around but dirt and bushes as far as the eye could see. Everyone gathered around.

"Go ahead and text Jacinda with these coordinates," said Rick as he showed Junior his iPhone.

Junior texted Jacinda. She didn't respond. Rick figured she was probably driving.

"All right, let's spread out and see if we can find the stash. I have no idea what we're looking for, but if it's here, it will probably be obvious."

They all spread out about ten feet apart and began to look. After thirty minutes, it seemed like a waste of time. They continued to search anyway. The sun was getting low in the sky, and they would be without light soon. This was not the way Rick had hoped it would turn out.

As they continued to walk the area, Jules shouted, "Look! Over there."

At the edge of the area they were searching, the ground sloped down and there lay a pile of branches leaning against the grade of the land. They all ran up to it and began to pull the large branches away. Beneath them, they revealed an opening in the dirt. It was just large enough for a man to crawl into.

"It's a warthog hole," said Junior.

"Why was it covered in branches?" asked Rick.

"There's only one way to find out. May I?" asked Junior.

"Be my guest."

Junior kneeled in front of the hole and shined his flashlight inside. The hole looked like it stopped and made a sharp right-hand turn. Not something warthogs would do. Junior climbed into the hole as they all gathered around.

"It's here! It's here, come on," yelled Junior.

Rick instructed Possum to get the IED out of the Overland. Jules and Gary drove both vehicles over to the area of the hole and turned on the headlights. The sun had gone below the horizon. Once inside, Rick knew it was not a warthog hole in any way. It was an old mine. The walls opened and were braced with large railroad-type ties. As he continued inside, the room expanded, and against the wall were stacks of ivory tusks. Piles and piles of them. More than he could count.

"It's the motherload!" exclaimed Rick.

Soon after, Jules, Gary, and Possum joined them. Chief was tucked under Jules's vest with his little white head peeking out.

"Okay everyone, help me search the pile of tusks. One will be different and have markings on it. It's the clue we have been looking for."

Everyone began to search. Junior had a couple of powerful LED lanterns in the Overland. He climbed out and returned with them, and they lit up the room nicely. As they all searched each piece of ivory and set them aside looking for the odd one out, a few hours passed. There must have been two thousand tusks in the room. It was sad that all these elephants were illegally killed by men with a lust for money.

Another fifteen minutes went by, and they heard the sound of vehicles approaching the site. Rick knew it was Jacinda. He climbed out of the hole to greet her. Behind her was her security detail. Five men, all toting Ak-47s.

"I'm glad you made it," said Rick.

"Well, I was planning on joining you guys for dinner, but Junior's friend said you had already left."

"Speak of the devil," said Rick as Junior dusted off his pants after exiting the hole.

"Hi, Jacinda, glad you could join us," said Junior.

"Yeah, I was a little shocked when I stopped at your friend's shop and you were all gone."

"Yep, he texted me. I don't remember giving you his address."

"It was you!" blurted out Rick.

"What?!" asked Jacinda.

"The only way you knew how to get to Junior's friend's shop was to follow the AirTag! You have an iPad too. When we left your house, the AirTag chimed. You were tracking us. There was no Zoom call. It all makes sense now. Your father was killed by a 30-06—*your* 30-06. The only reason you came back into Junior's life is because you found out he had hired me to find the ivory and find the murderer. Well, I have found both now."

"That's ludicrous!"

"Really? Then show me your iPad."

Jacinda glanced back at her Tacoma then raised her rifle. Her detail did the same.

"Bravo, Rick Waters, bravo! Very clever. Yes, I found my AirTag you hid behind the tires. It's safe and sound in my purse now. It doesn't matter now anyway. You all are going to die, and I am keeping the tusks and the secret of my father's death to myself."

"How could you do this? He was our dad!" exclaimed Junior.

"You were always much closer to Dad than I was. It was an accident, I swear. I am sad and distraught that it happened—I only meant to wing him. I planned on forcing him to show me the ivory. He was on to me. He confronted me a few days before I shot him. He refused to show me where the ivory was, and I had no choice but to make him show me. As you know, I'm an excellent shot, but as I slowly squeezed the trigger, my phone vibrated, and it made me jump. I pulled the trigger hard and hit him in the chest. I never intended to kill him. But what's done is done. The irony is the text was from Colin Mulenga. If he had just texted me a few second later, we could have found the ivory and avoided all this mess."

"So, you and Colin are partners in the resort?" asked Rick.

"Don't be so naive, Rick. It goes way higher than Colin Mulenga. Let me think. The judge, Lusaka police chief, many others in the force, and two more men in the UNPD. There's no stopping this. Dad was in the way. I admire him for trying to save the elephants, but the one thing he could stop was progress. He wanted to but there's too much money at stake. Dad was just too honest for his own good."

"You are a monster!" yelled Junior.

"What, are you gonna just shoot us all too?" asked Rick.

"Naw, I need you. You will help me get all the ivory out first. Then thanks to your buddy Possum, I will blow you all to smithereens."

Rick gritted his teeth. "You won't get away with this."

"Watch me!"

She motioned for her protective detail to escort Rick and Junior back into the mine. Once inside, they flanked the crew and made them form a human chain to remove all the ivory to the outside of the hole. Two armed guards on the outside loaded a large box truck that they backed up close to the hole's entrance. Jules, Gary, and Possum had no choice but to help once they realized what was happening. Rick stayed closest to the ivory and reluctantly handed each tusk to Gary, who passed it along to Jules, then Possum, and so on.

They were all sweating and exhausted as they continued to pass along the valuable ivory. Rick's heart was pounding with anger, but it didn't stop him from focusing on every piece he picked up. He soon spotted a small end piece of ivory that appeared much different than the rest, with a scribbled manmade marking across the side of it. It had to be the one he had been searching for.

As he grabbed another large tusk, he used his left foot to slide some dirt over the ivory. It took another thirty minutes for all the ivory to be removed from the mine and loaded onto the truck.

"Now what?!"

"Now, you die. Let's go, boys," said Jacinda.

"If you leave, what's to stop us from just climbing out of the hole?"

Jacinda just reached into her pocket and pulled out three sticks of dynamite, then smiled as she set the timer on Possum's bomb. As she exited the hole, she lit the dynamite and placed it at the edge of the hole. Rick and the gang moved as far away from the hole as they could.

Boom!

The entire mine shook as dust and dirt fell on top of them. They covered their heads with their arms to avoid the falling debris. The exit had been destroyed.

Once the dust settled, Possum moved over to the IED he had built. The timer read eight minutes and fifteen seconds and counting.

"Can you diffuse it?" asked Rick.

"No, no way. I built it so it could not be diffused. I love y'all. It's been one hell of a ride. We may as well hug each other and enjoy what little time together we have left."

"Fuck that!" exclaimed Jules.

"What?"

"I have an idea. See those timbers holding up the wall? If we move the bomb toward where the exit was and dig a little hole, we can then place all the timbers against the bomb, which will make the explosion go outward toward the exit. It's our only hope. I'd rather be hit by dusty old timbers than metal from a pipe bomb. We have seven minutes!"

Gary dug a deep hole in the fresh dirt that had covered the exit from the TNT and placed the bomb as high up as he could toward the surface. Rick and Possum grabbed a timber and started to pull it. The earth from the sides of the wall crumbled down as they pulled it away. Jules dragged the wooden pieces that were sideways on the wall and started to build a makeshift fence they could hide behind.

The ceiling vibrated above as the big truck pulled away.

They worked feverishly. Rick barely paused to catch his breath. Luckily, for whatever reason, Lucinda hadn't taken the LED lamps with her when she left, so they could see quite well. They had placed about fifteen heavy timbers against the bomb. The timer displayed three minutes left on the countdown.

They managed to get a couple more against the bomb as the timer went under a minute. They all climbed behind the blockade Jules had constructed and got as low to the ground as they could. Rick put his arm around Jules and kissed her and Chief on the beak.

"I love you, Jules. I love you too, Chief. I love you all!"

"We all love…"

Kaboom!

The blast sent wood and earth flying. Everything went black as the LED lamps disintegrated. The explosion pushed the fence into them, and dirt covered them up. The noise from the bomb made Rick's ears ring, and a silence fell over them.

"Are you all alive?" shouted Rick as he coughed dust out of his lungs.

"I'm here, Rick!" said Jules, coughing.

"Yep," said Possum.

"Junior?"

"I'm alive. I think my arm is broken though."

"Gary, are you okay?"

There was no response.

Rick pushed the dirt off him and pulled Jules to her feet. A sliver of light from near the exit was the only light inside the dark mine. Rick pulled out his iPhone and turned on the flashlight feature. He began to dig, trying to find Gary. He felt a wet spot in the dirt. It was blood. He reached down and felt Gary's shoulder. With all his force, he pulled Gary's limp body out from under the pile of earth. His head was bleeding profusely, and he had no pulse and wasn't breathing.

"Help me!" yelled Rick.

He flipped Gary over and began CPR. He continued CPR for several minutes and again checked for signs of life. Nothing.

Possum took over as Rick collapsed beside Gary's lifeless body. Jules helped Junior stabilize his injured arm. His bone had punctured his skin, and a large piece of wood was sticking out beside it. Tears were flowing down Jules's cheeks as Possum continued CPR.

"Please don't leave us, buddy," said Rick as he put his head in his hands and prayed.

"I don't know, Rick. I'm not getting anything," said Possum.

"Dammit, Gary, come back!" yelled Rick. He slammed his clenched hand into Gary's chest.

Dust blew out of his mouth, and he coughed.

His eyes slowly opened, and he took a gasping breath.

"Where am I?"

Rick collapsed over him and squeezed him tight.

"You're with us, Gary!"

Jules tore part of her shirt and wrapped it around Gary's head to slow down the bleeding He had a huge lump on it and a deep gash. He was confused and most likely had a concussion.

"We have to get out of here!" yelled Possum as he started digging in the area where the light was peeking through.

It took about a half an hour to dig their way out. The light was coming from the LED fog lights on Junior's Overland. Rick could hear the faint sound of an engine. It was the whisper-quiet sound of the Onan generator from the Overland. The Defender was gone.

"She took the Defender. Why didn't they take the Overland?"

"I have the keys," replied Junior. "The Defender was running when they got here to keep the headlights on the hold, but I used the generator on the Overland. She probably thought it was running too. Once she blew the hole with the dynamite, there was no way she could get the keys."

"Why didn't she turn off the lights and kill the generator?" asked Rick.

"She couldn't. It was all locked up."

"Let's get the fuck out of here."

Rick helped Jules and Chief out of the hole. Chief was so dirty he looked like a rare black cockatoo instead of a white umbrella cockatoo. All their ears were still ringing. Even Chief's, apparently, as he kept shaking his head and make a yawning motion with his beak.

Rick and Possum dug the hole wider and helped Junior out. They placed him in the passenger seat of the Overland once Rick retrieved the keys from his left pocket. Gary was able to climb out on his own. He was dizzy and disoriented but he seemed in fairly good shape.

Once they were all safe and sound in the Overland, Rick climbed back into the hole to try and find the unusual end piece of the tusk he had hidden. It took him a while, but he finally found it. Once outside, while standing in front of the fog light, he saw the etching on the side. It said one word: Jacinda.

Besides a few scratches and scrapes, Rick, Jules, and Possum were uninjured. Jules had saved all their lives.

CHAPTER SIXTEEN

Rick drove due south, away from Kafue National Park and more importantly away from Lusaka. Jacinda believed they were dead, and he planned to keep it that way for now. There was little between Lunda and Victoria Falls. Junior and Gary would just have to deal with the pain until they could reach the hospital in Victoria Falls. It would take them nine hours to get there.

Luckily, Junior's first-aid kit was well equipped with not only bandages and wraps, but also some heavy-duty pain-killers. Jules cleaned Gary's wound and managed to remove the small piece of wood jutting from Junior's arm. She gave him a wooden spoon to bite on as she pulled it out. The pain was so intense he passed out for a short while. She disinfected the open wound on his arm and lightly wrapped it to cover the exposed bone.

Gary was out of luck when it came to pain, though. It was far too risky to give him any kind of narcotic with a head injury. She cleaned up his cut and bandaged it. The lump on his head had gone down a bit about halfway through the trip, and he seemed to have his wits about him.

Rick called Renato and got him up to speed. They planned to meet the next day with a task force in Zimbabwe at a location to be determined. It would be somewhere near Victoria Falls. Time was of the essence, as they all knew Jacinda would be dumping the ivory on the black market as soon as she possibly could. Rick drove the entire way, sleep deprived and half deaf from the explosion. He was just happy to be alive and so proud of Jules for thinking on her feet so fast.

"How's my little black bird doing?" Rick asked Chief as he sat on top of the center console in between Rick and Junior.

Chief ruffled his feathers and gave Rick puppy dog eyes.

They arrived at Victoria Falls Hospital just after ten a.m. They gave false names to the registration at the ER and told them they had been involved in an auto accident. Gary indeed had a concussion, and they reset Junior's arm and put it in a cast. It was a clean break, and Jules had done such a good job removing the wood from inside his cut that they were none the wiser that it wasn't from a car wreck.

Once they left the hospital, Rick made reservations for them under false names at the Matetsi Hotel and paid cash so there would be no way to trace them. He knew Jacinda assumed they were all pushing up daisies and had no reason to check, but he took no chances. To make things easier, they arranged to meet with Renato at the hotel.

Jules took the longest shower of her life, followed by Rick, who also cleaned up his black bird Chief until he once again resembled a white bird.

Possum bunked with Gary so he could keep an eye on him, and Junior got his own suite. They were all in bed asleep before sundown.

The next morning when Rick woke up to go to the bathroom, the lingering pain from the explosion hit him all at once. He was sore all over. Jules said she was too. Rick checked on everyone after breakfast and they had the same experience. Luckily, their hearing was nearly back to normal except for a small bit of tinnitus. Rick changed clothes and decided to send out his and Jules's dirty clothes to be laundered. As he checked his pockets for receipts and change, he found the shell casing he had picked up when they all went to the shooting range with Jacinda. He had meant to give it back to her but forgot. It was a 30-06 casing.

Rick's phone rang at 9:15. It was Renato.

"Good morning, Renato. Are you here?"

"We are at the hotel. I have decided to put the command center at your hotel. We should be all set up within an hour. Can we meet at say…eleven a.m.?"

"Perfect. Just text me when you're ready."

"Ciao."

Rick's phone whistled at 10:55 a.m.

> We're here. Meet in the Strathearn Suite in five minutes.

See you then.

Rick, Jules, and Possum met outside the hotel restaurant and proceeded to the meeting.

"Buongiorno, I am Renato. It is my pleasure to meet you."

"I'm Rick. This is Possum and my girlfriend Jules."

"Please, sit down and let's go over what you have."

"Sure. Okay, so I'll skip some of the stuff you already know. We found an Apple AirTag hidden inside of a radar detector. I'm certain it was planted there by Jacinda. Her father had logged it into a receipt program called Neat and marked it as a gift. I would bet my bottom dollar that Jacinda bought it, hid the AirTag inside, and gave it to her now late father. He owned no Apple products and that is all Jacinda uses. If you can get ahold of her iPad, you will see that it is assigned to the AirTag I originally hid in a shop outside of Lusaka. I have the address and location of where I hid it in a notepad here."

"Okay, what else?"

"Besides admitting to the murder and trying to blow us up, what else do you need?"

"Do you have proof of that conversation? At this point it's just he said, she said."

"Wait." Rick reached into his pocket and pulled out the shell casing he had picked up at the gun range. "If you run ballistics on this, I guarantee it will match shell casings found by police near the murder scene as well as Jacinda's personal gun. She calls it Old Faithful. It's a 30-06, the same kind of weapon that was used in her father's murder."

"That's great. But it's still mostly circumstantial. I would love to have an open and shut case against her. Is there anything else?"

Rick thought for a moment then said, "Wait here, I'll be right back."

He jogged to his room and grabbed the keys to the Overland, then went down to it and grabbed the small piece of an elephant tusk he had found with her name etched in it. Once back at the suite, he handed it to Renato. "This is the piece of tusk Mr. Dlamini mentioned in a note he left for Junior."

Renato looked at the tusk and flipped it around, looking at both ends.

"It has her name on it. This means nothing."

Rick snatched the tusk back from Renato. "Son of a bitch. I'm giving her to you on a silver platter!" he exclaimed as he slammed it on the table.

When he did, small pieces of what looked like crumbled drywall fell out of the semi-hollow end. Renato leaned in for a closer look and picked up the tusk. He used his pen to dig around a little, then turned the tusk with the fat part facing down, and out fell a black flash drive. They all sat there staring at it for what seemed like an eternity. Renato dusted it off, pulled out his laptop, and plugged in the little drive.

Several documents popped up implicating Colin Mulenga and many others, and at the bottom of the folder was a video file. He clicked on it. The video looked like it was filmed from a hidden camera on Junior's dad's body. It was very clear, and the audio was perfect. They all gathered around, watched, and listened. The video started from inside his Defender while driving.

"My name is Bandile Dlamini. Today is March 28, at 9:37 a.m. I am headed to a meeting with my daughter, Jacinda Dlamani. She has gotten herself mixed up with some very bad people and I am going to try and talk her into getting away from them. She knows I stole the ivory from the poachers, and she is trying to convince me to give it back. I'm about a half a mile from the meeting place."

He kept driving in silence until the Defender came to a stop. He turned off the engine and stepped out while the camera continued to film.

"Good morning, Jacinda."

"Morning, Dad."

She hugged him and it blurred out the camera for a second, indicating it was probably a hidden pen camera in his shirt pocket.

"Listen, Jacinda. I know you think you are doing the right thing, but I will not return the ivory. I have spent my life defending these elephants and I am not about to stop now."

"Dad, you are making a big mistake. They will kill you if you don't return it. These men are ruthless."

"What men? Maybe I can talk some sense into them."

"They are high up in the government. The main guy needs this ivory to buy part of the park for his resort and he'll stop at nothing to get it. He has the police in his palm and some of the judges."

"You mean Colin Mulenga?"

Silence followed, and her mouth fell open.

"How did you know?"

"I know more than you think. I know what cops are involved and what judges. I've done my own snooping and I have documented it all. I just need to find the right agency to turn it all in. I've kept your name out of it so far, but if you continue, I will have to implicate you. I have no choice."

"Your own daughter?"

"Yes, my own daughter, who abandoned her entire family over a squabble about the parks and the elephant and the pursuit of money. You come back after all these years once you find out I have the ivory? I'm not stupid."

"It's not like that, Dad. It's all corrupt. If I don't go along, I'll be in danger myself."

"Please, Jacinda, join me. Let's take them down together. You once loved and protected the elephants just like your brother and me. There's still time."

"No, there's not. Colin needs this ivory, and he will get it. Over your dead body or not."

"So be it."

"So, that's it? You won't tell me?"

"I'm sorry, Jacinda, you know I can't."

"Okay, well, it's your funeral."

She turned and walked back to her car, and Bandile did the same. He waited until she drove off then stopped the video.

Renato whistled. "Damn, that's a slam dunk. With all these files Bandile put on this drive, we can take them all down."

"What about the ivory?" asked Rick.

"We are going to set up a sting. I have an informant on the inside who will pose as a potential buyer. We will have our task force there undercover. When she tries to make the sale, we'll nab her and the ivory. I will personally see that it is all destroyed."

"When?"

"It's already been set in motion. I'd say tomorrow or the next day. Once she's in custody, she'll probably want a deal to testify against Colin and the others. We have no death penalty in Zambia, but she may plead down to twenty-five years with a chance of parole in fifteen. If it were me, I'd lock her up and throw away the key. I mean damn, she murdered her own father."

"I agree. What can I do?"

"Rick, you have done more than I can possibly imagine. Don't you want to just get out of Africa?"

"You mean like the movie?"

"Huh?"

"Never mind."

"If you are determined to be involved, I can use you undercover. You can easily identify her security team, right?"

"Damn straight. I'll be there."

They shook hands and returned to their rooms.

"Listen, y'all," Rick told his friends. "I think I'm gonna do this one on my own. There's no sense in all y'all being here. It's too dangerous and the task force is gonna do all the heavy lifting anyway. I'll just have to testify against her and help identify her security detail."

"I want to stay, Rick!" said Jules.

"I know, baby, but I will be able to concentrate better on this sting if I know you are safe."

Rick thought for a minute. He hated being away from Jules as much as she did.

"I'll make you a deal. If you stay here at this resort in Zimbabwe, you can stay. But you're not going on the sting. Deal?"

"Okay," she said like a little kid who was just told they couldn't have ice cream until after dinner. She even kicked the floor with the toe of her shoe. It made Rick smile.

"Possum, I want you and Gary to head back to Florida in Gary's jet. Please take Chief with you. We will head back after the trial and fly commercial. Is that cool?"

"No problem, hombre. I wish we could help you, but it does make more sense to head back. I can help Gary and Johnie get the ship ready to retrieve the treasure we dumped near Key West."

"Good man."

"I'll go talk to Gary. He'll probably have his pilot bring the plane here. I bet Clay's going out of his mind being stuck at that damn hotel in Lusaka."

"You're probably right."

Rick called Johnie to let him know what was going down.

"Johnie, it's Rick."

"What's up, man?"

"How's the ship?"

"I've got good news and bad news."

"Okay, just spill it."

"The good news is all the repairs and upgrades to *Nine-Tenths* went faster than planned and she's ready."

"The bad news?"

"Well, because the yard wants her removed, I had to postpone the sea trial for the new ship."

"That's actually good news, Johnie. I'm sending Gary and Possum back, so they can go on the sea trial with you after you take *Nine-Tenths* back to Destin. Who's going to ride back with you?"

"Oh, no worries there. I hired a new deckhand who's a great little helper on the ship. He volunteered to head back with me. He wants all the sea time he can get. We can fly back in a couple of days."

"Perfect. I think Gary and Possum will be leaving tomorrow. They are bringing Chief with them. Jules will fly back with me commercial after this is all over. Hopefully in a few days. I may have to fly back to Africa for the trial, though, to testify. Time will tell."

"Okay, boss. I hope it all goes smooth as silk."

"Me too, Johnie. See ya soon hopefully."

After the call, Rick and Jules went to the hotel restaurant for lunch. It was a beautiful outdoor setting. The Cassia Restaurant got its name from the two bold and beautiful Cassia fistula trees poised in front of the hotel, facing the direction of the mighty Victoria Falls. As they sat down, the roar of the falls reached Rick's ears. A few impalas and warthogs grazed nearby on the hotel lawn. Victoria Falls was known by locals as the smoke that thundered.

Rick had a Cassia beef burger, and Jules went for the Thai chicken salad. Both were delicious. They decided to take a little stroll on the grounds after lunch. They were greeted by several warthogs and a small herd of ibex. In the trees was a group of playful vervet monkeys. Rick wished they had grabbed Chief before their walk. He was sure the cockatoo would be calling the monkeys.

After their walk, they changed into their bathing suits and spent a little time by the pool. The resort was incredibly beautiful and manicured. It was a far cry from out in the bush, as if two worlds had collided. He was growing to love Africa and beginning to feel more like a part of it than the ugly American. For the first time, he wasn't looking forward to leaving.

Gary rested on a lounge chair, while Possum made a grand entrance to the pool with a cannonball and splashed Jules as she was sunning. She just laughed. Boys would be boys.

"I called Clay and the jet is en route," remarked Gary. "He is stoked to get out of that airport hotel. He really has nothing to complain about with what I'm paying him to watch TV, but I get it. It's been a minute."

"What time are y'all lifting off tomorrow? Have you chosen a route yet?" asked Rick.

"We're gonna have wheels up around ten a.m. I think we're gonna make a stop in Frankfurt, then onto Miami, then Key West. We'll refuel in Frankfurt and probably stay overnight there and get some German beers. I've never been to Germany."

"That'll be nice. Try the schnitzel, you'll love it. Oh, how is Junior's arm? Is he feeling any better?"

"Physically, he's good. But he's having a bit of a rough time accepting what his sister did. It was a shock to the system, I guess."

"Yeah, that would be tough on anyone. Where is he now?"

"He's in his room. I tried to talk him into joining us, but he just wasn't into it."

"Damn, I hate to hear that. Maybe I'll go talk to him in a little while and try to cheer him up."

"He definitely needs some cheering."

With that being said, Gary stepped into the pool and dunked his head under the water to see how long he could hold his breath. Jules scolded him for overdoing it. He wasn't taking his concussion seriously, and she reminded him as only she could. He gave her a pouty face and went back to his lounge chair.

He hasn't changed a lick since high school, thought Rick with a chuckle.

Possum was making water fountains in the pool with his enclosed hands like an eight-year-old. Rick was glad his gang was intact and safe after their near-death experience in the mine. It reminded Rick how worn out he was. The warm water in the pool helped. Jules was content to soak up the beautiful warm Zimbabwean sun. She looked like a tan angel lying on the colorful lounge chair.

Rick climbed out of the pool and kissed her on the forehead. She opened one eye, as she wasn't wearing shades, and blew him a kiss.

"I'm gonna run and grab Chief. He loves water."

"Okay, can you grab me a diet coke too?"

"One diet coke and one white cockatoo coming up!"

After a few hours in the pool, they all settled into their rooms. Rick knocked on Junior's door.

"Come in," said Junior.

"Hey, man, how you feeling?"

"I'm good. Just watching a little TV."

"Possum said you're feeling a little down?"

"Yeah. I can't lie. I mean, my sister just came back into my life after the stupid fallout between her and my dad, and now I find out the only reason is because she wanted to get her greedy hands on the ivory. Not to mention she's the one who pulled the trigger on him. It's a little too much to handle all at once."

"I understand. I can't relate, but I get it. Listen, the best thing we can do for your father's memory is recover and destroy that ivory. You need to get up and get out of this room. It's beautiful but not good to be stuck inside here all day. We are thinking about taking a little sunset cruise on the Zambezi River in a couple hours. Gary and Possum are flying out tomorrow, so it will be the last time you'll get to see them. What do you say?"

"All right, I'll go. I want to thank them for helping. They're a couple great guys. So are you, Rick. I can't really begin to thank you for all you've done for me. I'll snap out of this. Don't worry."

"Okay, then it's settled. Meet us in the lobby at four. We're gonna see hippos! Woohoo!"

Junior just laughed at Rick's attempt to cheer him up. It was working, though.

They all met in the lobby and hopped into an excursion van. Pets weren't allowed, so Chief had to stay back at the resort. It bummed Rick out.

But once they boarded the beautiful Ra-Ikane boat, all was forgiven. The weather was perfect for the cruise. Besides Rick, Jules, and the crew, there were only two other couples on board, and the guide and first mate. They motored out as he spoke over a PA speaker, describing the flora and fauna.

They saw crocodiles, hippos, and every type of bird imaginable. Possum must have snapped a thousand pictures. Even Junior was smiling.

They all took a group photo as the sun set on the majestic Zambezi. It was a photo that would end up on Rick's desk when he returned home. A memory of his trip to Africa and its amazing people and animals. He would never forget it.

CHAPTER SEVENTEEN

Rick and Jules hugged Gary and Possum goodbye. Jules passed Chief to Possum, who would be his caretaker on the flight. Junior shook both of their hands and hugged them as well. Clay had already left for the airport to prep the plane for the long flight. At least they'd gotten to see him on the cruise and later at dinner. He was a good pilot and becoming an essential part of the gang.

As they drove away, Rick put his arm around Jules and they both waved. Rick's phone whistled. It was Renato.

Can you come to the
Strathearn Suite?

Be there in a couple
minutes.

"Come on, Jules. Let's go talk to Renato. Hopefully he has good news."

They strolled hand in hand through the lobby and over to Renato's suite. Before Rick could knock on the door, Renato opened it and waved them inside.

"We have a small problem."

"Great, what is it?!"

"We have intel that Jacinda may be selling the ivory tonight on the black market in Kafue. We need to break that up before it happens. I want to send a team to her home while she's away to confiscate that 30-06. I can get a warrant, but I don't want her to know we are on to her yet. I need to run a ballistics test on the rifle. Not only do we have the casing you gave me, but we have the original one found by the police outpost where Bandile was murdered. We also have the actual projectile removed from his body. It was largely damaged but still has a couple of identifiable grooves on it. The problem is her home is heavily guarded with surveillance cameras and armed security. We only have a small window to do this in," said Renato.

"So, you need to break in, steal the gun, and run ballistics on it?"

"Not steal, borrow. Plus, it must be returned in the same condition it was in and wiped clean."

"I've been to that house. We both have. Hell, we stayed there a few days. If anyone can get that gun, it's me."

Renato stared at the ceiling, pondering for a minute. "You're willing to do that?"

"Yes, I'm willing to break in, borrow the gun, test fire it, and return it. All in a day's work. I'll need a mobile unit nearby to run the test. Can you arrange that?"

"Yeah, we can put together a team for you for support. We have to do this off the record—and don't get caught, because I can't be a part of this."

"I'm down. I can't believe I'm about to say this, but I need a distraction, and Jules is the one I need. We're also gonna need a car with a spare tire. Jules, are you ready to go undercover? Feel like being a blonde for a day?"

She perked right up. "Yay! I hoped I was gonna be a part of this! I have the perfect outfit. But we need a nice car. Like a Jaguar or a Beamer."

"Done," said Renato.

"Rick, we can place you in a box truck with the team. It will look like a DHL delivery truck. We already have one for surveillance. We just need to add the water tank for the ballistics test, but that's not an issue. You'll have eyes and ears on Jacinda's place. Once she leaves, we can send Jules in with a flat tire in front of her property and she can draw out the guards. Then you will have a very short window to get in, grab the gun and test it, and then return it."

"What do you think?"

"I think I like my odds," said Rick as he rubbed his chin.

"Okay, we leave in an hour. We have a safe house near Kafue where you will meet the team. They are prepping the truck as we speak. Do you need anything from us, Jules?"

"Besides the car, a long blonde wig is all. I have the perfect dress."

"All right. Get packed and meet me in the lobby in an hour. We will take a chopper to Kafue. Oh, and don't worry, Rick. Anything you could possibly need to break in, we will have at the safe house. And if this goes sideways, I don't know you. Got it?"

"Of course. Just have bail money for me if I need it," he said with a laugh.

Jules packed a small bag for her and Rick. They would keep the room and Junior's until it was over. Rick caught up Junior on the plan; he wanted to help but knew with his arm in a cast, he'd just slow them down. So, he agreed to stay behind and rest.

Once in the lobby, they boarded a van bound for the airport.

The Sikorsky S-97 Raider sat on the tarmac. Rick recognized it instantly, being a huge fan of choppers. It was the second-fastest helicopter in the world next to the Bell Boeing V22 Osprey, which he didn't count because it could convert from a chopper to a plane. In his mind, the Sikorsky was the fastest true helicopter. It made sense too, since time was an issue and there were no direct flights from Victoria Falls to Kafue.

The flight took no time, but they were served a late breakfast/early lunch on board. They landed on the roof of the safe house. It was on the outskirts of Kafue and consisted of a hundred acres of fenced-off guarded property. It looked more like a military outpost than a safe house. Once inside the building, it felt like the scene from the James Bond movie *Goldfinger* where Q shows Bond all his new toys and the Aston Martin DB5 with a bulletproof windshield.

Renato introduced Jules and Rick to the team. In the background, several guys were putting the finishing touches on the faux DHL surveillance truck. Rick was filled with excitement. He could feel his blood flowing through his veins.

"What about the security cameras?" asked Rick.

"Come check this out," replied Renato.

They followed him over to a workbench where he picked up a large device that looked like a small satellite dish.

"What is it?" asked Jules.

"It's a scrambler. It will jam the entire security system. The cameras will still be operating, but the picture will look like the old days when the TV went off the air at midnight. The record time does not change and as soon as we turn it off, they will return to normal operation. Unless someone is monitoring the video feed at the exact same time, they will never know. That's where you come in. You'll need to coax the guards out to help you fix your flat tire and keep them there while Rick is inside."

"Easy peasy!"

"The device will be hidden behind a window on the DHL truck. See the truck? It looks like a solid truck, right? No side windows. Follow me."

They walked up to the truck, and Rick even touched the side of it. No windows. Then Renato opened the rear doors, and they stepped inside. Both sides of the entire truck were glass and covered in some sort of yellow film that made them look like metal. It was mind-blowing. They had already placed the water tank near the rear doors. Renato picked up what looked like a large PVC pipe, two inches wide by two feet long. He grabbed a 30-06 leaning against the side wall of the truck and screwed it on.

"Step back."

Rick and Jules covered their ears, and Renato shook his head and motioned to them to remove their hands from their ears. He chambered a round into the rifle, placed the gun in the opening of the water tank, and squeezed the trigger.

Pew!

The shot was almost undetectable.

"Won't that affect the grooves on the bullet?" asked Rick.

"Not this one. It's made with a sound-proofing polymer that NASA developed. Watch this."

Renato retrieved the wet bullet from the water tank, placed it on the workbench, donned a pair of ear protectors, and gave Rick and Jules a pair as he unscrewed the silencer.

"Fire in the hole!" he hollered.

All the guys in the James Bond-type room covered their ears.

Boom!

Even with ear protectors on, the sound was astonishingly loud inside the small area of the truck. He once again retrieved the bullet and held them both up together for Rick to examine. The grooves made in the bullet by the rifle's barrel were identical.

"Man, you guys are something else," proclaimed Rick.

"You can thank NASA and M16 for this one. Some tech guy over in London came up with the design. As far as we know, this is the only one in operation so far. A prototype, if you will."

"Color me impressed."

Renato motioned with his head for them to follow him.

"Rick and Jules, I want to introduce the team to you. This is Hans, our computer scientist. James here is our sound engineer, surveillance camera expert, and will also be firing the round from the gun you borrow. This is Henry and Joseph. They will be your weapons experts. Your snipers if things go sideways. They will both be equipped with DHL yellow Barrett M107A1's and will be positioned on the roof of the DHL truck," he said as he pointed in its direction.

Rick glanced over at the truck. "Can't they be spotted on the roof?"

"No, I forgot to tell you but there is an exit on the ceiling, and the side walls are two feet higher than the roof line. You see those tiny little discolorations in the front and rear of the top of the truck?"

Rick squinted and could barely see what he was referring to.

"Those are Judas holes. You will be covered quite well. We don't expect or want any gunfire. That's the whole point of this operation. In and out and back in and out. As quiet as possible," said Renato.

"Gotcha."

Rick and Jules shook all their hands and then followed Renato to the supply room. Rick was super stoked and almost giddy about getting his hands on some new weapons.

"All right, take anything you need. I've got to make a call. I'll be back in fifteen minutes or so. Oh, and there's a choice of wigs in that cabinet, Jules. Help yourself."

Jules opened the cabinet and tried on a few wigs. They were made from human hair and the highest quality she'd ever seen.

Rick began to fill a duffel with what he needed. A DHL uniform in his size was already hanging in the locker for him. He grabbed two matching Springfield XDM Elite 9mms with silencers, six loaded magazines, a Gerber Prodigy combat knife, another smaller KA-BAR Becker BK18 Short Harpoon knife that he would strap to the inside of his lower leg, the smallest pair of night-vison goggles he'd ever seen, which looked like regular sunglasses, and an earpiece that was already set to the frequency the team would use. Jules also took an earpiece. He brought his own lock-picking kit and hoped he wouldn't need it. He already had a pair of black gloves, but they had invisible gloves. He tried a pair on. They clung to his skin so tightly, and even when holding them up to his face, he couldn't see that he was wearing them.

"Wow! This is real James Bond shit, Jules. We need to step up our game when we get back to Destin."

"Maybe they'll let you keep some?"

"I doubt it, but you never know. We ain't getting paid, we ought to get something. After all, we are sort of working for national security now."

After everything was packed away, Renato came back.

"I've arranged for dinner in the great room. Your room is all set up. If you want to go get refreshed, why don't we meet back here at say, 1800 hours?"

"We'll see ya then."

Renato gave them directions and a key to their room. When they arrived in the room, they knew they wouldn't be able to do any hanky-panky. The room was wired for video and sound. They just lay down on the bed and relaxed. After a short while, they drifted off to sleep. Rick had set his alarm just in case for five p.m, so they could shower and change.

But Rick was awakened early, around four, by shuffling in the hallway. He peeked out of the door to see a couple members of the team in tank tops and shorts walking down the hall.

"Where are y'all going?"

"To the gym? Wanna go?"

"Y'all have a gym?"

"Ja, it's more of a spa," replied Hans.

"I'll be there shortly."

"It's just down the end of the hall, second door on the right," said Joseph.

Jules was now awake and watching Rick lean out of the door. He closed it and came back inside.

"You wanna work out, Jules? They have a gym here."

"Before dinner? I don't know...I'm hungry."

"Awe come on, don't be a wimp."

Jules popped out of bed. Rick knew his challenge would be accepted. They quickly changed into workout sweats and went down the hall. When Rick opened the door to the gym, his mouth fell open. It was bigger than any gym he'd ever seen and had equipment that looked like it came from the future. There was a self-serve smoothie bar and three types of coffee in silver airpots. It was late in the day for coffee, but Rick made them smoothies. Hans and Joseph were both on futuristic-looking half stair stepper/half treadmills. Rick strolled over to them, sipping his smoothie. He rubbed his arm, realizing he was still super sore.

"Those are some fancy treadmills," he said.

"Ya, state of the art," replied Han, half out of breath. "Who do you work with, Rick?"

"I normally run with a bunch of ragtag guys out of Florida, but they are flying back now. They're actually making a stop in Germany. You're German, right?"

"Ya, tell them to try some Weihenstephaner Original Premium. It's the only beer I drink. Hard to find here. I have it brought in by a guy who owns a liquor store in Lusaka."

"Okay, I can't even pronounce it, but I'll try and remember to tell them," said Rick as he rubbed his sore arms. "I'm pretty sore. Not gonna be able to do much today," he said to no one in particular.

"See Helga," said Hans, pointing to a room that said "Massage" on it.

"Want a massage, Jules?"

"Hell yeah!" she said as she took a sip of her smoothie.

Rick opened the door to the massage room. No people were inside. There was a large machine in the center that had one word on it: Helga. Rick laughed.

He set down his smoothie, took off his shoes, and lay down in the machine as Jules sat down to watch.

"Here goes nothing," said Rick.

Jules just grinned.

He picked a setting for soreness and pushed the "start" button. The clam shell closed over him, and water jets underneath two layers of plastic began to pulsate. Then rollers went up and down his body. He was in ecstasy. It was better than any human massage he had ever experienced. After twenty minutes, the clam shell opened. Rick turned and stood up.

"I gotta get me one of these. Hell, we need two of these! One for me and one for you," said Rick with a chuckle.

"My turn," exclaimed Jules.

Rick sat down and continued working on his smoothie as Jules pushed the same "start" button. Rick had to laugh when he heard her moaning from inside the clam shell.

She sounded a little like Meg Ryan in the *When Harry Met Sally* movie during the public orgasm scene. She must have moaned "Oh God" a dozen times. When it was done and the clam shell opened, she just lay there for a minute in silence.

"Yes, we need two of these!" she blurted out.

Rick laughed out loud.

They walked back into the main part of the gym, and both started on the fancy treadmills Hans and Joseph were using. There was a scanner facing them and as soon as they started walking, a screen displayed their weight, blood pressure, heart rate and oxygen levels. It was a full-body workout and after thirty minutes, they were all warmed up and loose. They did mostly their arms and upper body and went light. They needed to have all their strength for the mission.

After a shower, they both felt invigorated.

They headed back to the Bond room at ten minutes to six. Rick was wondering how Possum and Gary's trip was going and how Chief was doing, but he was unable to call out since Renato had made them turn off their phones and put them in a safe.

They took an elevator down a level to what Renato called the great room. It looked like the inside of a fabulous restaurant with head mounts of big game on the wall. The only difference was that the eyes of each mount had cameras inside. These guys took security seriously.

During dinner, Rick made small talk. The meal was exquisite. Roast lamb and several sides.

"I had no idea Interpol was so high-tech," expressed Rick.

"We're not just Interpol here, Rick. We are an elite unit. We work with MI6, the CIA, FBI, and your NSA, as well Italy's AISE. Plus, we have jurisdiction everywhere. World leaders call upon us to make arrests all over the world."

"Wow, I had no idea. It will be a pleasure to work with you. Let's stay in touch after this. I get cases all over myself."

Renato smirked but didn't respond and continued to eat dinner. After they were done, he stood up. "Let's go finish the final prep before you leave."

"Oh, Renato. I forgot to ask. What about the sale Jacinda is going to try and do tonight while I'm 'borrowing' her gun?" asked Rick, making finger quotes while saying the word "borrow".

"We have an entire team on that. Just focus on your job and they will disrupt the sale."

"Sounds like a plan."

They all headed out of the great room to change into their outfits and make sure everything was ready. Jules snickered a few times when she looked at Rick in his DHL uniform. She couldn't help it.

They were both getting pumped up for the mission. They put their game faces on as they rejoined the others.

"Okay, let's do this thing and all come back as a team," said Renato in the garage. "Our second team is in position for the sale. If this all goes well, we should be able to complete both missions and be well on the way to recovering the ivory and taking down Jacinda and everyone involved."

All they could hope for was that Jacinda would leave Old Faithful behind at her house and rely on her security detail, instead of bringing it with her to the meet-up.

Rick climbed into the driver's seat of the DHL truck, and Jules got into the metallic-gray Jaguar F-Type R75 convertible. On the dash was a highlighted button that said only two words: flat tire. Rick exited the garage, and Jules followed close behind. It was go-time.

CHAPTER EIGHTEEN

Jacinda put on her lipstick and mussed up her hair in the vanity mirror. If the sale went as expected, she would make more money than she had ever seen in her life, even with the 50/50 split with Colin. She still planned to invest some in his development project, as she knew it would be a big hit with tourists. She felt a little remorse for killing her father and brother, but she shrugged it off. *Life goes on.*

She looked at her watch, then climbed into her Range Rover Defender, courtesy of her brother. As she pulled out of the driveway, three of her security detail followed her in a white van. They drove past a DHL truck to the stop sign and turned left.

"Jules, the mark has left, are you reading?"

"10-4, I'm en route, two minutes to location."

Jules looked in the mirror and winked at her blonde self. She drove past the DHL truck, slowed down, and pushed the highlighted button. A loud pop came from the driver's side front tire, and the car came to a stop directly across from Jacinda's house. The streetlight above her lit her blonde hair up like a torch.

She climbed out of the car and yelled, "Dammit!" as she leaned over in her tight red dress, revealing her curves to the onlooking security guys.

The non-prescription glasses she wore made her look like a sexy librarian. She continued to whine loudly and opened the trunk. She held her Interpol-issued phone up in the air, pretending that she had no signal. Rick watched through binoculars as the two guards began to walk toward the front gate.

"You need some help, ma'am?" yelled one of the guards.

"Yeah, I don't know how to change this stupid tire. Can you come help me?" she hollered back with a desperate-sounding voice.

"I can call you a tow truck," he responded.

She sexily walked toward him. "I'm so late for a meeting. It'll only take a minute." She licked her lips and reached for his biceps. "I bet a strong guy like you could fix it in no time. Pretty please."

The other guard had walked up as well and was eyeing every inch of her perfectly sculpted body. "If you both help me, it will take half the time," she said with a childish giggle.

The first guard pondered for a minute and looked up and down the street.

"Let's go. It won't take long," he said to the other guard as he slung his AK-47 behind him.

The other guard followed him with his AK-47 in his hands. He stood at the edge of the car, keeping an eye on Jacinda's house and the street.

The two snipers were in place on the roof of the DHL truck. Inside the truck, James clicked on the surveillance jammer. Rick climbed out of the truck with a fake DHL package and strolled right past Jules and the two guards, whistling as he walked. He walked to the house next to Jacinda's and up the driveway. When he was out of view of the two guards, he dropped the box and scaled the fence. He ran to the back of the mansion and put on his invisible gloves. He took out his lock-picking kit and was about to start unlocking the double French doors, but he paused, deciding to try the handle first. It was unlocked.

Holy shit! That'll save some time.

He opened the door and made a beeline for Jacinda's bedroom. In the corner of the room was the gun safe. *It better be in there*, he thought. If she'd taken it with her to the sale, they were screwed.

With calm precision, he used his years of experience to crack the safe, trying not to think about what could be going wrong with Jules and the guards outside.

Inside the safe was Jacinda's 30-06. He breathed a sigh of relief.

He picked it up and checked to see if it was loaded. There was a bullet in the chamber. He ran to the back of the house to the opposite neighbor's yard and scaled the fence with the gun strap around his shoulders.

"I've got it," he whispered in his earpiece.

As he approached the end of the driveway of the neighbor's house, the one guard standing watching the other guard was facing the same direction as Rick was standing.

"Get the guard to look the other way," he told Jules.

The other guard had just finished changing the tire and stood up. Jules walked to the front of the car and put her purse on the hood. She started to pull out some money, then pretended to drop it on accident. It drifted down the street away from Rick. The two guards scrambled to catch it.

Rick bolted full speed across the street and entered in through the rear door of the truck. He handed the rifle to James, who placed the barrel into the water tank.

Pew!

He quickly wiped down the gun with oil and jammed an aluminum rod with a special cloth-covered solvent into the barrel, then passed the gun back to Rick. The two guards were about to walk back to the house. There was no way Rick could get back in time.

"Need distraction, Jules. Now!"

"Let me pay you boys for the help," Jules said as she tried to hand the money back to them.

They waved it off, and she took a step and faked a fall. She landed on the ground with her purse in hand. They both bent over to help her.

"These high heels will be the death of me," she said as she watched Rick run across the road.

She lay there rubbing her ankle.

"Are you okay?" one guard asked.

"I think I sprained my ankle."

Rick placed the gun back where he'd found it, climbed the original fence he'd used to enter the grounds, and walked back toward the DHL truck, still whistling. The guards had helped Jules to her feet as Rick walked by and winked at her.

"Thank you, guys, so much. You sure I can't pay you?"

"We're good, have a nice day. We must get back to work."

They strolled back to Jacinda's compound, and Jules drove off, honked, and waved at them.

Rick climbed into the DHL truck and drove off thirty seconds behind her. He threw his DHL hat in the seat and yelled, "Hell yeah, that's how it's done!"

He slowed down and stopped around the corner as Henry and Joseph climbed back into the truck from the roof.

"Great job, Rick. You too, Jules," said Hans.

"Thank you, boys," she responded.

They drove back to the compound, parked the vehicles, and celebrated.

"That was exactly how I wanted it to work," said Renato. "Great job, you two. And good news. The second team thwarted the sale. They posed as local police, and Jacinda got spooked and called it off. She is returning home as we speak. Now we just have to convince her to sell it to us instead. She's greedy, so we are going to offer a substantial amount more. If she takes the bait, we are going to bust her ass once and for all!"

Rick and Jules changed out of their undercover outfits and into street clothes. Rick decided to call Junior and see how he was doing and let him know how the mission went. He didn't answer, probably because he didn't recognize the number, since the phone was Interpol-issued. Rick texted him but he didn't respond to that either. He figured he must be eating a late dinner. He'd try him in the morning.

They walked down to the great room and were surprised by the celebration at hand. Even though they'd had dinner earlier, apparently a whole second meal awaited them. Which was fine with Rick; the mission had made him hungry again.

"Sit down, Rick, sit down. We ran the ballistics and it's a perfect match. We have Jacinda dead to rights. Now we just need to get her to bite on our offer. One of our operatives is making the contact now. We may know something before the night is over. We owe a lot to you and Jules. So, I'm breaking protocol and I'm gonna allow alcohol for one night at the compound," said Renato.

He opened a bag and pulled out a bottle of thirty-year-old Flor de Caña and a bottle of Jules's favorite aguardiente.

"How did you know?"

Renato laughed.

"You know who we are?"

"Oh yeah, I forgot," said Rick as he patted Renato on the shoulder.

They all sat down at the big table. In the center were two bottles of Camus Cabernet.

"You ready for some cow, Jules?"

"Okay, you're starting to freak me out," said Rick, reflecting on how much they knew about Jules's and Rick's favorite beverages and sayings.

"You've heard of Big Brother?" asked Renato.

"You mean, like from the book *1984*?"

"Exactly. It's real, only far more intrusive than even they predicted," replied Renato.

"Makes me nervous."

"Don't worry, you're on the right team."

"That's what scares me."

"Touché."

They started with bacon-wrapped scallops, Rick's favorite. Followed by steaks, which came out exactly the way they both liked them. Rick's was medium and Jules's was still mooing. Just as dessert was about to be served, Renato glanced down at his phone then raised his glass.

"She took the bait. Let's go fishing, boys!"

"That calls for some ha-ha, clink-clink," added Rick.

"Ha-ha, clink-clink?" asked Renato.

"Oh, so Big Brother missed that one huh? It means laughs and drinks."

"I love it. Ha-ha, clink-clink. I'm gonna remember that one."

After the celebration, Rick and Jules settled into their room for the rest of the night. He wasn't sure if Renato needed them anymore, but he was still high from the mission and ready to continue.

Rick woke up feeling better than he had in years. Partly because of the success of the mission but mostly because of Helga. He and Jules got dressed to work out and did a total repeat of the afternoon before. After they showered, they met Renato in the great room for breakfast.

"Good morning, Renato."

"Buongiorno, Rick. I mean, good morning. Sorry I slip in and out of Italian so much. I just got off the phone with my wife in Milan. How are you feeling this morning. And you, Jules?"

"We both feel amazing. I'd give my left nut to have a Helga in Florida."

"He would. And I'd let him. Ha-ha," added Jules.

"It's an amazing machine for sure. Sometimes I wonder with all the technology if humans will even matter much anymore. I mean, AI does some insane stuff. We are keeping our eye on that. ChatGPT is coming out soon, according to our intel. It's a writing tool that learns. In the wrong hands, it could be very destructive."

"Hmmm, never heard of it."

"You will. It's open source so it's constantly evolving. Many governments are concerned about its potential."

"Interesting. Listen, I was wondering if you would be needing us anymore. Jules and I are kinda ready to get out of Africa. Ha-ha, yes, like the movie."

"Huh?"

"Never mind. Anyway, what's the plan, Stan, with the next sting? Will you need us? I mean, we can stay if you want us to."

"I appreciate it, Rick, but all my assets are in place for that one. It should be happening tomorrow night. We will probably need you to testify, but just like in the states, the justice system here moves at a snail's pace."

"You can count on me to testify. Junior as well."

"That's great, Rick. On behalf of Interpol, Italy, and Africa, we want to thank both you and Jules. We can't legally pay you because you were officially never here, if you know what I mean. But feel free to keep any of the items you used on your mission. Jules, did you enjoy driving the Jaguar?"

"Yes. That thing was sweet!"

"Quella è una bella macchina. I mean, that is a fine machine. It's yours. We will ship it to Florida or wherever you want it."

"¡Ay, Dios mío! I mean, Oh my God. Ha-ha. Are you serious?"

"Dead serious," replied Renato. "Don't worry, Rick. We are giving you the DHL truck as well."

The look on Rick's face was priceless. Renato busted out laughing so hard he almost fell out of his chair.

"I'm just kidding. We have something for you too. It's nothing major and we already shipped it to Destin. You'll love it."

"Wow, thanks, Renato. I don't know what to say."

"It's all good. Nothing to say. If you two wanna head back to Victoria Falls after breakfast, we can give you a lift in the chopper. I will get your phones back to you once we are in the air."

Rick and Jules shook Renato's hand and said goodbye to the team. Even though they had only worked together on one sting, they felt a kindred spirit. They packed their things and came back down to board the chopper. The pilot let Rick ride shotgun. It wasn't every day he got to fly in the world's second-fastest helicopter. He wanted one of those too and secretly wished that. was what Renato was shipping him back to Florida. But he knew it was just a pipe dream.

After they landed, they thanked the pilot and then the driver, who dropped them off back at the resort. Jules went to their room. Rick told her he'd be there in a second, and walked straight to Junior's room and knocked on the door. It opened.

"May I help you?" said a man Rick had never seen before in his life.

"Who are you?"

"Who are you?!"

"I'm sorry. I'm Rick. My friend was staying in this room."

"We checked in yesterday. Maybe he changed rooms?"

"Okay, sorry to bother you."

"No problem," said the man as he closed the door.

That's freaking weird.

Rick went to the front desk.

"Hi, I was looking for my friend Junior who was in Executive Suite 103."

The man behind the desk started typing. "We have no one here by that name. What was his last name?"

Rick remembered they had checked in with aliases and tried to remember what Junior's was.

"Oh, it's Smythe. Adrian Smythe. Junior is his nickname," said Rick, thinking quickly.

"Mr. Smythe checked out yesterday."

"Did he leave a note?"

"Let me check."

He walked into the back office and returned shortly.

"No, I'm sorry. He did not leave a note."

"Okay, well, thank you."

Rick strolled back to his room, scratching his head, trying to figure out why Junior had left.

"Rick, Rick, read this. I found it on the floor. It was slid under the door," exclaimed Jules.

Rick,

I want to thank you, Jules, and the rest of the guys for all you've done. After you left to go on your sting, I had a lot of alone time to think. I just couldn't sit here and do nothing. I must avenge my father's murder. If it means killing my sister, so be it. Eye for an eye, right? Please don't try and stop me and don't tell the authorities. I know where she lives, and she thinks I'm dead anyway. What could go wrong? If you read about or see her death in the news, you'll know why. Prison is too good for her. She needs to pay for what she's done. I love you like a brother and Jules like a sister. When this is all said and done, maybe I can come visit you in Florida.

Your friend,
Junior.
P.S. Take care of Jules. She's a special lady.

"Son of a bitch! He's gonna get his ass killed!" exclaimed Rick.

Jules eyes were wet with worry. "What are we gonna do, Rick?"

"I don't know. He's right, though; she doesn't know he's alive, so he has the jump on her. But her security detail is packing automatic weapons and they are highly trained, as you know. Plus, he's at a huge disadvantage with that cast on his arm. Not to mention he could get caught right in the middle of the sting. There's no way he can pull it off."

"We have to stop him," said Jules.

Rick pulled his iPhone out of his back pocket and called Junior. It went straight to voicemail.

"His phone is off. I'm gonna leave him a message. Maybe I can talk him out of it."

"Good idea."

Rick hit redial again.

"Junior, it's Rick. I got your note. Please don't do this, man. Call me first. There's something big going down tomorrow night with her. I can't tell you want it is now, but it's big. Call me. Please."

"Should you let Renato know?" asked Jules after Rick ended the call.

"I don't know. I need to think. If I tell Renato, he's gonna be pissed and worry Junior may screw up the sting. If I don't tell Renato, he's gonna be pissed because he probably would want to use some of his guys to track down Junior and bring him in until after the sting. Dammit! The only thing positive is that Renato is gonna be pissed!" said Rick, giving a fake grin, trying to put a little levity on the situation.

"I think you should call him."

"Maybe you're right, Jules."

Rick was just about to call Renato when his phone rang.

"Rick, did you make it to the hotel? I have news."

"So do I," replied Rick.

"We are meeting with Jacinda sooner than we thought. It's gonna happen in a couple of hours. We've got intel that Colin Mulenga will be at the switch as well. Apparently, he was very upset that last sale didn't go through."

Shit, thought Rick. That timing really wouldn't bode well for Junior.

"That's great, Renato. Although, we may have a problem. When I arrived at the hotel, I got a note from Junior. He is going to try and kill Jacinda. Hang on—I'll snap a photo of the note and text it to you."

"Are you kidding me? If he interferes with this operation, we could be screwed."

Renato's phone pinged, indicating the text went through.

"Once you read the note, you'll see he mentions Jacinda's house. Maybe you can stake it out and catch him before he makes his assault."

"That's exactly what we are going to do, Rick. Thanks for the heads-up. I'll keep you posted if we nab him or if the sale goes down."

"Thanks, Renato. I hate that I had to rain on you parade."

"You did the right thing. Hang tight and I'll be in touch soon. Ciao."

"What did he say?" asked Jules once Rick hung up.

"He's happy that I let him know, and they are going to stake out Jacinda's place and try to catch Junior in the act. If they catch him though, and he's armed, he has intent, and they could arrest him for attempted murder. We need to stop him. If we hurry, maybe we can intercept him. I don't think Renato would want us to get involved, but I don't give a damn."

"Let's go!" said Jules.

Rick and Jules headed for Jacinda's place. Their only hope was to get there in time before Junior went too far.

CHAPTER NINETEEN

Junior sat in the rented van at the end of Jacinda's street. He wrung his hands together over and over, nervous about what he was about to do. With a spotting scope, he looked down the street to determine what cars were at her house. He could clearly see her Tacoma in the driveway and could also see two guards at each side of her house. Some head-lights came up behind him in his side mirrors, and he ducked down in the seat a little.

"That bitch!"

As she turned into her driveway, he could see she was the person driving and realized the car was his dad's Defender. He wanted to jump out of the van and just go running down the street firing at her, but he stopped himself.

Taking a deep breath, he gathered himself and went over the plan in his head. He would call Jacinda and ask for a truce and pretend to be on her side. It would take some con-vincing since she'd tried to blow him up, but he would tell her blood is thicker than water and blah, blah, blah. She was always gullible and a bit naive and would eventfully fall in line. Once she met him at the door, he'd unload on her. His unregistered semi-automatic 9mm held fifteen rounds. With any luck, he'd take her out with several up-close shots and have a few more left for the guards.

He tucked the pistol under his loose shirt and picked up his phone. It was now or never. She picked up on the third ring.

"Jacinda, it's Junior."

A silence fell over the phone for what seemed like an eternity.

"But I..."

"I know, you thought I was dead. So did I at first. The rest of the crew is dead. When the blast went off, I was in the rear behind everyone. Their bodies took most of the impact and shrapnel. All I got was a broken arm. Look, don't hang up. I'm not mad."

She didn't say anything, so he continued, "After I dug my way out and made it to the hospital, I had a lot of time to think. You and I are blood. It's way stronger than anything else. I want to help you now. They all think I'm against you, but if we work together, I can help you get the inside jump on where the money is, and we can take their money and then you can still sell the ivory to someone else. A double dip. What do you say? All I ask for is 25 percent of the first take. I want a fresh start. I'm gonna take that money and move to America. I know in my heart I can't follow in Dad's footsteps and protect the elephants anymore. He was wrong. Progress is good and it can't be stopped. It's a fool's game."

He was laying it on thick. He could almost hear the little hamster running on the wheel in her head.

"When do you want to meet?" she asked.

"Now. I'm nearby and unarmed. Jacinda, we were ripped apart by Dad's ridiculous way of thinking and wanting to protect the elephants. I mean, who chooses elephants over their own daughter? We are all each other has and we should be together. I missed you so much when you left. Let's not let the past once again ruin our future. I love you, Jacinda. You are my sister and it's time we team up for good."

He heard what he thought was a whimper and then silence. He didn't say anything else, waiting for it all to sink in for her.

"Okay, Junior, come on over. No offense, but I'll have to have the guards frisk you."

"No problem."

Damn. I'll have to kill her with my bare hands.

He put his pistol in the glove box and drove up the street, parking right in front of her house. As he stepped out of the van, two armed guards approached him. He raised his arms and shirt and let one frisk him. It wasn't the way he'd planned for this to go down, but he would improvise. Even if he died trying, he would get to Jacinda. The guards followed him to the door, which opened as he stepped onto the porch.

"Hi, Jacinda."

"Hey, Junior."

He was reaching out to hug her, with every intention of strangling her or breaking her neck, when he felt a burning sensation in his neck. He reached up and pulled out the dart just before he hit the ground.

"Dammit!" said Jules.

She and Rick had just parked down the street from Jacinda's house when she saw Junior fall to the ground through her pair of binoculars. She'd texted him again while they were on their way to try and stop him, but either he hadn't seen the text or he'd ignored it. And now they were too late.

"Rick, someone just hit him with a tranquilizer dart. He fell!"

"Let me see!" exclaimed Rick as he took the binoculars from her.

Two men grabbed Junior's arms and dragged him into the house. One stepped back out and picked up the dart that lay on the porch.

"Well, they didn't kill him. We need to get in there and get him out. I just don't know how," said Rick.

Jules bit her lip, thinking hard. "I have an idea."

"Wait until I'm in position and I give you the signal," Rick said. "You got it?"

"Got it!" said Jules. She gave him a quick peck on the lips and took off for Jacinda's house.

Rick had parked the car a ways down the street from Jacinda's, out of sight but still close by. He waited until Jules was on her way before getting out of the car with the sniper rifle and moving closer to the house. He would set up in a spot where he couldn't be seen. The plan was for Jules to approached Jacinda's house under the guise of her car breaking down and her cell phone being dead. She'd ask if she could use their phone to call for help. Then Rick would use the sniper to shoot as many of Jacinda's security team as possible, and they would get inside and go from there to get Junior out alive.

It was risky as all get out, and part of him had wanted to tell Jules no way, but he didn't have a better idea. All he could do was trust that she would keep herself safe, like she had so many times before.

In between some bushes, Rick got down on his stomach with the rifle and put the binoculars up to his eyes.

Jules was already at the compound gate and talking to one of the guards. She flung her hair over her shoulder flirtatiously, saying something Rick couldn't hear. She was moving faster than he'd anticipated, not waiting for his signal.

He quickly set the binoculars down and went to prep the rifle.

He'd barely lifted the rifle to look through the sight when both of the guards grabbed Jules by her arms and pulled her through the gate.

Rick cursed under his breath. "Dammit!"

They were wrenching her up the driveway, out of sight, dragging her all the way up to the house. Already too far away for Rick to get a good shot—he might hit Jules instead. They must have recognized her, even though last time she pulled a stunt like this, she was wearing a disguise. Before Rick knew it, Jules was inside the house. Gone.

"No, no, no, dammit!"

Rick got up from the ground and slammed the rifle down in anger. Now Jacinda had her, and he had to get her back and save Junior as well.

Renato's team assembled in a warehouse in Lusaka, a mile from the exchange point. He'd brought in the best snipers he could acquire from the UK. He wasn't taking any chances this time. The meet would be in an alley between two old meal factories. The meet time was six p.m., which Renato didn't like because the sun would be going down and it could cause a glare for the snipers. His regular team was assembled along with the new snipers, and they'd cased the site earlier that morning.

Jacinda said she would come with Colin and no one else to make the exchange. The ivory was inside of a moving truck at an undisclosed location that she would give them once she had the money. Renato wanted proof, so she texted him a photo of the truck with the back door wide open. It was filled to the brim with elephant tusks. He had no choice but to trust her.

He planted a tracking device deep inside the almost nearly 800 million kwacha, roughly equivalent to forty million US dollars. Even if she got the money, they would track it. The device was far higher tech than anything like an Apple AirTag. It was tiny, flat, and implanted inside of one of the bills. It was so thin it couldn't be seen even if the bill was held up to the light; it was intertwined in the holographic strip next to the African fish eagle on the face of the bill. The device sent a signal detectable by satellite, and the only way they could lose it would be if it were blocked somehow by concrete or lead.

"On my command, you take your shot if you have it," said Renato.

The two snipers rode street bikes and were deep undercover. They parked behind one of the buildings and went separately into a coffee shop. Once they were certain they weren't made, the first on the left would make his way to the top floor of the east building, followed by the other to the west a few minutes later.

"*Bird dog one in position.*"

A few minutes later, another voice came on the radio.

"*Bird dog two in position.*"

With that, Renato and the team took two cars to the location. One was an old bread delivery truck containing the pallet of money, and the other was a government-issued limo complete with Zambian flags. Renato and his top aide would be in the back with a highly trained third sniper driving. The two other snipers had already assembled their rifles from inside their North Face backpacks.

Once parked near the alley, Renato texted Jacinda that he was ready to make the switch. Within a couple of minutes, she turned up the street in her Tacoma with Colin sitting beside her.

What the hell? thought Renato.

She had no security detail with her, just her and Colin alone together. It made no sense. She parked directly in front of the alley, and they both walked a few yards inside. Renato followed with his aide to the meeting spot.

"Jacinda, Colin."

They both greeted Renato.

"Do you have the money?" asked Jacinda.

"Yes, do you have the location of the ivory?"

She held up her phone, revealing a video feed from behind the truck in an undisclosed warehouse. The tusks could clearly be seen in the video. She then handed him a GPS location of the truck on a piece of paper. Renato took it and held it up over his head in the light to see it better.

"Let's do this," she said.

Renato handed her the keys to the bread truck and told his team to exit the truck and get in the limo. After a few minutes, he heard in his earpiece:

"*Team in limo.*"

He was about to give the snipers the signal to take their shot when she held up the phone again, showing a video of Junior and Jules sitting in a chair with TNT and a cell phone strapped around their bodies.

"*Hold position.*"

"If you follow me, or try to hurt me, I will call the number of the cell phone strapped to them, and both Junior and Jules will become thousands of little pieces all over the walls."

Renato gritted his teeth. *How the hell did she kidnap Jules?* Rick and Jules must have gotten involved again, without his permission.

He almost gave the signal for the snipers to take the shot anyway, but his conscious wouldn't let him. Junior was more than just collateral damage. He was the reason they had taken the case in the first place at Rick's request. And he knew how much Rick cared for Jules.

"So, how is this gonna go down?" asked Renato.

"Simple. I'll take the money. Colin will drive my Tacoma, and if you don't follow me, I will release them and give you the ivory location."

What she didn't know was that one of Renato's team had given the GPS coordinates to a third team assembled nearby, and they were minutes away from the location.

When Renato had held up the pieces of paper for a better view, a member of his team with a Canon EOS-1D X Mark III camera and a long-range lens had snapped a photo of it.

He tried to stall her now, but she walked past him, bumping his shoulder with attitude, and drove off in the bread truck. At least they would have the ivory and they could track the money anyway, so Renato wasn't worried.

In his earpiece, he heard, "*At location, ivory not here.*"

"What?!"

"*Sending video.*"

Renato's phone pinged and he clicked on the text. He hit "play" on the video. It showed a member of his team walking in front the camera she had placed there. He reached up to the open rear doors of the truck, revealing the tusks, and slapped it. It was a cardboard photo of the tusks in a pile, attached to the inside of the truck. It folded up and fell to ground, leaving behind an empty box truck.

Son of a bitch! Clever!

"Abort mission, back to base," said Renato.

James was tracking the money as it drove out of Lusaka toward Jacinda's house. Renato joined them in the limo.

"Where is she now?"

"She's about seven kilometers from her house," said James.

"She's not stupid enough to take the money to her house, is she?"

Suddenly, James's mouth fell open. "I lost her. She was headed east on T4 and about three kilometers from Lusaka University, not far from her place, and it just stopped. Like immediately."

"How? Maybe she drove the truck underground?" asked Renato.

"Impossible. I was tracking her in real time, and it literally disappeared from my tracker as she was going 110 km per hour. She never slowed down."

Renato slammed his fist against the wall of the limo. "This is a nightmare!"

His phone rang. It was Jacinda.

"Put me on speaker," she said.

He did as they all listened.

"Nice try, Renato. I knew you'd track the money. I know you have people on the inside, but so do I. Ha-ha, you have a mole. You should really pay your boys more money. Remember, money talks and bullshit walks."

Renato clenched his teeth and looked up at his men, eyeballing them to see if one had a tell that he was the mole. They all just shrugged and shook their heads.

"So, what now?" he asked.

"I say redux. I want another 800 million kwacha. Wait, no, this time I want it in US currency. Let's round it up to $50 million. Otherwise, I'll sell the ivory to the black market and end Junior and Jules's lives. Do we have a deal?"

"Deal. It will take me a few days to get the US currency."

"You have twenty-four hours."

"One question. How did you stop the tracker? We were clocking you at 110 km an hour."

"Simple, stupid. A tiny EMP."

She hung up.

"She used a tiny EMP?" asked Renato aloud.

"How did she get one of those?" asked one of the snipers.

"From one of us," said Renato in disgust.

The limo driver headed back to base camp as they all rode in silence. Renato knew he had a mole, he just didn't know which one. For all he knew, it could be one of the snipers he'd recruited.

Once back at the compound, he made them all turn in their cell phones and go to their rooms. He organized an outside team to do a forensics deep dive on the phones, and brought the rest of the team in from the field and placed them on sort of a house arrest. He didn't know who to trust. But he had an idea. He called the chopper pilot and told him to fuel a Sikorsky S-97 Raider, load two scooters onboard, and meet him on the roof in thirty minutes.

"Let's go," said Renato. The pilot fired up the chopper, and Renato climbed in beside him.

"Where to?" asked the pilot.

"Head toward Victoria Falls, but don't log a flight plan or use GPS. Just fly southwest. I'll tell you where to set her down."

The pilot did as he was told. About an hour into the flight, Renato pulled out a pair of night-vision binoculars and began looking down. They were flying almost parallel with highway T1.

"Right there," said Renato as he pointed at an empty field beside the highway.

The pilot landed, looking confused about what was going on.

"Help me unload the scooters and leave your phone in the chopper," said Renato.

"Am I in trouble or something?" asked the pilot.

"No. I'm just taking precautions. Follow me."

The pilot jumped on his scooter and followed Renato across the highway to a dirt road. They continued to ride for another ten minutes, then stopped by an old, abandoned barn. Renato donned a different pair of night-vision goggles and handed a pair to the pilot. "Put them on," he said.

They walked into the dusty old barn. When they got to the far-right corner, Renato moved several bales of hay and dusted the floor with his boot until it revealed something hard and flat. He dug around a little, then pulled up a lock and opened it with a key around his neck.

"What is this?" asked the pilot.

"A safe house."

Renato instructed the pilot to go down the stairs first after he turned on the lights.

"Sit down at that table. I have a few questions for you."

The pilot was clearly upset and began to sweat. Renato paced around and asked him some questions unrelated to the case and he answered. After a few questions, Renato walked over to the kettle on the stove behind the pilot and filled it with water. The safe house hidden under an old barn looked like a modern apartment in the city. Renato had had it constructed himself when he was working on a case in Zimbabwe a few years back. It wasn't even an official safe house and was unknown to Interpol.

As he let the water run, he approached the pilot from behind, pulled out a hypodermic needle, and plunged it into his neck. He slumped over on the table.

"Sorry, buddy. I couldn't take any chances."

He walked up the stairs and locked the hidden door, covered it with dirt and hay, then cut the fuel line on one of the scooters and hid it under some more hay bales. The chances of the pilot escaping were slim to none. The lock and door were made of ABUS Granit and stainless steel with a tensile strength of six tons. There were plenty of C-rations and fresh water in the safe house, so if the pilot wasn't involved, he wouldn't starve to death or die of dehydration.

Renato jumped back on the scooter and headed toward the chopper. He was an experienced chopper pilot trained by the Italian Special Forces known as Esercito Italiano, under the Aeronautica Militare. He had just gotten his rating recently for the Sikorsky for an event just like this. Once back at the chopper, he unpackaged a burner phone he had taken from his desk, copied down Rick's number, and turned off both his and the pilot's phones to be safe. No one except the pilot even knew he had left the compound anyway.

Rick picked up on the third ring. He rarely answered numbers he wasn't familiar with, but he saw it was a Lusaka number.

"Hello?"

"Rick, it's Renato. I'm calling from a burner phone. Where are you?"

"I'm a few miles away from Jacinda's house." He'd driven the car away to make sure none of her guards would come looking for him after they caught Jules. He was still trying to figure out a solid plan to save her and Junior, but he knew he needed Renato's help.

"I told you not to get involved—"

"I know, and I apologize. But she has Jules and Junior."

"I know. Too much to say on the phone. I'm headed back to Lusaka. Meet me at these coordinates." He gave Rick the coordinates of a location on the outskirts of the city. "I'll be there in about three hours. I'll explain everything when I get there. Turn off your phone and Jules's phone as soon as we hang up. Under no circumstances should you turn them back on. Understand?"

"Got it. See ya soon. If she harms a single hair on Jules head, I'll kill her myself."

Rick turned off his phone and drove off.

The coordinates led Rick to a landing strip on the edge of Lusaka. It was nothing more than a crop duster field and had no staff or tower. His palms sweated as he impatiently waited. All he could think about was Jules and Junior, and hope they were both still alive.

Finally, Renato's chopper appeared in the sky and landed on the tarmac.

As soon as he came outside, Renato told Rick everything that had happened.

"How did they get Jules?" asked Renato.

"We were trying to intercept Junior from killing Jacinda. Jules got caught up in the heat of the moment and approached a guard before I could set up my sniper rifle. Once they had her, I had to abort. We need to go in strong and get them out!" demanded Rick.

"Try and remain calm, Rick. We'll get them back. I need to find out who this mole is on my team. We are gonna work close together now and stay covert. Leave your car here for now, just bring your things. We'll get a taxi out on the main road."

CHAPTER TWENTY

The cab took them to the Twalumba Lodge just south of the edge of Lusaka. Renato rented two adjoining rooms under aliases, and they made their way to the rooms.

"What's the plan?"

"Late tonight, or I should say early in the morning, I will return the chopper to the compound and see if forensics has found anything that would indicate the mole. No one knows I left, and no one will know when I return. The entire team is under house arrest. I have no idea who I can trust but you. We need to make a move on Jacinda. She thinks she has the upper hand. I don't trust her as far as I can throw her. There's nothing to stop her from selling the ivory out from under us. I will lure her out to a location, and you need to find Jules and Junior. Take a look at this. It's a still I blew up from the video she sent of him tied to a chair with dynamite strapped to his chest."

Rick looked at it and winced. The idea of her blowing Jules and Junior to bits hit him hard.

"Do you have the video image on your phone I can blow up?"

"I can't turn on my phone. Wait, I saved it to the cloud. Do you have your laptop here?"

Rick jogged into his room and came back with his MacBook. Renato signed Rick out of his iCloud password and signed into his own, then downloaded the video on the lodge's Wi-Fi. He quickly signed out again.

"Here you go."

Rick moved the curser frame by frame, and as Junior turned his head to the side, he could see a reflection in his glasses.

"I know where that is. Son of a bitch! It's in her reload room. I recognize the Dirty Harry poster!"

"That's great work, Rick. Now we just need to lure her out. This must be a completely covert operation. Only the two of us. No one else," said Renato. "Let's get some sleep, and I will return to the compound in the early hours and come back with the motherload of an arsenal."

"Now that's what I'm talking about. Can I keep the toys?" said Rick with a wink.

"I don't care. Keep 'em. See you in the morning."

A smile crept over Rick's face, but it vanished once he was alone in his room, thinking of Jules tied up in that room.

I'm coming for you, baby. Don't you worry.

At 9:30, Rick's new burner phone pinged with a text.

> *Meet me in the breakfast room in five minutes.*

Rick quickly got dressed and brushed his teeth. Renato was sitting at a corner table sipping a cup of coffee. A second empty cup and a large insulated coffee dispenser were sitting on the table. He sat down, and Rick poured himself a hot cup of java. The only other people in the breakfast room were a young couple and their two kids, and they were far from earshot.

"It's all in motion. Everything you could possibly need is inside the DHL truck. Here are instructions on how to scramble the security cameras at Jacinda's. I plan to meet her at eleven a.m. It will take her about fifteen minutes to drive to the location where we are doing the swap. She is getting greedy. I talked her into coming alone and keeping Colin out of it. She jumped on it like a bug to a bug light. I believe she thinks she is invincible."

"I bet she does."

"In the truck, there's a tranquilizer gun with a dialed-in scope. Here is a satellite phone I just printed this morning. There are two outside guards on each end of her property. They haven't changed positions in hours. They just keep rotating. I watched for several hours and believe there are five guards on the property total. Two outside, two inside, and one in the reload room. They rotate every half hour. Once you take out the two outside, jam the surveillance cameras. You can do it with a timer or manually. It's all explained on the note. Any questions?" asked Renato.

"Just one. Are you really gonna pay Jacinda another $50 million?" asked Rick.

"Hell no. I will have it with me, but once you give me the signal that Jules and Junior are safe, I will take her down. Timing is everything here."

"Oh, one more question. How did you get the DHL truck out of the compound without arousing suspicion?"

"Easy. It was due for an oil change, so I checked it out in the logbook after I loaded all the toys in it and drove it straight here. No one will be any the wiser."

"That works," said Rick.

Renato glanced down at his watch.

"It's time. Your DHL uniform is in the truck. Take it to the same spot in front of Jacinda's and wait for her to exit the property. I will already be waiting for her at the swap point. Good luck. For all of us. Their lives depend on this."

Rick parked the DHL truck near Jacinda's. He could see the outside guards clearly from his vantage point. He stepped between the seats into the back and waited.

After about twenty minutes, Jacinda pulled out of the driveway in the Defender. She was alone in the SUV. He climbed onto the roof of the truck with the tranq gun. He took out the guard closest to the truck first, then quickly took out the farther one.

The silenced rounds went off within microseconds of each other. Both guards fell to the ground in under two seconds.

"Hit!" exclaimed Rick to himself.

He quickly climbed back into the truck and started the surveillance camera jammer. On the way out, he grabbed a fake DHL package. He ran across the street and scaled Jacinda's fence, then dragged the sleeping guards' bodies into the bushes.

"DHL, delivery!" yelled Rick.

A guard answered with an AK-47 pointed out of the door in Rick's direction.

"How did you get in here?"

"That guard let me in," replied Rick as he pointed toward the area where one guard was supposed to be.

The man leaned out to get a better look. "What guard?"

"He's right..."

As the inside guard took his eyes off Rick, he fired the taser sitting under the box. The man shook violently and fell to the floor. Rick shot him in the neck with a tranquilizer handgun. The other inside guard heard the commotion and began to run toward Rick, firing the AK-47. Rick fired as he dove out of the way and shot him dead as he ran.

Rick got up, grabbed the dead man's AK-47, and ran toward the reload room. Another guard came out firing. Rick rolled on the ground, shooting the AK in his direction. He missed and his gun jammed.

The guard took aim at him. *Shit.*

Before he could squeeze off a round, Rick pulled out his duck knife and flung it at the man's neck. He fell to the ground with his finger still squeezing off rounds. Rick quickly finished him off and busted down the door to the reload room.

"Jules, are you okay? You, Junior?"

Jules nodded her head, unable to speak with tape covering her mouth. Rick took off the tape and then took a hard look at the explosive vests they were both wearing.

"Boy am I glad to see you," said Junior. "We gotta hurry—when the guard heard the gunfire, he set the timer like Jacinda told him to if anyone tried to rescue me."

Rick looked down at Junior's chest at the digital timer next to the cell phone.

One minute forty-nine seconds and counting. Jules has the same time.

"I have to diffuse this thing," yelled Rick.

"There's no way. You'll have to cut it off of us!"

Rick looked over toward the work bench, and across the entire length of the wall in a large pile were the ivory tusks. He ran and fell on top of them, desperately trying to find a cutting tool. He opened all the cabinets and in the last one was a pair of snips. He almost fell on his face trying to get back to them.

"Jules, don't breathe!" yelled Rick as he began to cut the tight vest from her.

Jules sat frozen in the middle of the room next to Junior, her body trembling with fear and uncertainty. The vest seemed to weigh her down more with every passing moment. But this was no ordinary vest—it was laden with sticks of dynamite, each one ready to explode with an earth-shattering force.

Rick feverishly cut the vest with the snips. He got her left arm out and moved over to the right. Once she was free, he moved over to Junior. Time was running out.

"Get out of here, Jules!" yelled Rick.

She moved toward the exit but didn't leave.

Fifty-five seconds.

He cut as fast as he could as time wound down. He was almost to the end of it, and the timer started beeping.

Ten, nine, eight...

He made the last cut with four seconds remaining, jerked Junior out of the chair, and ran out the door just behind Jules.

"Pool, pool!" yelled Rick.

Jules dove into the pool headfirst, and Rick and Junior hit the water feet first, plunging under the cold water.

Kaboom, boom, boom!

A massive fireball flew fifty feet high, resembling a mushroom cloud. Fire from the blast lit up the water as pieces of the reload building splashed in and around the pool. They all held their breath and finally surfaced. A hole the size of a Volkswagen was all that remained where the reload room used to be.

Rick climbed out of the pool and ran full speed toward the DHL truck, and scaled the fence faster than a spider monkey. He snatched the burner phone he had placed on the dash and hit "send" on the pre-typed words he had set up:

TAKE HER NOW!

Renato had his phone in his left hand and the duffel bag of money in his right. He glanced down at his phone and then swung the duffel hard, hitting Jacinda in the face, knocking her to the ground. He dove on top of her with all his weight, flipped her over, and handcuffed her.

"You are under arrest for the murder of Bandile Dlamani and too many other charges to say now. You have the right to remain silent; anything you say or do can be used against you in a court of law. You have the right to an attorney. If you can't afford an attorney, one will be appointed for you. Do you understand your rights?" asked Renato.

She nodded, unable to speak.

"I need a verbal yes," he said.

In an airy voice, she blurted out, "Yes!"

Renato looked back down at his phone and typed, *Got her!*

Out of breath, Rick stumbled back inside the compound to pool.

Jules had already helped Junior out of the water, and they sat on the concrete surrounding the pool. The guard who was inside the reload house was nowhere to be found. He had been completely obliterated, just like the reload room and all the ivory.

"Are y'all okay?" asked Rick.

They both nodded, unable to speak because of their cotton mouths.

"Let's go inside, tie up the remaining guards, and get something to drink," said Rick.

They both got to their feet and followed him into Jacinda's bullet-riddled mansion.

Rick secured all the guards with zip ties. They were asleep in dreamland because of the animal tranquillizer in their system.

Rick's phone rang.

"Hey, Renato. Where are you?"

"I'm on my way to you. I'm dropping Jacinda off at the main detention center. I can be there in about a half an hour. How are Jules and Junior?"

"They're fine. We all are. I can't say the same thing for a few of her guards, or her reload room and the ivory. There's a giant hole in the ground where her room used to be. She never had any intention of selling the ivory. She was just gonna double dip and say her room blew up because of a gunpowder incident. It was a good plan, but she didn't count on us."

"I heard about the explosion over the scanner. There will be lots of black and whites to you shortly. Just hold tight and put down your weapons. I'll sort it all out with the local authorities when I get there. She won't give up the location of the money. She probably thinks she can take a plea and have a nest egg when she is paroled. She'll be an old lady by then. Too bad the tracker was terminated."

Rick suddenly remembered what Possum had told him about Tiles. He glanced over at her key hooks hanging by the door, remembering seeing a little square Tile on one of the sets of keys. Over on the coffee table sat her iPad.

"Does she have her purse with her?" asked Rick.

"Yeah, it's sitting right beside me. Why?"

"See if her car keys are in it. And let me know if there is a Tile attached."

"A Tile?"

"It's a little square thingamabob that will be attacked to the keychain. Squeeze it."

Rick ran over to her iPad and picked it up.

A few seconds went by.

"Okay, yeah, I see that. I'm gonna squeeze it now."

As he did, the Tile notification lit up on her iPad, started playing a little song, and Rick touched it quickly.

"I know where the money is! All we need is her iPad password."

"Are you serious?"

"Dead serious. As long as we get into the Tile data within thirty days of her hiding the truck, we got it. Hang on, Renato. We're all parched. I'm gonna grab some water out of the fridge."

"No problem."

Rick put down the phone and walked over to the fridge. He grabbed a large container of water. Behind it were a couple of beers: Weihenstephaner Original Premium. He grinned and walked back to the phone.

"Oh, and I know who the mole is."

"Who?"

"It's Hans. I guarantee it. If you check his apartment, I bet you every last penny to my name he has some Weihenstephaner Original Premium beers in his fridge. If you check them against the lot numbers, they will be from the same case I'm looking at right now. I bet you can even pull his DNA off the ones in Jacinda's fridge."

"Oh man, that is genius. The team is still under house arrest at the compound. I'll get forensics on it immediately and a search warrant for Han's apartment. See you shortly."

Rick and Jules sat in their first-class seats, sharing a glass of champagne. It was hard to believe they were finally going home. Rick turned on the viewing screen in front of him and scrolled through the movies as the plane lifted off. Suddenly, he stopped and winked at Jules as *Out of Africa* began to play. They were still wired and watched the entire movie.

Afterward, they slept on most of the flight to Newark and changed planes. Once they arrived in Destin, Johnie was there to greet them.

"Man, am I glad to see y'all."

"Us too. You have no idea."

The new mate is polishing stainless on *Nine-Tenths*. I bet y'all are gonna be glad to sleep in your own beds tonight," said Johnie. "Oh, you had two large packages delivered a couple days ago from Africa. I had the maintenance guys at your condo let them into your place. I hope that's okay."

"No worries, Johnie. We're gonna take a few days to catch our breath and then we'll all head to Key West. How's Chief?"

"He's good. So are Gary and Possum. Gary's been doing the Duval crawl ever since they got here."

Johnie dropped them off at the condo, hugged them, and headed back to Destin HarborWalk. Rick fumbled with his keys, trying to get the door open. It had been so long since they'd been home, he had to try several keys before he got it right.

When the door swung open, sitting in the center of the living room were two giant crates. Stamped on their sides were two labels:

Helga One and *Helga Two*.

Epilogue

Jacinda took a plea and was given twenty-five years to life for the murder of Bandile Dlamini. She testified against Colin Mulenga and several others in the government, including two judges and several high-ranking officers in the SAPD., Kelvin Marcus and Yuusf among them, for their part in the illegal attempt to overtake part of Kafue National

Park. They were also convicted for the sale and attempted sale of illegal ivory on the black market.

Hans was charged with espionage and selling national security secrets. As he awaited trial, his lawyer got him out on twenty million Zambian kwachas, or the rough equivalent of one million US dollars bail. He was forced to wear an ankle monitor. A few days after not checking in with his pre-trial officer, his body was found floating near the bank of the mighty Zambezi with a single gunshot wound to the back of his head. No one was charged with the crime, although Renato Bianchi remained a person of interest.

An elephant rehab facility was built and named the Bandile Dlamini Center. Junior Dlamini was awarded the highest civilian medal in Zambia for his efforts in capturing the poachers who had been wreaking havoc on the elephants.

Rick was paid a 10 percent finder's fee for the return of the 800 million kwachas to Interpol, as well as the reward for finding the killer of Bandile Dlamini. All in total, he netted 6.2 million US dollars. He donated half to the new sanctuary after paying his crew. He built Junior a new house and a safari center near the park, and still had several million left over.

Before he and Jules headed to Key West, he had the photo they took on the hippo cruise framed, and he put it proudly on his desk. He told Jules he would never forget Africa and hoped they could visit the continent again someday. But for now, he was just happy to be home and out of Africa.

THE END

ACKNOWLEDGMENTS

'd like to thank my beta readers Ron Dalton, Bavette & Dennis Battern, Mike Keevil, Carroll Shroyer, Chuck and Linda Reed.

I'd like to thank my amazing editor, Stephanie Diaz Slagle.

I'd like to thank my proofreader, Carroll Shroyer.

Thanks to my graphic artist Les.

Special thanks to Nick Sullivan, Wayne Stinnett, Cap Daniels for all their input and advise.

I like to especially thank all the readers of my novels. It's all about the readers. I appreciate your continued support on this journey.

ABOUT THE AUTHOR

Eric Chance Stone was born and raised on the gulf coast of Southeast Texas. An avid surfer, sailor, scuba diver, fisherman and treasure hunter, Eric met many bigger than life characters on his adventures across the globe. Wanting to travel after college, he got a job with Northwest Airlines and moved to Florida. Shortly thereafter transferred to Hawaii, then Nashville. After years of being a staff songwriter in Nashville, he released his first album, Songs For Sail in 1999, a tropically inspired collection of songs. He continued to write songs and tour and eventually landed a gig with Sail America and Show Management to perform at all international boat shows where his list of characters continued to grow.

He moved to the Virgin Islands in 2007 and became the official entertainer for Pusser's Marina Cay in the BVI. After several years in the Caribbean, his fate for telling stories was sealed.

Upon release of his 15th CD, All The Rest, he was inspired to become a novelist after a chance meeting with Wayne Stinnett. Wayne along with Cap Daniels, Chip Bell and a few others, became his mentors and they are all good friends now. Eric currently resides in Destin, Florida with his three exotic birds, Harley, Marley and Ozzy.

Inspired by the likes of Clive Cussler's Dirk Pitt, Wayne Stinnett's Jesse McDermitt, Cap Daniels Chase Fulton, Chip Bell's Jake Sullivan and many more, Eric's tales are sprinkled with Voodoo, Hoodoo and kinds of weird stuff. From the bayous of Texas to the Voodoo dens of Haiti, his twist of reality will take you for a ride. His main character Rick Waters is a down to earth good ol' boy, adventurist turned private eye, who uses his treasure hunting skills and street smarts to solve mysteries.

FOLLOW ERIC CHANCE STONE

WEBSITE:
EricChanceStone.com

FACEBOOK:
facebook.com/RickWatersSeries

Printed in Great Britain
by Amazon

47165923R00155